JESUS CAN'T DRIVE

Ray Doherty

PANDA PRESS

(C) 2022

ISBN: 978-0645893014

DISCLAIMER

ACKNOWLEDGEMENTS

To my family and friends and to those who inspire me – thank you.

"Welcome to my home
furry little wanderer
relax till home found."
By Adam Hapworth

Special mention:

To the men and women of the Prince Charles Hospital, Brisbane, Queensland, who saved my life during the time I was writing this book. Thank you and God bless all of you.

Jesus Can't Drive
Written by Ray Doherty © 2022
Published by Panda Press
ABN: 26 186514 635
Edited by Lynne Lloyd – Lloyd Moss editing and publishing
Story consultant - Buck Buckingham & Peter Standen
Beta readers - Rod Benfield & Peter Standen
Cover design by Ray Doherty
Cover photo from pexels.com/markvegera

A special thanks to my team, without you, this doesn't happen – thank you.

Special thanks and acknowledgment to the Tarlka Matuwa Piarku Aboriginal Corporation.

Australia

1979

CHAPTER ONE

How quickly one's life can change. In a blink of an eye. It was only three weeks ago that Ken and Carol saw her specialist. He will never forget that day, the day his life shattered. The clang of old wooden doors sounded like a shotgun being fired as Dr Andrew Billings burst into the office carrying with him an encyclopaedia of notes and test results. As a suburban doctor, Ken knew who was the best oncologist and had wasted no time in getting Carol in to see him. Andrew Billings was the best in the country, not to mention a friend of Ken's for over 15 years.

The tall, bald doctor leaned over to shake both their hands, "G'day Carol, G'day Ken," he said in an upbeat tone. "How are you feeling today, Carol?" he asked, knowing full well what the answer would be.

"I've been better Andrew," she replied, forcing a smile, and trying to be strong. But she's so tired from fighting the good fight and all she wants is for this to be over, one way or other.

"So, Andrew, how did we go with the tests?" Ken asked impatiently, anxious to hear the news. The smile on the specialist's face when he walked in disappeared and was replaced by a more serious expression that sapped Ken's confidence. He knew that look all too well, he's had it himself: the daunting task of telling someone they are going to die.

As a medical professional, Ken had learnt to detach himself, but as a human being, it doesn't make the task any easier to tell someone their life is coming to an end. Ken and his family now find themselves in an unfamiliar position of being on the other side of the desk.

"I wish I had better news," the doctor said flatly, "your suspicions were correct, the cancer has returned, and I'm sorry to say it has returned at an unprecedented rate of growth."

"What do you mean, 'an unprecedented rate of growth'?" Ken asked nervously, as Carol sat quietly, waiting to ask her one question, 'How long?'

The specialist frowned, contemplating how to deliver his reply.

"There's no easy way to say this, Carol, the cancer has spread throughout your entire body, I'm sorry to say, there is nothing more we can do," he tells them, realising the impact this news will have.

"What are you saying?" Ken asked with a quiver in his voice.

"What I'm saying is that regretfully Carol, your cancer is terminal. There isn't anything more I can do."

Carol processes the doctor's words, confirming what she already knew within herself, time's up. But Ken can't believe what he's hearing.

"There has to be something more we can do, something else to try?" he pleads, but Andrew has nothing for them.

"I'm sorry, Carol, Ken...further treatments may help for a while, extend things for a few months maybe, but ultimately, it's not going to make much difference. I understand how shocking this news is...."

Ken cuts him off before he can finish his sentence.

"You understand?" His voice trembles and falters as his friend tries to calm him down.

"Ken, please, try to stay calm. As a doctor, you've been in this position yourself, you know it isn't easy to give you this prognosis, especially when it's people I love."

Ken knows he overstepped the line. The stress is getting the better of him.

"I do, Andrew, I'm sorry...but it's not your wife!" he said sharply. There's an expectant silence in the room until Carol breaks the tension, finally being able to ask her question.

"How long do I have, Andrew?" Once again, the doctor steadies himself to deliver more bad news.

"It depends: with additional treatment, maybe a few months; without treatment, a couple of weeks at most."

"A couple of weeks?" Ken scoffs, shaking his head, not believing they have reached the limit of medical science. He's the first to admit oncology is not his specialty, but he can't just give up – they won't give up!

"Carol, I don't know what else to say, other than if you wish to continue treatment, we need to start you today, back in hospital," Andrew states, imparting a sense of urgency.

"There will be no more treatments, Andrew," Carol says firmly, "no more."

"What!" a stunned Ken asks, "What do you mean no more treatments? Carol, are you out of your mind?"

Andrew nods, understanding her wishes without the need to exchange words. His face and tone are sombre, "That is your choice, Carol."

"Shut up Andrew!" Ken lashed out, "Help me here, don't tell her stuff like that, it's crazy talk, tell her more treatment is going to help."

Carol glares at her husband for speaking to their friend in an aggressive way. "Don't you talk to Andrew like that," she responded to her husband, "at the end of the day it's my choice, not yours, mine!" She knows he loves her, but she's tired of him dictating her care options. As a doctor, he is only trying to do what's best for her, but as a husband, she knows he's really pushing what's best for him.

Carol continued, speaking in a soft, calm voice, making her wishes crystal clear, "It's not Andrew's fault I'm going to die, everyone has done what they can, people get sick, it just happens."

However, Ken was convinced it must be the painkillers making her say these ridiculous things. Was his wife even in her own mind?

"Carol, please, we can talk about this... yes?" Ken begged, holding her hand. "There are things we can do, things to try, Andrew even said there are some treatments we can still try, right, maybe even some of those experimental treatments we read about overseas, right Andrew?"

Andrew shrugged his shoulders, "Maybe, perhaps, I don't know, I'd have to look into it."

But Carol wasn't having any of it, she'd made up her mind; whether her husband liked it or not. "Ken, look at me," she softly asked her husband, "we are not giving up. I've had enough, my love; I have nothing left to give."

Ken heard the words come out of his wife's mouth but they didn't register. "Carol...please." He begged her again, kneeling in front of her as she placed her arms around him, pulling his head onto her lap, comforting him as a mother would a child, "I know this will be hard for you," she said, "I know you don't want to be alone, and you will struggle without me, but only for a while. You have your work, you have Gemma, you will be OK."

⇒⇒⇒⇒ ⇐⇐⇐⇐

One by one, the well-wishers began to leave, offering their condolences and support, seen off by Gemma and Kevin, the perfect hosts. Ken slowly sipped the afternoon away with his bottle... As the last of the people exit the front gate, Kevin finally lets out a loud yawn.

"We should get back to the hotel, honey," he says to his wife who is also exhausted from such a big day. She consults the watch her mother gave her, and agrees.

"Yeah, I suppose we should get going," she replies, looking at the lonely figure of her father, still sitting there in the pale light staring into the darkness.

4

"I don't want to leave him alone, I'm worried about him."

Kevin nods, he understands how his wife feels, he'd felt the same way when he lost his father two years earlier. "I know, but sometimes you just have to let people work through things on their own and knowing your dad, I think this is one of those times."

Gemma agrees. "You're right...I'll go talk to him; tell him we're leaving."

"And I'll call us a taxi, and let you two say good-night."

Gemma followed her father into the medical world, not as a doctor but as a Registered Nurse (RN). There wasn't enough room in the family for two doctors apparently. Like her father, she loves her job of helping people to heal, she was born for it and is naturally maternal.

She walks down the beautifully cobbled path and through the Japanese junipers that drape over the side. Ken spots his daughter walking towards him. She always amazes him when he sees her, her strength and grit, he has nothing but absolute love for her in his heart. Gemma always finds a way of getting through to him, despite how indifferent and prickly he can be. She knows how to approach him, as her mother did; in truth, he could never refuse either of them.

"Hey Dad, sitting out here with all your friends?" she teases, trying to be light-hearted to lift his mood even a little. She sits next to him on the long bench, placing her head gently on his shoulder. They sit silently.

This section of the garden was designed as a quiet place of reflection. It's a paved, circular area which has a large iron bowl as a fire pit in the centre, an elegant setting. On one side is the large garden bench, where they are sitting; on the other, a large five-foot-tall water fountain of Jesus with cherubs on his shoulders. Water cascades from the cherubs' mouths and circulates into a pond, highlighted by small lights. Ken always thought the fountain was creepy looking but Carol loved it. She said it gave her peace. The private area was finished off with a large row of azaleas, purposely grown tall as a privacy screen so she could pray or meditate without prying eyes.

He places his arm around his daughter's shoulders, hugging her, "I'm fine," he eventually replies, unconvincingly, smelling of bourbon, still in his funeral suit.

"You have been out here all afternoon by yourself, not engaging with anyone," she comments, trying to drag him out his mental quagmire.

"Yeah, I know, Gem," he replies with a big sigh, "I just couldn't do it."

"You didn't even say hello to Aunt Ruby."

Ken scoffs and chuckles. "Well thank goodness, that woman can talk the leg off an iron chair." They both share in what is a family in-joke.

His tone lowers. "Thank you for carrying the day, I don't know what I would do without you, sweetie."

As much as she wants to rip into him for being selfish and indulgent, she can't do it. She only feels pity and love for the man who raised her, for he too is all she has left, other than Kevin of course.

"It's OK, Dad, it's what I do. By-the-way, is Aunt Ruby even my aunt?"

"Oh God no!" he replies with a laugh, "She was your mother's lifelong school friend, you knew that."

"Yes, that's right. Are you hungry?" she asks, knowing he hasn't eaten all day, "because if you are, I can make something for you before I go. There's a ton of food left over in the fridge."

Ken shakes his head.

"No, thank you, darling, I'm OK, I'll get something later."

Gemma smiles.

"We both know that's a fib, Dad."

"Yes, but only a little one," he quips.

Although her father seems a little better, she's sure it's the booze talking. She's seen him like this before; on those occasions, he was distant and melancholy. Usually, it was when he returned home from one of his overseas trips. Over time, he usually worked his way through emotional stuff but this was so much more than they had previously experienced. He will need a lot of time and a lot of healing.

"Kevin and I are going back to the hotel unless you want me to stay the night?"

Ken interrupts her, "Oh shit! I forgot all about Kevin, I'm so sorry Gem, is he OK?"

"Yeah Dad, he's fine, he understands what you're going through," she replied which eased her father's mind.

"Oh, thank him for me, will you?" He feels awful that he has ignored his son-in-law all day.

"I will, Dad, don't worry," Gemma says.

He shook his head as if trying to wake himself up. He can't believe he was so forgetful.

"Back to your question," he replies, "no, I don't need you to stay, you should go with your husband, that's where you need to be. I will stay here a while longer and then I'll be off to bed."

Another statement they both knew wasn't true.

"Are you sure, Dad?"

"Absolutely, I'm fine, but thank you for asking and thank you for offering, but you should go," Ken assures his daughter, wanting her to leave so he could be on his own, "All is well."

"So long as you're sure, I hate the idea of you being alone tonight."

"For God's sake, Gem, I'm fine," he remonstrates, becoming tired of repeating himself, but he understands her concern. "Now off you go with your husband and don't give it another thought."

"Thanks Dad, Kevin's leaving for Perth tomorrow; he has to be back at work, it would be good to spend some time together."

"Well tell him I said to travel safe. Now go, go and make me a grand-child, will you?" Ken says jokingly.

"Eeewww Dad!" she replies, blushing, slapping him playfully on the shoulder as they share a real laugh for the first time in weeks.

Carol kept the fire pit stocked with a good assortment of dry wood, the scent of burning spotted gum was a smell she adored, as did he. Thanks to a constant sea breeze, the neighbours were never bothered by the smell or smoke. Gemma grabbed the long BBQ matches and fire starters, which were nothing more than Styrofoam blocks her mother kept nearby.

She lit the fire starter before throwing it into the pit. Ken looks at his daughter quizzically to which she smiles.

"We both know that you're going to be here for more than a little while."

Ken looks into her eyes, conceding with a slight smile.

"I don't want you to catch cold," she adds, as the smaller sticks begin igniting the larger pieces.

"Thank you," he replies, giving her hand a slight squeeze.

"I'll be back in the morning after Kevin leaves for the airport, and we will go to the funeral home, hey?"

"The funeral home?' He asks, confused as to why they had to revisit that place so soon, "Why do we need to go there?"

"To get Mum," she answers matter-of-factly, "remember we paid extra for a priority turnaround? They said she would be ready tomorrow." Ken nods, he can't believe he forgot that as well.

The loud beep of a car horn can be heard coming from the front of the house, "The taxi is here, Dad." she still sounds reluctant to leave.

"You better go." He gives her a quick peck on the cheek and she heads for the gate.

"Love you, Dad, see you in the morning."

"Love you too," he calls after her, "See you tomorrow."

Gemma makes her way up the pathway, guided by the garden lights towards her waiting husband who waves good-bye to his father-in-law. Ken can barely see him in the dark, but waves back. He hears the sound of the taxi's 6-cylinder engine driving off down the street, and breathes a sigh of relief; finally, he's alone.

Ken feels the warmth of the fire radiating against his body. Undoing his tie, he reaches into his coat pocket for the small flask Carol gave him as a present. He looks at it, contemplating whether or not to continue drinking. He's already had a few and wonders if he's had enough but who's here to say otherwise. He was once a heavy drinker, not out of desire, nor was it a reflection of how he grew up. He used alcohol to self-medicate when he came home from his overseas trips. Like many others who experienced the horrors of war, it was the only thing that helped him to forget what he had witnessed.

He hadn't drunk throughout Carol's sickness, not a drop. When she was first diagnosed, he stopped. As if some internal mechanism inside of him had turned off the urge, he hadn't touched it since, until today. But now there is no Carol, there's no sickness and there's no reason not to. There's only him which terrifies him.

He opens the flask and takes a deep sniff, "Ah," he says aloud, the smell of it providing instant respite. He looks towards the creepy statue of Jesus which, for a moment, seems to stare back at him. He raises his flask in tribute.

"Well, here's to you, my friend, you've certainly excelled yourself this time," he says, taking a quick swig. "She gave her life to you and this is how you repay her, by taking hers; well done!"

There isn't much more for him to worry about tonight, other than exacerbating his misery. He slumps further into the bench seat, getting set for a prolonged stay. 'So, this is my life now!' he tells himself, "We'll just have to see about that!" Again, he raises his flask to the statue with another swig.

He recalls an odd conversation he had with his wife just before she passed. Carol confessed things she would not normally even consider talking to him about. Knowing he didn't believe, she certainly never discussed anything of a spiritual nature with him.

Towards the end, she would often have to take heavy painkillers to help her sleep, so on this night in her delirium she shared an experience she had in the very garden in which he now sits. She told him she swore she could hear children's voices and laughter as well as soft gentle music surrounding her. Yet there was no apparent source of the sounds. She occasionally heard voices that would speak to her, telling her everything was going to be alright. At first, she thought it was the neighbours but it couldn't have been them. They weren't even home at the times it happened. Ken dismissed her experiences as medicated incoherence, rather than anything supernatural. Now sitting where she sat a short time ago, her words come the forefront of his mind.

He stares at the statue; his anger builds for what it represented to Carol. It reminds him how God failed him in Africa and has failed him again now. He stews on that thought. His rage boils up from nowhere. He staggers up and throws the half empty flask at the statue with all the force he can muster. It's a direct hit and breaks off the nose on the statue's face, sending it flying somewhere across the grounds. Glaring at the nose-less statue with venom, he picks up his flask which now has a large dent and scoffs at his handy work.

He rummages through the house on the hunt for more alcohol. He knows he stashed a bottle around here somewhere, but can't find it, throwing things out of drawers, taking little care. He turns his attention towards an antique chest of drawers and ransacks the first two with no luck. He opens the third drawer and finally, he finds what he is looking for, "Ah, there you are my friend," he says gleefully. Grabbing hold of the bottle, he dislodges what appears to be an old birthday card. It falls on the floor. He picks it up and walks over to a nearby chair. He takes a small swig before opening the card. It's from Carol on his 48th birthday, some 10 years prior. He was away in Africa at the time, tending to the victims of a civil war. The dedication in the card reads:

"My dearest Ken,
You will never understand just how much I love you.
May God bless you and protect you in your travels,
Happy 48th birthday, darling.

All my love
Carol"

Tears are again released and course down his cheeks. He stares at her handwriting, touching the ink gently as if trying to make contact with her in some way. After everything he put her though, all the moods and drama over the years, she loved him more than he ever deserved.

He reads the card several more times whilst taking the occasional swig. He sees a picture of his wife, sitting in a small, antique frame on top of the set of drawers. He picks it up and returns to his seat, trying to understand why Carol was dealt this hand. He spirals further down a well of self-loathing and self-pity.

He reads the card one more time and a line that stands out to him:

"May God bless you."

"God huh? You kept me safe, but what about her, you buggered that up, didn't you?" he yells as if God was in the room with him.

"I am sick to death of hearing about you! I am sick to death of being told she's in a better place, and I am especially sick of hearing about how it's all part of your fucking plan!" his eyes bulge and spittle falls from his lips as his rant escalates.

For only the second time in his life, he wants to punch something, he wants someone else to feel his pain and his grief! He wants someone to blame and, in this moment, it's God! He lurches out of the chair and throws the small picture frame across the room. It crashes into the wall, glass shattering into dozens of pieces across the floor. Swaying slightly, he realises what he's done, he's hurt her all over again in that one stupid action. He can't be here right now; he needs to get out of the house. He cannot be surrounded by all her stuff for another minute. He has to go!

Mumbling to himself, Ken staggers to the front door and leaves the house. He heads towards the beach, a short walk away. He trips and stumbles his way down the dark road before he reaches the soft sand. With the bottle of bourbon firmly secured, somehow he finds his way to the spot where she died. Plonking himself down on the sand, he raises

11

his head and breathes the sea air into his lungs. He instantly feels better and not as claustrophobic.

At this time of night, the beach is deserted, the mournful waves and the blustery sea breeze are all he can hear. In a drunken stupor, he begins to talk, commiserating with himself, like two old men in a pub whose team just lost a football grand final.

He pulls out the birthday card from his pocket. Even though it's dark there is some moonlight, but he can't see anything through his bourbon goggles. He can only feel the card, pretending he's touching her hand. He feels his temper rising and taking hold of him again.

"Why did you take her from me?" he screams at the top of his lungs, demanding the universe acknowledge him, as if a voice will come out of a celestial port-hole with a reply. But there are no other voices, just his, alone, on the beach.

He screams into the wind, demanding an answer until he can scream no more. He slumps, weak and exhausted, as the tears continue to roll down his face, grains of sand blowing into him. With all of his emotion spent, he collapses backward onto the soft sand, stretching his body out and staring up to the stars, 'Is she out there somewhere?'

"How can all of this be for nothing?" he whispers into the black void of space, listening to the beating of his own heart. He can feel his energy beginning to fade, he's losing consciousness; he hopes it's death coming to claim him.

With a final burst of energy, he cries out, almost taunting God, "Show me you're real! Show me her faith in you was, was ...."

His voice dies down to a whimper as sleep claims him.

CHAPTER TWO

Seagulls scour along the shoreline for any morsel of breakfast they can find. Ken snores into the sand, oblivious to the world and the array of early morning recreational users, all of whom look at him as though he was a vagrant. Two tall men in blue uniforms approach his position from across the beach. They see a well-dressed, middle-aged man with a beard, blissfully asleep without a care.

As they arrive, they find his half-empty bottle of bourbon still firmly in his grasp. A person does not need to be Sherlock Holmes to figure out what took place here. The younger of the two constables, Brown, decides to wake him. If they can't, they will take him off to the watch house until he sobers up. He bends down to jolt the sleeper awake but stops himself just before he does so.

"I know this bloke," he says to his partner, Constable Davidson, "he's the local GP, he's the one who came out and helped my wife that Christmas day. Why would a man of his stature be asleep on the beach like a bum?' He recalls his name. "Burton, Dr Burton, that's his name, he has a practice down the road not far from here."

"Then what's he doing here, boozing it up on the beach?" Davidson asks.

"I have no idea, but let's find out," Brown replies as he shakes Ken by the shoulder while calling out his name, "Doctor Burton!...Doctor

Burton!" he shouts for all to hear, with no effect. He tries one more time, otherwise it's off to the watch house,

"Doctor Burton!" This time he shakes the life out of him, finally causing him to stir.

"Yes, yes?" Ken replies in a drunken mumble, as he struggles to open his eyes, the direct sunlight obstructing his view. His head pounds, he looks around and doesn't know where he is or what's going on.

"Where am I?" he asks the men, who he still hasn't identified although it doesn't take long for the previous night to come rushing back to him, "Oh, that's right."

He blinks and opens his eyes and sees two police officers standing over him which gets his attention. The sight snaps him out of his drunken haze, he quickly rises to his feet, standing almost to attention.

"Good morning, constables, what can I do for you?" he asks, acting as though everything is perfectly fine. Out of the corner of his eye, he notices some locals gawking at him. At this point, he's feeling beyond embarrassed.

"Good morning, Doctor Burton," Constable Brown says, "we wanted to make sure you are OK?"

Ken is surprised the younger officer knows who he is. "You know my name?" he queries, hoping he isn't in any kind of trouble.

"Yes, I do. You probably don't remember, but you helped my wife last Christmas day. We had problems with our baby when she was pregnant. I was stuck at work, but you came over and took her to the hospital -"

Ken interrupts.

"Jessica...Brown, breech baby," he says, showing his memory is as sharp as a tack despite being terribly hungover.

"Yes, that's right, doctor," the policeman replies, impressed that Ken remembers, "You have a great memory."

"I try not to forget my patients." Ken answers with a smile, "How is your wife and child now?"

The constable nods and smiles back at him. "They are both very well, doctor, thanks to you. How is your family?"

Ken pauses before giving a reply. His voice cracks.

"Um!" he clears his throat, "Mrs. Burton passed away a few days ago, we had her funeral yesterday."

"Oh," Brown says, it all makes sense to the officers now, "I'm sorry to hear that."

"Thank you very much, I appreciate it." All three men stand there, awkwardly looking at each other. "Well, if there is nothing else, officers, I should be on my way, I have a lot to do today, if that's alright?" Ken asks coyly, knowing full well they could easily lock him up for vagrancy.

The policemen look at each other. They will not make things any worse for the man who saved the Brown baby.

"Of course, you're free to go, please try to have a better day, doctor." Ken nods with a smile and begins to walk off briskly, hoping no one else will see him in this state.

"Ah, doctor!" Constable Brown calls out, picking up the bottle of bourbon and passing it to Ken, "You forgot this,"

"Thanks." He takes the bottle from the officer, knowing the news of his unceremonious fall from grace will be doing the rounds of the suburb by lunch-time, compounding his self-perceived disgrace.

In a way, he's glad Carol isn't here to see his behaviour; she'd be having a fit. Luckily, he has a good reputation, built on many years of community service which meant he didn't go to the watch house. He needs to make sure it doesn't happen again, if for no other reason than to protect his wife's memory. The last thing he wants people to think of is his lovely wife and her drunken no-good husband. He leaves the beach, immediately throwing the bottle into the rubbish bin, feeling the eyes of the older ladies upon him. They are walking their dogs; give it time, wagging tails and wagging tongues.

※※※ ※※※

He walks into the house to find an almighty mess. He's shocked that he has caused such carnage. It was bad enough he slept on the beach, now he finds his house trashed by his own hand, he must have really let go. He looks at his watch 7 a.m. and he's already spent. He needs a shower and to clean the place up before Gemma gets back. He doesn't want her to learn of his bender. He still needs at least one person to hold him in good esteem. Besides, he wouldn't hear the end of it; she is her mother's daughter in that regard.

After a lightening quick shower and a shave, he starts cleaning up the mess and, in short time, the house looks respectable again. He notices the small photo and its frame lying at the bottom of the wall. It is beyond repair. He remembers what he did and cringes at the thought of doing something so stupid. He picks up the shattered pieces of glass and the frame. "The photo is still intact, thank goodness! Sorry my love," he says, placing the photo and the glassless frame back on top of the antique drawers, "I'll get a new frame." He looks at his watch again, 8.50 a.m., "Gem shouldn't be far off," he tells himself, as his stomach rumbles.

He can't recall the last time he ate and goes into the kitchen to see what's on offer. Opening the fridge, he sees that it's filled to the top with the obligatory ham, cheese and tomato sandwiches, packed nicely in plastic Tupperware containers. Gemma wasn't kidding when she said there was plenty of food. He also notices a large plate of party pies and sausage rolls, another plate with pikelets, jam and cream. He's hungry, but this food makes him feel sick. He closes the door, dissatisfied, and returns to the lounge room for a rest while he waits for Gemma.

He sits on the couch in the lounge room, it's large and comfortable. He puts his feet up and extends the entire length of his body on it, with a small cheeky smile. Carol would never allow anyone to lie on her precious couches; he feels like a school boy sneaking an extra biscuit when no one is looking. He places his head on the fluffy pillows making himself completely at home.

"You would be having a fit if you could see this," he says out loud, allowing his body to relax as he feels a wave of sleep beginning to wash over him.

"Surely, a short nap can't hurt, even if it is the morning," he tells himself, sinking further into the soft upholstery. As he drifts off, images begin to fill his head, Carol, Gemma, he feels content. However, his feeling is short-lived as other images filter into his subconscious mind. A cross mounted to a large pile of rocks on a desolate dirt road is one image. The images flicker in quick succession, a crow and one of a large dog, a ghastly-looking animal growling at him and drooling in his face.

Ken opens his eyes and realizes it was a dream, of sorts. He looks at his watch, "Shit! It's 1.30 p.m. Where did four hours go?" The last thing he remembered was lying on the couch and drifting off. He recalls the strange imagery but has no clue as to their meaning, especially that ugly dog. He's confused. How could he have slept for four hours, but he has. His thoughts turn towards his daughter.

"Gemma!" he calls out, as he swings his legs to the floor and slowly stands up, "Are you home?" Surely, she must be back by now, but there's no answer. He checks the entire house with no luck. He walks past the dining table where he notices a piece of paper, it's a note, with Dad scribbled on it. It reads:

'Dad,

I saw you sleeping and I didn't want to wake you. I have gone to get Mum from the funeral home so you don't have to deal with it. I've taken Mum's car; hope you don't mind. Oh, and BTW, you know you are not allowed to lie on the couch, right?

Be home later.

Love Gem'

"Just like her mother," he chuckles to himself, feeling a little better, although his stomach still rumbles, he has to eat something. He returns to the refrigerator for a second look, still uninspired he decides to seek culinary options elsewhere.

He takes a short walk to the local shops, a good old-fashioned pie with peas is in order, he buys two of them, one for him and one for Gemma. He knows she doesn't eat them so he will have to have both, or at least that is his excuse.

He heads for home when a nearby bottle shop grabs his attention. He walks towards the store, tossing up whether or not to restock his supply of alcohol. After some procrastination, he purchases a bottle of bourbon, places it into a customary brown paper bag which he pops into his bakery bag, leaving the store hastily before anyone spots him.

Arriving back at the house, he can hear the phone ringing. He fiddles with his keys as he rushes to open the door and jogs down the hallway, well, the 58-year-old version of jogging at least, picking up the phone before the call ends.

"Hello?" he answers, panting heavily from his short run.

"Hey Dad, it's me."

"Ah Gem, are you far from home? I just went to the bakery and bought you a pie."

"Urgh, a pie, really Dad? You know I don't like pies."

"What a shame," Ken says with a hint of sarcasm. Gemma is slightly buoyed, her father sounds a little better. Perhaps Kevin was right, that he just needs time.

"Well, by the sound of your breathing, Dad, you might have to lay off the pies for a while," she says, "Anyway, I've already been home and have dropped Mum's urn off."

His heart instantly sinks, he isn't ready to face it.

"You've what?" Did he mishear her? He expected to have more time to prepare, it's come too fast for him to get his head around it. His lovely Carol is gone.

"Dad, I dropped Mum's urn off this morning. I wasn't sure where you wanted me to...put her," Gemma gasps and chokes as she tries to squash her emotions, "I put, Mum, on her bedside table." There's a long pause in the conversation, no immediate reply comes from Ken as he prepares himself to deal with it.

"Thanks Gem," he says, finally, in a lower tone, and another short pause ensues before he speaks again, "Where are you now?"

"To be honest Dad, I need a bit of a break. It's been a lot to deal with. If it's OK with you, I'm going to hang out with Sandra for a while. You remember Sandra, don't you?"

"Of course, I do, how could I forget," he replies, rolling his eyes, remembering the trouble the pair of them would get into as young girls. Sandra was a handful, but so too was his child.

"I'm going to have a few drinks with her tonight and I might stay over, I'm not sure yet." It sounds like his daughter needs a night to let go like the one he just had.

"That's fine, I'll see you when I see you," he replies, grateful for some more alone time. Besides, he's more focused on what awaits him in the bedroom. He needs to be alone for that, adding "Have a good time."

"Thanks Dad, you're the best, see you tom -"

The line goes dead before she could finish her sentence which is fine by her, she knows he has to be alone for this next part as she was. She was crying in the car for 40 minutes with the urn sitting on the passenger seat. Having the urn at home makes the loss more real than before. You try to reconcile how a living, breathing person you loved has been reduced to nothing more than a pile of powdery ashes.

Ken stands motionless next to the phone, staring at the bedroom door, wondering if he's ready to deal with seeing it. For a moment, fear grips him and paralyses his body, stopping him from taking another step. Common sense returns, "Don't be stupid man!" he tells himself, remembering the phrases his father would use on him at times of emotional distress, "Harden up and get on with it!"

He takes a deep breath, "Get on with it then," he says, egging himself onwards. He gently pushes the door open, peeks inside and sees the urn sitting on the side table, just as Gemma said it would be. Carol had arranged for a modest pewter container and not one of those cheap and nasty plastic ones. She had wanted something better than plastic, even if her spirit was elsewhere.

The lamp on the side table shines brightly onto the urn, it glistens like a beacon, standing alone, in the darkened room. Carol didn't want a permanent interment anywhere. They had discussed some ideas of how to proceed when the time came, but the end came quicker than they expected. Hence, they never got around to making a final decision.

He walks over to the urn, hovering for a short time, before sitting on the side of their king-sized bed.

"Hello luv," he says nonchalantly, "Welcome home." It sinks in, she's not coming home. "Oh God, Carol," he erupts, covering his face with his hands, as tears stream through his fingers. After a short time, he slowly lifts his head, sniffling and wiping his eyes dry with his shirt.

"Thank goodness Gemma isn't here to see me like this, hey?" Ken says, talking to his wife. "Thank goodness, you can't see me like this either."

He lies down on Carol's side of the bed, staring at the pewter container. "I hope you can hear me; I hope there is a heaven for you, I hope you're there, my love," he says, trusting that she lives on somehow, as impossible as that is to him, "I hope you're having a good laugh at me for being a big cry-baby," he says, embarrassed he hasn't been as stoic as he intended to be. It's engrained in Australian society of that era that men are supposed to be tough, not show their emotions and certainly would not cry. But he can't help it.

He thinks about their life together, reflecting on their highs and lows, cringing when he thinks about the things he did wrong. Again, he has the urge to sleep, everything has just taken a toll, hitting him hard. Unable to keep his stinging eyes open any longer, he closes them and images of his wife appear again in his mind.

Nothing specific at first, lots of random images, words and events which occurred over their life together. It's like watching a movie that transitions from one frame to another. He recounts these memories and his resting face smiles; he is in a happier place.

The images stop flashing and settle on a particular time when he, Carol and Gemma were at the beach, the same beach close by their home. Gemma was only seven in this vivid memory; Ken is aware he's dreaming, but a part of him isn't so sure. It seems so real, he could swear he's there.

It's a beautiful sunny day, not too hot and not too cold, but warm enough for a swim. Carol is reading her magazines and laughing at Gemma who's trying to bury her father in a mound of wet sand. Eventually, Gemma succeeds in burying her father from head to toe, he couldn't move any part of his body, he's trapped under the sand. Gemma moves onto her next activity, as kids do, leaving her father stranded.

"Excuse me, madam," he calls out playfully to his wife, "could I trouble you for some assistance?" Carol can't contain her amusement.

"You can get up, can't you, it's only sand?" she replies cheekily.

"Yes, well, it's only sand, but your daughter is quite adept at burying things, including me, and I can't move at all. So, if you wouldn't mind rendering me some assistance, I would appreciate it."

Of course, he can move, he just wants Carol to come over to him so he can pull her on to the sand with him, sharing the fun, it's all part of his plan to kiss her.

"Very well sir, I will assist you. I've always tried to help those less fortunate, and besides, you've always said I'm good at digging thing up," she replies, laughing as she walks slowly towards him.

He admires how beautiful she is, tall, graceful and elegant, not to mention desirable. She kneels beside him, smiling with contentment.

"Well, I'm here, shall I dig you out?" she asks.

Ken shakes his head, "I'm in a serious condition, I may require the kiss of life."

"Oh, it does sound serious." Knowing exactly what her husband is up to, she plays along, "I guess I don't have a choice?"

"No, I don't see that you do." He smiles at her, as she slowly leans in to kiss him.

Just before their lips touch, her image starts to falter like static through a television, Ken becomes concerned, he wants his kiss! Her image and that of the beach fades, as he's transported somewhere else, to a place he's never visited.

The image of his beautiful Carol is replaced by that of a desert, he finds himself standing there, in different clothes. Like his previous dream, these feel even more vivid, more real, than the previous vision. He can even feel the hot air rolling off the rocky hills, hitting him in his face. This is no dream, but what is it?

He sees a man, standing a short distance away, the man is unfamiliar to him, "What's he doing here in my dream?" Ken asks out loud. The younger, bearded man with long hair and a deep olive complexion is trying to speak to him, but he can't make out what he's saying. The man is mouthing words, but Ken can't understand him, yet the stranger continues talking.

Frustrated, he yells, "What are you saying?"

But the man just looks at him, bearing a goofy-looking smile, and while he seems disarming, Ken remains in the dark.

Suddenly, a powerful voice booms through his mind and vibrates through his entire body. "Wake up!" it says, with so much force it jolts him forward and upright on the bed.

His heart is racing. He looks around the dark room, certain someone is there with him. He can feel a presence, but he can't see anyone. Adrenaline runs through his body as his mind goes on alert – the presence is strong.

"Carol, is that you?" he calls out, allowing himself a split second to believe his dead wife has come to visit him. He hears the floorboards in hallway creak; it sounds as though someone is walking around the rooms. He runs out of the room to catch whoever has invited themselves inside his house.

"Gemma!" he calls out but there's no reply.

The entire house is in darkness, it's night and the only light he can see is from the dining room lamp, shining brightly, guiding him to that room. Like a moth to the flame, he follows the light, cautiously creeping down the hallway towards the lamp on the antique set of drawers. The first thing he sees is the broken photo frame where he left it. Only, it's no longer broken, it's as good as new.

He examines the frame, wondering how the glass could have been replaced. Carol bought that frame twenty years ago from markets in Victoria. It was one-of-a-kind, a custom piece. Gemma could not have possibly found the exact same frame. He knew he would have to get a glazier to cut and match a specific piece of glass. Who fixed it?

Confident he's in the house alone, his heart rate slowly returns to normal. He glances at his watch, the illuminated hands tell him he has, once again, slept for hours, yet his body feels as though it was only seconds. His senses are now back with him, and those vivid dreams have recessed into his subconscious. The whole experience has left him feeling shaky; he needs something to calm his nerves – he knows just the thing.

He retrieves the new bottle of bourbon, placing it on the dining room table before collecting two whisky glasses from the kitchen. He retrieves the urn from the bedroom and places it in the spot where Carol would normally sit, along with one of the glasses.

He takes his usual seat, at the head of the table. "Well, my dear," he says, "let's have a little drink, shall we?" He pours the bourbon into both glasses, before raising his, proposing a toast, "To our wonderful life together, that is now over." He sculls the drink and immediately refills another shot, scoffing it down, before slamming the glass on the table.

He randomly thinks of that younger man in his dreams, it perturbs him, so too does the image of the beast. It has not left him all day. He has no idea what the imagery means, who the young man is or where any of it comes from. All he knows is that those visions, if you will, seemed very real.

He swore he could feel her there with him in that moment and everything was normal again. But he woke up, back to the real world and back to his misery. He wants to go back as they once were, or at the very least, to be back in that dream where he can pretend. He could be happy in that dream.

He knocks down a third and then a fourth drink in quick succession. As he does, something occurs to him, something he had never considered, until now. He knows she's gone, but if heaven is real and she can't come back to him, then maybe, just maybe, he can go to her.

It dawns upon him that, if he doesn't like his situation, he can change it. In a split second, he realises he wants to die. He pours another drink, but this time, sips it slowly. The cogs are turning in his head, "This is a great idea" he drunkenly tells himself, "This could really work!" It's all the booze talking, half a bottle of bourbon is already gone on an empty stomach. "We could be together again in a few seconds, sweetheart, and all of our pain and all of our misery will be over."

He walks to his study, and returns with a dark brown leather bag, like an old toiletry bag. He places it on the table with a slight thud, suggesting something of weight is inside. Excitedly, he opens it, revealing a 0.38 snub nose revolver, or a "Snubby" as it's called in the trade.

His heart rate begins to race as he opens the cylinder, it's empty. His hands begin to shake as he tips the bullets out of the leather bag and onto the table. Five bullets fall out, he only requires one. "Am I really going to do this?" he asks himself, as he chambers the bullets and closes the cylinder.

The gun belonged to his father who served as a medic in World War Two, but he never knew where or how his father obtained it. This is the first time Ken has taken it out of the bag. He hated guns growing up, and as an adult and a doctor, he swore he would live by the Hippocratic oath 'To do no harm.' But now, he intends to become a hypocrite and do himself harm.

He sculls the remainder of his drink and reloads with another glass of Dutch courage.

"Well, my love," he says calmly, "I am hoping we will be together shortly, otherwise it will be for nothing and we will never know." His Catholic upbringing tells him that if takes his own life, he will be dammed straight to hell, but he doesn't care. He doesn't believe in an afterlife. In Ken's mind, there is no God, so if there is no God, there is no hell, just a void of nothingness. It's a chance he is willing to take.

He cocks the gun and places it in front of him, staring at it, making sure it is what he wants to do. He sculls his last drink and picks up the gun, immediately placing it firmly against his right temple, he doesn't want to miss and end up with brain damage, rotting away in some nursing home for the rest of his life. He needs to do the job right the first time.

His eyes are closed, his finger is on the trigger, the safety is off and he has taken up the pre-fire slack in the mechanism. All he needs to do now is squeeze the grip gently and his problems will be over. His heart is racing, "Come on, you chicken shit, pull the fucking trigger," he goads himself. Suddenly, the tension leaves his body, and a calmness overtakes him, his heart rate slows, he knows he can do it, right now is the time.

"Bugger it," he says, squeezing the trigger, releasing the hammer, as it strikes the round in the chamber, in a nano second, he'll be with his beloved again. However, instead of a loud bang, he hears a click - it didn't fire!

"What!" he exclaims in frustration, he fires again and again, wanting to finish the job before he changes his mind.

'Click...Click...Click, is all that happens. "SHIT!" he roars, not understanding why it didn't work. He needs to hurry, he doesn't want to lose his momentum He's no gun expert, but after a quick look, it seems fine. He opens the chamber, all the bullets are there, they're seated properly, the ammo doesn't seem to be too old, not that he would know.

Satisfied the gun is in good working order he places it against his head once again, "OK, no mucking around, let's go, sorry Gem," he says, bracing himself, as he pulls the trigger without hesitation. Again, there is no fire.

He yells and curses, throwing the gun down onto the dining room table. He doesn't understand why it didn't work, it all looked good, but there's more than one way to skin a cat. Suddenly, the loud sound of the phone rings out throughout the house. It startles him as he jumps in his seat.

He walks to the phone, answering it, taking his mind off his failed suicide.

"Hello," he says in a defeated tone but there is no immediate reply. "Hello, whose there?" He asks again, huffing, aggravated. He can hear some kind of static or interference but he can't make heads nor tails of it, maybe it's Gemma with a bad line? He asks for a third time, "Hello, is there anyone there, Gem is that you?" He pauses, as the static intensifies, "If you're trying to play silly buggers, I'm going to hang up."

As if on cue, a female voice breaks through the crackle, "Ken!"

He instantly recognizes it, it's Carol's! He drops the phone in shock and staggers backwards, "Who the hell is that?" he says, frightened by what he heard. He slowly picks the phone back up, tentatively placing his ear to the receiver. As he listens, he's relieved to hear the beeps of the discontinued call tone, whoever it was hung up.

He breathes a sigh of relief, "I'm too drunk for this crap, that couldn't have been Carol." He puts it down to the drink, and a lot of wishful thinking and places the receiver back on the phone. As he turns away, the phone rings again, stopping him in his tracks. A cold feeling overtakes his body. He's unsure of what to do as it rings over and over.

"Bugger it," he says, slowly lifting up the receiver to his ear once more, "Hello?" he says cautiously.

"Hi Dad, did I wake you?" the slurring female voice asks. It's Gemma. Ken breathes a sigh of relief, obviously she was the previous caller with a bad line. He just heard wrong because he's so drunk.

"No, you didn't, darling, what's wrong? Is everything OK?" he is also slurring his words which goes unnoticed by his daughter.

"Everything is fine, Daddy; I've just been having a few drinks. I'm not drunk."

"OK," he replies, still very much shaken.

"I'm ringing to let you know I will stay over at Sandra's tonight. I will be home tomorrow, and you can drive me to the airport in the afternoon, if that's OK? Ken had forgotten she's going home tomorrow; he's been preoccupied.

"No problems, that's fine." he states, realising he can put that previous call to bed in his mind, "By the way, Gem, did you just try calling me before?"

"No, I didn't," she replies, slurring, "Why do you ask?"

"I had a call before, but it was a bad line, I thought it may have been you," he says, convinced only that he was inebriated.

"Well, anyway, I'll see you in the morning," Gemma says, his explanation going completely over her head.

The previous call bothers him, drunk or not, he knows his wife's voice, and it was definitely Carol's voice, he's sure of it! Someone is playing games with him, however it's a mystery he can't solve tonight. He's too drained to deal with it, he needs sleep.

He walks back to the dining room and tucks the bourbon away in one of the drawers of the antique cupboard. He picks up his gun, unloads the ammunition and packs everything back into the brown case, placing it back in the desk drawer of his study. Picking up the urn, Ken heads back to the bedroom and returns it to Carol's side of the bed.

He lies down, hoping to clear his mind of the strange incidents tonight, but they keep circling constantly in his head. He can't believe he tried to end his own life. *What if Gemma had found him, what would that have done to her?* He can't believe he was so selfish. And now that phone call, "What the hell was that?" He's overthinking everything and he has to stop. If ending his life is the path he is to follow, then he can't do it here, he can't put Gemma through that horror. He'll have to find another way.

CHAPTER THREE

S unlight streams through the bedroom curtains, striking the urn with a single ray of light. Ken lies in the bed, awake, listening to the birds flying around the row of bottlebrush trees outside the bedroom window; he's barely slept. He's always found the chirps and songs of the birds soothing and today is no exception. It's the one small enjoyment he has left. The thought of getting up and dealing with the day does not appeal to him in the slightest, but what's he going to do, try to kill himself again?

He's consumed almost a full bottle of bourbon each night for the last two nights. It hasn't helped one bit, if anything, it's made things worse. He feels sick. His attempt to shoot himself was a failure. He couldn't even do that right. He isn't giving up on the idea of being with Carol again, he just needs a better plan.

"Let's see what the day brings," he tells himself, deciding not to spend it lying in bed, feeling sorry for himself.

After a shower, he's ready for the day and starts cleaning the house which is in another big mess. Gemma is going home today and he wanted to have a good day with her before taking her to the airport. Perhaps she'll be hung-over and not notice the house isn't perfect. He can't be bothered cleaning but will make some kind of effort.

As he vacuums around the dining room, he looks over at the phone and thinks about that call, trying to make sense of it. The voice on the other end said, "Hello Ken" in the exact tone of voice and mannerism as his late wife, but how could that be, she's dead? He shakes his head, 'You're reading too much into it, Ken, you were drunk and it was someone else, that's the answer, simple.'

Another idea comes to him out of the blue. There is a gunsmith, just ten minutes away from his house. He could take the gun in for a service to check it is functioning properly. After all, it could simply be operator error, a quick check will confirm that.

He hears the sound of a key turning in the front door, Gemma was home earlier than he thought, but he's glad to see her although his gut knots at the thought of her finding him dead. It didn't happen, but it could have.

"Hi Dad," she says, struggling through the door with her overnight bag. She lumbers down the hallway, sporting dark sunglasses. Ken meets her halfway, taking her bag.

"How are you feeling?" he asks, kissing her on the cheek as she looks ready to collapse.

"Not too good, big night, how about you?" She looks as if she could sleep for a week.

"I'm fine," Ken answers, "Why don't you go and rest for a while, your flight isn't until later," he suggests, taking pity on her.

"Are you sure, I wanted to spend some time with you before I left?" She looks guilty about having drunk the night away.

"It's fine. I have a couple of errands to run anyway, and we have all afternoon. So, go rest in the spare room, it's quieter there."

"Thanks Dad," she says, reluctantly taking his advice, "I'll see you later then?" she asks, to which he nods. He watches her walk down the hallway to the room. His head is woozy, way too much bourbon! However, practice makes him more adept at hiding it. The door to the spare room closes with a soft thud. Wasting no time, he goes to his study and retrieves the brown leather case, now it's time to get some answers.

Ken parks his Landcruiser outside the small shopping centre which is more of a strip mall, than a shopping mecca. Sporting sunglasses, he takes a long look around to make sure he can't see anyone who could recognize him. His efforts at the beach the other morning will still be a topic of conversation in the area. Satisfied the coast is clear, he enters the gunsmiths' shop through the main door, triggering an infra-red door buzzer.

A short young man walks out from the back of the shop with an eager expression on his face, "Can I help you, sir?" he asks cordially.

"Yes, thank you. I want to have my gun checked; I think there maybe something wrong with it," Ken replies, placing the leather case on the counter.

"May I take a look?" the young smith asks.

"Yes, of course," Ken gestures to him to open the bag, "Be careful," he warns, "I can't remember if it's still loaded or not, that's poor of me, I know, but I just can't recall."

"No worries, sir," he replies, unzipping the bag and revealing the gun, "Oh, a 38 snubby, nice gun," he states, "do you happen to know how old it is?"

"No, sorry, not exactly, it was my father's, he'd had it for many years," Ken replies, as the gunsmith examines it closely, opening the chamber, ensuring the gun is empty. He cocks the hammer and releases it several times to check everything works as it should.

"Well, it looks to be in great shape and well cared for. What exactly seems to be the problem?

Ken isn't sure how to answer the question, he couldn't tell him the truth, *'Yes young man, I tried shooting myself and it wouldn't fire.'* "I was on my property and tried shooting some targets, but it wouldn't fire, I don't know if the problem is with the gun, the ammunition or perhaps me," he says pasting a pleasant smile on his face.

"Well, it looks perfectly serviceable to me, I tell you what, I have a test tank out the back, would you mind if I test fired it?

"Whatever you need to do is fine," Ken quickly replies, nodding, of course he wants him to fire it; he wants to make sure it will work, "I would like to know why it wouldn't work for me."

"Great, it'll take about ten minutes, feel free to wait if you like." He picks up the gun and the case and hurries back out to what must be the workshop.

Ken is suffering the mother of a hangover and is also decidedly uncomfortable to be in a shop dedicated to death. Yet again, he feels like a hypocrite and can't wait to leave the place.

After ten minutes, the young gunsmith returns to the front counter with the gun tucked away safely and discreetly inside the bag. He's also holding a tray with a tea towel covering it. He places everything on the counter. "Well," the gunsmith says, "There's nothing wrong with the gun, it performed fantastically, no problem at all."

"So why wouldn't it fire?" Ken asks, curious as to the diagnosis.

"Well, you were right, there was a problem with the ammunition."

"What kind of problem?"

"Sir, with all due respect, I think someone has played a joke on you," the gunsmith replies, sliding the tray over and removing the towel. Ken sees that his bullets have been pulled apart.

He looks at the man in confusion, "How can this be?" Ken asks, stunned by what he's looking at.

The gunsmith shakes his head once more. "I don't know, but someone removed the gun-powder from the shells and replaced it with sand."

Ken's even more confused than when he walked in. His brain is ticking over furiously, trying to figure it out but no ideas spring to mind. This discovery only adds to the strangeness of the last 24 hours.

He must get out of this shop so he can think, he turns his attention back to the gunsmith, making out it's no big deal.

"Well, I guess it will remain a mystery. How much do I owe you?" he enquires, playing the whole thing down.

"Just fifty dollars, thank you sir," Ken nods, taking a fifty dollar note out of his wallet.

"Many thanks for your help," he says, handing the money across the counter as the gunsmith slides the brown bag over, "I appreciate it."

"Oh, I've also replaced your defective bullets for you, free of charge."

"Thanks," Ken replies, "that's very kind, perhaps all isn't lost after all."

"I have some 38 special cartridges on hand, if you would like a box?"

"No thanks," he says, quickly collecting his things for a rapid escape, "I only need one."

None of this makes any sense to him. How did sand get into the bullets, and who did it? Unless, it was some kind of joke by his late father? A final prank played on his son, who he knew hated guns? That wouldn't surprise him in the least.

⟶≫⟩ ⟨≪⟵

Back in the car, he sets off for home, convinced someone is messing with him, and it's wearing a bit thin. However, in hindsight, a part of him was glad his plan failed. He thinks of Gemma, and what she would have gone through. He scolds himself for his selfish intentions. He was only thinking of his own pain and not of their only child. What if he had shot himself dead, Gemma would have lost her mother and her father. He winces at the thought of it.

He vows to do better, to be better, for Gemma. As for wanting to die? The suicidal thoughts are still there, the idea of not having to deal with this daily anguish is attractive to him; however, for the first time he realises that life isn't just about him, or his deceased wife, it's about

Gemma and Kevin, they're what's important. His own plans need to go on the back-burner for a while.

After several minutes of driving, Ken arrives home, turning into his driveway and parking in the garage. . He turns off the engine and sits there, looking at his reflection in the rear vision mirror, "Wake up to yourself!" he rebukes himself, "Your daughter needs her Dad, understand?" He nods. It's unspoken, but he makes a pact with himself to be the father she needs, what she's always needed.

He will die one day, maybe at his own hand, maybe not, but it isn't going to be today. "OK," he utters, getting out of the car, resolute about his direction. He has to be there for Gemma, and that commitment will get him through. He hopes he still feels the same way after she leaves. Even though he craves solitude, it can also be the worst time. When a person is alone, they generally have too much time to think, little spot fires of overthinking can break out and turn into a raging bush fire. Concealed therein is the double-edged sword of solitude.

>>>>> <<<<<

He enters the house and hears a harsh gasping noise rising and falling. It is coming from the spare room where he finds his daughter fast asleep and snoring. He's never heard her snore before. Watching her, the tension in him gives up momentarily and he smiles. Even though she is grown up and married, she is still his little girl.

He heads to the lounge room. He has to rest and the couch looks inviting. He lies down and closes his eyes. Within seconds, he is transported back to that place in the desert. The young man, whose face has recently haunted him, reappears and once again he can feel the heat of the desert. Wherever this place is, he is there.

As before, the younger man is trying to speak to him but Ken cannot hear anything. He is unafraid and calm but frustrated that he can't hear the man who is talking and gesticulating at him, still with the same goofy smile.

The man approaches him, walking slowly. They stare at each other, he seems to know him but Ken has no clue as to his identity. The man stops just short of him, moving his mouth before reaching out to touch him on the shoulder in a friendly gesture. It is an instant jolt to his body almost like an electrical shock, stunning him, forcing him out of his dream and back into the real world.

He opens his eyes to see his daughter standing over him, trying to wake him. He sits up, surveying where he is, confused and dazed at first, before remembering he's at home.

"You right, Dad?" she asks, as he tries to wake up, feeling as though he's been whacked with a sledgehammer.

"I'm fine," he mutters groggily.

His daughter isn't convinced, "Whatever you were dreaming about must have been full of action. You were tossing and turning all over the couch," she says, helping him to stand, "Come on, I've made us some afternoon tea."

A large assortment of food is spread out on the dining table. There are ham and cheese croissants, some blueberry muffins, tasty treats even if they are two-day-old leftovers.

"Thanks, honey." He slowly gets up from the couch and looks at his watch. Two hours have passed in what seemed like seconds, *"This has to stop,"* he tells himself, *"I'll never get any sleep!"*

"Coffee, Dad?" Gemma asks, to which he nods, taking a seat at the table, half a blueberry muffin disappearing into his mouth. She joins him, and for the first time in days they both eat ravenously.

In a short time, all the food is gone and father and daughter are feeling satisfied. Ken pours them another coffee. Now, they can focus on conversation without being distracted by their growling stomachs and splitting hangovers. They had barely spoken over the last few days; the situation made it hard for them to catch up. To be fair, she had tried to talk to him a few times before the funeral and he wasn't very communicative. She had wanted to make the most of her time in Sydney, seeing old friends, which was part of her healing process.

However, now they have both come up for air and have found time to be with each other. Perhaps today is the day when the healing really begins, for both of them.

"That was great, thanks Gem, just what we needed," he says, sitting forward in his chair with a grateful smile.

"My pleasure, the food was in the fridge the whole time, you know?" she replies, happy he is on a more even keel. It made her feel good to do something for him.

"Yeah, I know, I just couldn't be bothered," he replies.

"Are you alright? That dream you were having seemed pretty intense?"

He wouldn't know how to explain it to her. "Dunno, can't remember much about it." They both know it is a lie.

She doesn't press him about it and instead changes the topic to more immediate matters.

"So, Dad, what are you going to do with yourself now?" she asks bluntly, "Now that everything is...you know, done." He's been waiting for this chat and it's typical of his daughter not to be backward in coming forward.

"Honestly, I don't know, go back to work eventually, I suppose," his voice betrays his uncertainty. He realises he hasn't thought about it. He's been caught in the present, trying to get through from one day to the next. He has no idea really.

"How about you?" he asks in return, steering the conversation away from himself.

"Well, aside from going home tonight, I have to be back at work the day after tomorrow, so I guess I'll be straight back into it."

Ken nods, remembering her personal leave is fast running out.

Gemma is worried about what will become of her father once she leaves. In hospital, she has seen how it is not uncommon when one partner passes away, their spouse follows shortly afterwards. No one knows why this happens, perhaps it's a broken heart, perhaps it's grief, or perhaps they've taken matters into their own hands. Since her mother's passing, she fears that this fate will befall her father, although he seems better today.

She knows he's not the sit still type. Even when his own parents died, he went back to work almost straight away. He needs to be busy.

"Have you thought about going on a holiday?" she suggests, trying to give him something to look forward to. "Perhaps getting out of the country for a while, a change of scenery, taking some photos would be good for you?"

Ken hadn't thought about it, "Not a bad idea, but where would I go by myself?"

Gemma's eyes shoot upwards, trying to think of a destination.

"Africa!" she blurts out, "What about going back to do some work in Africa again like you used to?"

Ken sees how Gemma is excited by the idea of Africa. She has no idea what that place means to him, the horrors he witnessed. A place he never wants to visit again.

"No!" he says sharply, "I'm never going back there."

"But why? You loved it, the work you did, the friends you made?" she states, unaware what his years of service there cost her family. He only ever revealed some details to his wife; he certainly won't be revealing any to his daughter.

"I've done all I can do there, and let's leave it at that, next idea please," he asks politely with a smile.

She always believed it was a place where he had the best of times; clearly, she was wrong.

"Well," she says gingerly, not wanting to hit another nerve, "there is one other idea, I'm not sure if Mum discussed it with you?"

"And what would that be?" he asks, interested to see if his daughter comes up with any other brilliant ideas.

"Mum told me that before, you know, that you were planning a trip over to see me and Kevin."

"Yes, that's right," he replies, "we were going to drive over and see the sights along the way, camp out, you know, take our time and relax."

"One last trip, Mum would say."

His tone suddenly changes, remembering yet another of their plans that was not realized. "Yeah, one last trip," he says softly.

"Well, why don't you still do the trip?" she asks, "The caravan, everything is just sitting there, why not?"

He'd forgotten all about it, having put everything on hold when Carol relapsed. The thought appeals to him, but he couldn't even consider it without Carol.

"I couldn't, Gem, not without your Mum," he states firmly, "it wouldn't be right."

"Why not?" she asks again, not understanding the issue.

"It was something your Mum and I had planned, and doing that trip without her doesn't seem right. It's a good idea, but not without her."

"Who says you would be alone? Take Mum with you, take her on the trip."

Ken is appalled. "What, take her ashes?"

"Why not?" Gemma replies, "Think of it as Mum being there with you, in spirit at least," she says, continuing to sell the idea, "When you arrive, all three of us could go down to Burns Beach and spread her ashes. You know she loved that place; it would be a fitting tribute."

Ken reflects on the suggestion, damn his daughter for making so much sense, how dare she! It's a great idea, and it could be a great trip, however the idea of travelling around with her ashes makes him uneasy. To suggest she is travelling with him in some kind of supernatural state is preposterous, as far as he's concerned.

"You know I don't believe in that stuff, once you're dead, you're dead; end of story."

Her father's attitude really gets under her skin at times and she snaps back at him, "Well, you know what, Dad, it isn't always about you. Whether you believe in life after death is irrelevant, it was Mum who believed, and it was Mum who kept this family together."

A dam of emotion gives way and tears stream down Gemma's face, tears she had kept private. "It was Mum who was with me when I had my first period, it was Mum who was with me when I had my first broken heart. It was my Mum who taught me how to drive. Where were you, Dad?" she asks as she lets go of years of built-up anger and hurt.

Ken had no idea she harboured such resentment towards him for those 'missed years' but he isn't surprised. It can be painful to hear the truth which is why many people lie to themselves; he did. His arrogance got in the way. He doesn't know what to say to her right now; it's better that he just listens, and he lets her get it all out.

"I know you weren't a gambler or a womanizer, you are a local doctor, a pillar of the community. That meant everything to you, we understood that, but everyone else in this family took a backseat to your patients, to your causes, especially me," she recalls, trying to regain her composure.

Ken knows she's right in what she says, it's the source of his guilt, but it is different when you see the impact your actions have caused, especially on your children. He goes over to the chest, picks up the antique picture of Carol, and returns to his chair. Looking deeply at the photo, as they both sit quietly. He thinks about her words, he can feel her emotion. He missed so much of her life, how misguided and self-centred had he been? Even that young police officer from the beach remembered him, why? Because he stayed with his pregnant wife all Christmas day while his own family waited for him to come home. Carol would often say that the greatest gift you can give is to be in service of others. Gemma's outburst only stated facts, that he'd got the balance wrong.

There's no point in arguing with her, he can't change the past, he can only control what happens in the future.

"You're right," he says softly, "I know the sacrifices you and your mother made for my work. For me. I'm truly sorry for what I've done."

She takes his hand, "I know you are, Dad," she replies, "it's been written all over your face ever since Mum became sick." He feels ashamed, he was kidding himself if he thought this day wasn't coming.

"I don't know what else to say at present," a dejected Ken says. "Excuse me, would you?" He gets up from his chair and walks out the back door and into the garden.

Gemma instantly regrets saying the things she did, but for her, it needed to be said.

>>>>> <<<<<

Gemma has packed her bags and is ready for her flight home to Perth. Ken's been sitting in the garden, quietly reflecting on their chat for over an hour. She had been spying on him through the kitchen window, as she cleaned up after lunch. She can't help but feel compassion for him, knowing he will be lonely. Touching her watch, she closes her eyes and whispers, "Please look after him, Mum, if you can." As she finishes those words, a warmth passes over her, a soothing and calming, yet familiar, feeling. She allows herself to go with it, sensing all will be well. It's not words per se, but rather a knowing, and in this instant, she knows her mother is with her.

Ken ponders the weight of everything that's happened, he has no clue how he's come this far, let alone what tomorrow will bring.

"Maybe I should take the trip, for us." he mutters to himself. It would be a great opportunity to get out of the house. Carol would have loved the trip. If he allows himself a brief moment to believe what she believed, she would be there with him. "Maybe this is something I can do?" he tells the wind, as though he's talking to her. However, if he does this, there will be no rush, he will take his time to stop and enjoy various places, that's what Carol would have wanted.

He can't help but think of the mechanics of it, he knows it's only a 4-day straight drive, via western New South Wales, Victoria, then onto the Nullarbor. He doesn't want to do it quickly, maybe he can drag it out. If he goes the outback way, it would take 7 to 10 days, which would give him longer to say goodbye to his wife.

Gemma joins him on the long chair they've shared since she was born. Once again, she places her head on her father's shoulder and gently takes his hand.

"I'm sorry, I shouldn't have spoken to you like that," she says, seeking his forgiveness, Ken immediately kisses her hand.

"It's alright," he replies, smiling at her.

"No, it's not, I had no right to say those things to you – "

Ken cuts her off in turn, "You had every right," he tells her, making direct eye contact to emphasize his point, "I took you both for granted and sacrificed our family for some misguided notion that I was serving the greater good and everyone would just have to play their part," he says painfully, "The worst thing is that by the time I realized it, I had already lost my family. Your mother was dying and you were married and moved away...."

She feels terrible that it took her harsh words for him to finally admit his shortcomings; now they can move forward. She squeezes her father's hand tightly, "I'm still here, Dad."

They sit in silence, contemplating the meaning of her words before Ken speaks, "I think the idea of this trip is a good one and that's what I want to do."

Gemma is surprised, she didn't think he would go for it, knowing how stubborn he can be. He's really taken her words on board. "That is great, I'm glad, you really want to do it?" she asks enthusiastically.

"Yes, absolutely," he replies, "the only thing is, I will take my time. I won't rush. I'll be camping and stopping to see whatever sights there are. I think your mother would like that, even if she is only with me in spirit.'"

Gemma smiles broadly and hugs him.

"So how long do you think it will take?" she asks inquisitively, wanting to know the details.

"Well, it's all very preliminary, of course; at this stage I'll give myself somewhere between 7 and 10 days, perhaps longer, if I choose, who knows?" He says, smiling. It is his first genuine smile in weeks.

"By the way, before I forget, I must thank you for having your Mum's picture frame repaired. I accidently broke it. I don't know how you found a new piece of glass so quickly, but thank you."

Gemma looks confused. "What broken picture?" she asks, not having a clue what he's talking about.

Now he is confused. "The antique frame, with your mum's picture in it, the one on the chest of drawers in the dining room, you had the photo frame repaired?"

She shakes her head. "No, I didn't. I have no idea what you're talking about."

He's puzzled, "Well, if you didn't, who did? As though on cue, the alarm on his watch sounds. He realises that time has beaten them. They have to go.

"I need to get you to the airport, or you'll miss your flight," he says, pushing the mystery of the repaired frame to the back of his mind. He stands up, extending his hand to his daughter, which she takes as if she was ten years old again. "Come on, let's get you home."

CHAPTER FOUR

It has been several days since Gemma left for Perth. Ken has been busily preparing for his trip, in fact, he's thought of nothing else. He's been studying maps, obtaining supplies and making sure the car and caravan are in tip-top shape. His mood has steadily improved with only a few patches of despair. However, the thought of ending his life still hasn't left him.

He's cut back the drinking to a swig here and there, and has been eating regularly, however the dreams haven't stopped. Every night, it's the same series of images. Wildly vivid dreams of Carol, only to be interrupted by the image of the wooden cross on top of a pile of rocks with an old weathered farm house in the background before shifting to images of the man in the desert.

Even after several dreams, he's no closer to finding out what the man is trying to say, let alone who he is. There is also the beast who manages to find a way to interrupt his sleep. He has no idea what any of it means, of course, other than it being some kind of subconscious figments which are part of his grieving.

Of course, Carol has been with him, never leaving his thoughts. As he's been preparing for the trip, he's caught himself calling out to her a few times, only to realise the reality of her absence and the shock of it. He could swear she really was there with him once or twice, if he believed in such things, but he's sure he felt her presence. He's convinced himself that this trip will not only appease Gemma, but also give him the opportunity to take matters into his own hands on the return leg, if he still wanted to. That way, if he just disappeared in the desert, no one else would have to clean up his mess.

The 1978 Viscount Supreme caravan is packed and ready to go, so too is his 78 Landcruiser, both are more or less brand new. He has removed a year's worth of dust and the caravan is clean and habitable. The water and gas tanks are full; he's added new linen and stored a large quantity of food, water and of course medical supplies; in fact, he has enough of everything to run a small hospital for a few days.

He's always carried medical supplies when travelling. As a doctor, he believes he should be prepared for anything, especially on a long trip like this. He calculates the route he's selected will take 7 days, give or take. He will limit his driving to 4 to 5 hours per day, making sure he has time for sightseeing.

He's chosen a route to take him near the great inland lakes which is one of the places Carol always wanted to see. He will stop and spread some of her ashes there.

He sits on the back steps, eating his lunch before he commences what they called the trip of a lifetime. Carol's ashes are next to him as he sips on his coffee, looking into the backyard, admiring the garden. Twenty-five years ago, Carol planted a mango tree. It's an unusual tree to have in Sydney, unlike Queensland where it's commonplace. It's quite large now, having grown strong and tall under Carol's expert care.

He notices a lower limb, around 10 feet off the ground. He's impressed by how strong it looks. Abstractly, he wonders whether it could take the weight of a body? For a moment, he finds it an interesting option, instead using of a gun, he could just just fade off into an unconscious realm, when your oxygen supply runs out, like going to sleep.

With a loud cracking sound and a gigantic thud, the limb he was admiring breaks off and falls to the ground, right in front him. He jumps to his feet, slopping coffee over himself. *"How the hell did that happen?"*

He stares wide-eyed and open-mouthed, it is astounding. It is another strange happening to add to the list which he is starting to believe is not coincidental.

It's time to go, he needs to be on the road before peak hour. In the kitchen, he washes his cup and plate as well as wiping his shirt and pants with a damp tea towel. He gives the house one final inspection, finding everything secure. He'll deal with that branch later. He picks up the phone and dials Gemma to let her know he's leaving.

It rings out with no answer. He'll try again later on from the road. Walking out the front door, locking the house behind him, he takes a moment to look back at it for what could be the last time. For a short moment, he sees and hears the ghosts of the past times of his family, Carol pottering around in the yard, Gemma shouting and running through the house like a lunatic, as kids do, and of course him, sitting there in the garden, reading the paper. The memories bring a fleeting smile to his face.

⟶⟫⟫ ⟪⟪⟵

Michael Stewart is a 37-year-old career criminal. Addicted to drugs from a young age, he has chalked up a record thicker than the Sydney Yellow Pages. He's spent more time in jail than he has on the streets, and by all accounts, his life is a complete waste. He has achieved nothing, other than bringing pain to his family and those who once loved him, not to mention his victims, like the near-death bashing robbery of an old homeless man. He was charged for that crime, robbery & attempted murder, but somehow beat the charge in court.

In the years since that case, he's escaped justice more times than he's faced it, and has opted to lie low in various towns and places in and around country New South Wales. He uses and abuses anyone who has the misfortune of crossing paths with him, however this day will be different. On this day, his life will change forever. Having stolen and sponged off the people and other low-life crims in the region, his time is up and he knows it. Whatever goodwill he had is gone, and the not-so-nice people of the area are looking for him.

He's stolen his pregnant girlfriend's car, a 1971 Valiant VH hardtop, a lumbering mass of metal on wheels. Today, he's on his way to see Scotty, his former dealer, to whom he owes a large amount of money. Michael has no intention of paying him, he has other ideas. He plans to convince Scotty that he has his money, only to gain entry into the house. Once inside, he'll rob him of his drugs and cash before absconding to Western Australia; leaving behind an empty-handed drug dealer and a car-less, pregnant girlfriend.

He approaches the dilapidated wooden house that sits on five desolate acres on the western side of Dubbo. It's an unusually hot day for early autumn, summer hasn't stopped and everyone is staying out of the heat. Michael's been planning this job for over for a week, ever since Scotty spread the word about him around town. He intends to make him pay dearly for his betrayal.

He's so strung out, he hasn't had a hit in over a week and isn't thinking straight, he sees this as his only move. He sits in the car, watching the house closely from the road, his target appears to be alone, there's only one car in the yard. The front door's closed, but that's common practice for a drug dealer. He knows he'll need to show some cash to get into the front door which is why he also cleaned out his girlfriend's purse before he left, that's the bait.

The Valiant slowly creeps up the driveway and parks directly behind Scotty's car, trapping him, before he quietly turns the engine off. He also leaves the keys in the ignition for a quick getaway, just in case. He slowly walks towards the front door, nerves on edge, looking around to make sure no one is lying in wait.

He rattles loudly on the wooden door and waits but no one comes. He knocks again, this time faster, more impatiently and louder. Finally, he hears a faint voice.

"Who is it?" Scotty snarls, having been woken up from a midday sleep.

"Scotty, it's me Michael, mate, I have your money," he yells through the wooden door, desperate to get in.

"What do you want?" Scotty yells back.

"I need some gear, mate," Michael replies submissively, "I have your money."

"Piss off!" Scotty yells, wanting to be rid of the freeloader.

"Come on, mate, I have cash, come on, let us in," he pleads. After a few moments, the door creaks open slightly; protruding though the gap is the half barrel of a sawn-off shotgun.

"Show me the cash, ya dog!" Scotty barks, not taking any chances.

Michael uses the old cardboard in the middle of the roll trick to make it look like he's carrying a bundle of cash when it is far less. He raises his hand with the thick roll tucked into his palm. Scotty looks closely, is impressed, and agrees to let him in.

"Hang on a sec," he says, before closing the door, releasing the dead-lock chains. Michael's goal is within his grasp, if he can keep it together and stop bouncing around.

The door opens and Scotty, a diminutive, but heavy-set figure covered in tattoos, stands in the doorway, wearing only a pair of ratty jeans with a white singlet, and a shotgun tucked into the front of his pants.

"Come on then," he says, allowing Michael into the house. Once inside, the rotten, musky smell of sweat and unwashed kitchen plates blasts through the house, fanned by the hot air coming through the kitchen windows. It's disgusting and makes Michael gag. Scotty gestures to him to take a seat and holds his hand out.

"Cash," he demands, which Michael slowly gives over, concerned he hasn't had a chance to take the cardboard out of the roll. Thankfully, Scotty, is still coming down from his own session and stuffs it in his jeans without looking.

"Where's the gear?" Michael asks impatiently, while Scotty looks down on him and scoffs before flicking him a small bag of heroin from a nearby shelf. Michael dips his finger into the bag and rubs it in his mouth greedily, as the chemical quickly takes the edge off his withdrawal, but he wants a full dose.

Scotty looks at him with disgust, "Bloody junkies," he says, "don't think you're doing that shit here, the wife will be home soon, do it at your own bloody place!" Michael nods, but he's running out of time and has to move to the next part of his plan.

He knows where the money and drugs are kept, he's seen the stash spots several times, he just needs to take care of Scotty somehow. Looking around the room, he spies a large kitchen knife on the edge of the sink. If he can grab it, then he's half a chance.

"Can I get a drink of water, mate?" Michael asks.

"Scotty huffs, "If you can find a glass," he replies, without taking his gaze off the TV screen.

He walks to the kitchen and finds a dirty glass amongst the mess. As he fills it with water, he grabs the knife off the sink and slips it into his denim shirt. He sculls the water before returning to the TV room, standing nervously behind Scotty who is slouched in his single seater couch.

Scotty looks up at him impatiently, "What now?" he growls, not wanting to be interrupted, "You're not getting any more stuff, so you can forget that idea, sunshine." Michael knows it's now or never to make his move, either way one of them is going to die, and as far as he's concerned, it won't be him.

Michael pulls out the knife and points it at Scotty,

"I want all your fucking money and gear, right now," he awkwardly demands, sure he has the upper hand but he's scared to death.

"You, fuckin' want what, dickhead?" Scotty spits out angrily. Hyper aggressive, he wants to rip Michael's heart out through his mouth for even thinking of trying to rip him off.

"I want all your fuckin' cash and fuckin' gear, right fuckin' now!" Michael demands again, becoming more agitated and nervous with each passing second.

Scotty smiles in disbelief. "You cheeky prick, you wait until I get up." Gobsmacked that this junkie has the balls to try and rip him off. Scotty slowly drop his right hand to the side of the couch, *'He's going for the gun'* Michael thinks and lunges forward, jumping on to the dealer and plunging the knife into his arm, pinning it to the couch. Scotty screams in agony from the blade driving through his shoulder.

Blood gushes everywhere, soaking the white singlet. Michael grabs the gun and points it at his foe. A screaming Scotty, pulls the knife from his shoulder and charges at Michael, aiming the tip of the blade at his chest. Michael pulls the trigger. A deafening bang. The force of the shot propels Scotty back into the couch, with a gaping hole in his chest.

Michael takes a moment to look at Scotty's lifeless body, his eyes look out in total surprise. "Fuck you!" Michael screams, spitting on the dead man's body. His brain switches gear, he doesn't have much time to get what he came for and Scotty said his wife would be home soon. He has to move it.

He spends the next few minutes raiding all the spots he knows, taking everything he can find, even the roll of cash from Scotty's jeans. All together he has three kilograms of heroin and five thousand cash, enough to start new life anywhere he wants. He throws the booty into a small leather bag that is next to the body. It looks like a woman's bag, but he isn't fussy. He also takes the shotgun and scurries out the front door.

The Valiant tears off at breakneck speed, leaving a trail of dust behind. His heart is racing, his plan actually worked; he's over the moon. He doesn't feel one bit of regret or remorse for the life he's just taken. Killing the dealer wasn't part of the plan, it just happened. It was a means to an end, that's all.

In what seems like only moments, he's travelled several kilometres away from the house, a safe distance. He pulls over behind a thick row of trees, just off the main road, bordering a national park. He takes a moment to catch his breath, his actions mean nothing to him, he can only think about one thing: drugs.

He prepares the injection he's been desperately craving. Using his lighter and spoon, he melts the drug into a liquid before loading a dirty syringe he found in the glove box. He doesn't care about hygiene; he just wants to feel good again. All he cares about is what he wants and what he needs, he couldn't care less what it cost.

Using his seat-belt, he ties his left arm off, trying to find a usable vein on his pockmarked arms. He finds one and quickly injects the drug into his body, instantly feeling the rush overtake him. His relief is swift and evident. The euphoria of the drug surges through his system. He slithers down in the driver's seat, blissfully passing out.

The next morning, he wakes to find himself still in the car. The injection was so large, he'd slept through the entire night. While it is unseasonably warm during the day, the nights are still freezing. He doesn't even recall dreaming; his mind was completely blank. He's lucky he didn't kill himself. He looks into the bag and sees the cash and drugs; he smiles and begins laughing, he has what he needs.

Feeling more normal,' he prepares another shot, a smaller one this time, just enough to get him through the next few hours, while he drives towards his destination, Western Australia. He will take the back roads to avoid the police. He has to put as much distance between himself and this area as fast as he can. He takes the shot, feels the rush once more, and his equilibrium kicks in. He starts the car, next stop Cobar.

A few kilometres outside the town of Nyngan, Sandy Piper and her daughter Stella are leaving home for a day of shopping in Dubbo. For nine-year-old Stella, it's much needed mother and daughter time as her mother, a part-time nurse and roadhouse worker, is a working single mother. Their home is on a side road which leads to the highway with a train line intersecting that road. Sandy's car pulls up to the boom gates as a long freight train, laden with equipment, roars past towards an outback destination. As they wait for the train to snake past, Stella plays quietly with her dolls while Sandy, excited about her day off work, blasts the local radio station. They sing along to the songs together.

Sally grew up in the area and had moved back to help care for her father who had cancer. He died three years ago, five years after her mother, but she decided to stay, and not return to Sydney. She didn't want the big city life for her daughter, and she didn't want a big hospital career again. No, the bottom line is she loves the region, she loves the people and so does Stella. It's home.

If he wanted to avoid attention from the police, Michael was going the wrong way about it. Flying along the precarious outback roads at 140 kph isn't exactly keeping a low-profile. He doesn't care; he's just enjoying the ride and his high. In this carefree state, he blows through a police radar at 142, a single officer gives chase in his police 4WD. Michael sees the blue light of the police car in the rear-view mirror, it's a fair way back. He looks down at the speedometer and increases his speed to 150, confident the heavy police vehicle can't catch him. In response, the police officer increases his speed, pushing the four-wheel-drive to its limits, gaining slightly, as both vehicles thunder dangerously down the highway.

The train passes by, the warning lights stop flashing and the boom gate goes up, allowing Sandy's car to proceed out onto the road. Her right turn view is slightly obscured by the gates themselves, but, luckily, there isn't much traffic as she accelerates on to the highway.

She does not see or hear the Valiant hurtling towards her and never had a chance. The metal monster ploughs through her small sedan, smashing into the rear quarter panel, and sending it spinning violently across the road. The entire passenger side slams into a large eucalypt tree.

The Valiant carries on, hurtling through the air, as Michael loses control. It happens so fast, he rides the car as it flies into a ditch where it impacts with the ground, and rolls several times. The car finally stops rolling, lying upside down on the downward slope of the ditch. Steam from its smashed radiator rises into the sky.

Witnessing the horrific accident unfold in front of him, Glen Standen, the young police constable, slams on his brakes, bringing his police truck to a screeching halt. He immediately calls for backup, the nearest being either Dubbo or his station at Cobar; either way, it could take some time for help to arrive.

He quickly alights from his vehicle, the smell of rubber and smoke mixed with fuel fills his nose. Debris from both vehicles is scattered across the asphalt.

He runs to the Datsun; an horrific sight greets him. There's no movement from either passenger, no cries or yells for help, no moaning, as far as he can tell, they are both dead. Angered, he wants the man who just killed a mother and her daughter.

He runs with all the speed he can muster to the wrecked Valiant, jumping down the slope to the overturned car. He looks inside to find what appears to be another body. A man is lying there with a gaping wound to his stomach. Blood is everywhere, the body is slumped and lifeless. Standen is certain he is gone as well.

With no time to think, his training kicks in: first, call for help, second, secure the scene. He returns to his police vehicle, again radioing in for assistance, before setting flares on the road to block the traffic in all directions.

From his perspective, he has three dead bodies, limited medical training and no immediate support. These are overwhelming odds for anyone, let alone a junior constable.

Two of his more experienced colleagues from Cobar arrive quickly with lights and sirens blaring. They immediately go about diverting traffic and moving the rubberneckers along.

Ken starts the second day of his trip in Dubbo, after stopping for the night. The first day was uneventful, other than trying to remember how to tow a caravan on the open road, so he's taken his time. This has allowed him more time to process everything, without being surrounded by the reminders at the house, even though the urn is with him, secured in the back-seat.

After a hearty breakfast, he decides to take a drive around town, having a good look for what could be his last time. To be frank, he feels a sense of relief being out of Sydney. Gemma was right, this is what he needed. He's tried calling her twice more, but each time, there was no answer and he isn't sure when he'll be able to call again.

His plan for the day is simple: make it to Cobar, only three and half hours away and camp there for the night. He sets off, keen to take some sunset shots with his old camera. There was a time when he loved photography.

When he first arrived in Africa, he would photograph everything and send the rolls back to Carol to be developed, so they could share in his experience. However, with each successive trip, the photo rolls were fewer, his correspondence became infrequent and his resistance in discussing the trips increased. So too did his drinking.

He's been keeping a good pace on day two. By his estimation, the small town of Nyngan should only be a few kilometres ahead. For the first time in months, he finds himself looking forward to getting into Cobar, away from everything and being able to relax.

He ascends the rise in the road and at the apex he sees a build-up of vehicles ahead. Trucks are stopped, and he can also see the flashing of the police lights; it looks like an accident, a bad one.

As he arrives at the scene, the carnage is evident, debris is scattered everywhere. Dismayed by the destruction, he falls in line with the traffic, where he observes there are only a small number of police controlling everything, he can't see any other emergency services. He has to help!

He breaks traffic formation, driving his car and caravan up the side of the road, circumventing the crash scene, and stopping close to the Valiant. He gets out, grabbing his medical kit from the backseat and hurries in the direction of the policemen, much to their displeasure.

"Sir, you can't park there," Standen politely tells him.

"I'm a doctor," he retorts with urgency, "Does anyone need help?"

The officer shakes his head.

"They're all gone." Sadness is evident in his voice.

"Well, it's a good thing that I'm the doctor and you're the policeman. Now if you don't mind, let me have a look," Ken says with authority.

Standen immediately ushers him towards the Datsun. "I should warn you, doctor, it's pretty gruesome in there."

Ken reassures him, "Don't worry yourself, gruesome and I are old friends."

Ken peers inside and sees what he assumes is a mother and daughter. He puts on his surgical gloves and can see from the severity of the injuries that the young girl bore the brunt of the impact. The Datsun 180B has a small, cramped interior which makes working in it difficult, to say the least.

Before working on the girl, he dashes around to the driver's side to the mother, reaching in to check her pulse. Touching her neck, he instantly kicks into high gear, "They're both alive!" he yells, prompting Standen to run over.

"They're alive?" Standen repeats, astonished by this miracle.

"Barely, I have pulses." He quickly checks on the mother's wounds. Ken swings into action or he could easily lose both of them. He's determined that won't happen, not now he's on the scene.

"Alright Constable, do you have any blankets in your vehicle?"

"I think so, doctor, and first aid kits if you need them."

"I will," he nods, "get everything you have and bring it over as quickly as you can. How far away is help?" he asks. ,

The officers are unsure and shrug their shoulders. "We don't know," Standen answers, disappointed he was wrong, "I thought they were all dead."

Ken ignores the comment, he doesn't have time for such indulgences, he has lives to save. "Well, find out, will you? Tell them at least two people are alive and that a doctor is on the scene. We need ambulances here now!" Both officers run to the closest vehicle, updating their request for help.

Ken starts on the daughter, working frantically to stem the bleeding from her head. Both police officers can tell this isn't the first time he's experienced such a calamity, his calmness under pressure is something they could learn.

The girl's bleeding is severe, he's soaking up as much blood as he can, however, without proper hospital equipment, he can't tell the true extent of her injuries. She's lost so much blood that without a transfusion, and soon, she may not survive.

After some time, he manages to stop the bleeding, and has dressed her wounds. The policeman returns with the blankets as he moves over to the mother.

"Cover the girl in the blanket until we are ready to move her." Ken orders.

"What will that do?" Standen asks.

"It will help her body with shock," he replies, as the mother moans, she's beginning to come around which is a good sign.

Soon, the pain will be too intense for her, so he administers some morphine to take the edge off and to keep her semi-sedated.

"What's your name, love?" he asks, as the woman stirs, "Can you hear me, what's your name?" He repeats the question several more times before he gets a faint response.

"Sandy...Sandy Piper," she utters, delirious. Ken smiles, she's alive and slowly coming around. This is his reward; it isn't every day you save a life, let alone two.

"Hello Sandy, I'm doctor Ken, you're going to be OK," he assures her, as he holds her head still in his hands. Her moment of consciousness doesn't last long as she passes out from the medication.

>>>>>   <<<<<

Michael wakes to find himself on the roof of the car, he's upside down. The first thing he feels is intense pain throughout his entire body. He tries to cry out, but the only sound he makes is a painful cough as blood splutters everywhere. He knows he's badly hurt; he touches where the pain is most intense, his stomach, but strangely that area feels numb, probably due to the drugs in his system. The rest of his body feels like it's on fire. He sees the flashing blue lights of the police car behind him and knows he has to get out of here. He tries to move but the pain intensifies. Touching the wound with his fingers, he feels a large deep gash, and knows he's in trouble.

In the distance, he can hear some men talking, he manages a brief look by tilting his head. It's the police, they're at the other car. An older, grey-bearded man is with them, focused on the other passenger. He wiggles his toes and legs, they still work, he's relieved, he's sure he can walk. He reaches for the bag containing the drugs and cash, some of which has spread through the interior of the cabin. He grabs a small bag, snorting it immediately, hoping it will numb the pain and slow the bleeding, it's only a guess.

He slowly tries to wriggle his way out of the wreck. Luckily for him, the Valiant is like a tank, and the damage was largely confined to the front of the car. Despite the roll, he can still crawl out the window, taking his bag with him. He slides down, and instantly feels the sharp bite of pain in his lower body. The pain is so severe he's convinced he's going to die; he can't go any further.

Suddenly, a voice radiates inside his head. 'Get Up!' the voice says, in a loud whisper. He looks around and can't see anyone nearby, the police are at the other car, so it wasn't them.

"Who said that?" he whispers back. There is no reply. He dismisses it and keeps trying to get out of the car.

Inch by inch, he struggles painfully, somehow managing to get onto the surrounding grass. With no time for rest, he gingerly reaches back inside the car for the gun. Now free from the wreck, he surveys the surroundings through dying eyes, looking for a way out. He sees the Landcruiser, about 20 feet away, that's it, if he can hide inside, that's his escape.

Using his bag to cover his stomach, he crawls on his side to the four-wheel drive where he reaches up to grab the door handle, pulling himself to his feet. He enters the vehicle through the rear passenger side. Sliding the front seat as far forward as it will go, he makes room for his slight frame to hide on the floor.

The drugs are barely keeping him functioning, he can't be bothered to try and look for the keys. He'll just wait for the owner, shove the shotgun in their face and get them to drive him some place safe. He doesn't care where, just some place he can hold up and recuperate. At that moment, he notices the urn.

'Go to the desert,' he hears in his mind as he did a few minutes ago. It sends his paranoia into overdrive. Someone is talking to him but he doesn't know who although he could swear the voice was coming from the urn.

He points the gun at it while frantically looking around.

"Who are you? What do you want from me?" but all he hears is the same message, repeated over and over.

'Go to the desert, go to the desert, go to the desert.'

He places his hands on his ears but it's inside his head, it's relentless, it won't stop and he can't take it.

"OK, OK, stop!" he screams, "I'll get them to take me to the desert!"

After a few moments, he slowly removes his hands from his ears, hoping that he doesn't hear that creepy voice again. Satisfied it's stopped, he breathes a sigh of relief. He doesn't know what's happening to him, or who is communicating with him. Perhaps it's the drugs, all he knows is he has to do what it says and go to the desert, or else it'll be back.

⟫⟫⟩ ⟨⟨⟨⟨

The ambulances have finally arrived, two of them, with lights flashing, under police direction, the big F100s drive right up to Sandy's car. Ken and the officers have managed to extricate the women from the car. They lie on the ground, patched up, collared and covered in blankets. The ambulance officers need to move swiftly and immediately transfer them onto spine boards. He updates them as to their conditions, what their stats and vitals are, and what treatment he has already administered. Ken assists with preparing the injured mother and daughter and soon, one after the other, they are slid into the two ambulances. They hit their lights and sirens, heading for the nearest hospital.

Ken walks over to Standen and interrupts his conversation with his colleagues.

"What about the driver of the other car, is he dead too?" he asks tersely, frustrated by the officer's earlier fumble.

"I was pretty sure doctor, yes," he replies, still kicking himself for getting it wrong.

"Well, you were pretty sure about the first car as well, weren't you?" Ken asks, pointing to the Datsun.

Ken doesn't wait for a reply, striding off towards the second car on his own. He eases himself down the slope and sticks his head inside the cabin for a look, seeing blood, white powder and cash everywhere but no body.

To attract their attention, he frantically waves his arms at the two police officers. Eventually they see him and wave back. They stroll over to Ken.

"Yes doctor, what is it now?" Standen asks dryly, his voice having taken on an exasperated edge.

"I thought you said there was another body in here?" Ken queries.

"There is," the policeman replies in an elevated tone, slightly concerned by the question, "He should be lying in there," pointing to the front of the wrecked Valiant.

Ken shakes his head. "Well, he isn't. It looks like you now have a manhunt on your hands."

Alarmed, the two officers slide down and look inside to see for themselves and the doctor's right, it's empty! A large pool of blood is all that remains of the occupant.

Standen is speechless, and stammers, "I was positive he was...!"

"What, dead?" Ken interjects,

"Yes."

"Well, clearly not," he replies with raised eyebrows.

"Shit!" Standen exclaims, rushing off to tell his colleagues what has happened as more police from the surrounding areas arrive, including the local area commander. After some discussions, several cars leave the scene with sirens and lights blaring to comb the area for the injured driver.

Ken sees the commander berating the young officer who had done his best, given the circumstances. Ken feels a twinge of regret for being harder on him than he meant to be, but he couldn't help it. He's a professional and can't stand mistakes, let alone such potentially costly ones.

Standen leans against a squad car, dejected; seems the injured are not the only ones who need some healing today. He sees the doctor walking towards him and rolls his eyes, not needing another lecture after the mouthful he just received from his boss.

"What's your name?" Ken asks gently, taking a different tack with the young man.

"Why, so you can report me for being incompetent?" Standen demands in an impertinent tone. "Too late, someone else has beaten you to it."

Ken shakes his head, maintaining eye contact and staring until he answers the question.

"I'm sorry doctor. Glen, my name is Junior Constable Glen Standen," he replies flatly.

"And how long have you been a policeman, Glen?"

"Almost two years. I normally deal with thieves and drunks, you know, petty crime. I've never encountered anything like this before," his voice begins to shake, recalling the horror of his first major car accident.

A pack of cigarettes and lighter sits on the dash of the police car he's leaning on. He picks it up, lights one, his hands still shaking from shock. He takes a puff, immediately coughing.

"I don't normally smoke," he mutters as the incessant coughing finally trails off.

"Let me tell you something, Glen," Ken says calmly, "I have been a doctor for over 30 years. I have seen everything from a nail through someone's foot, through to a person who was hacked to death with a machete, I can tell you, there is no getting used to it. A scene like this, injuries like theirs, it's very confronting for trained professionals, let alone the untrained. Don't be too hard on yourself, you did the best you could."

Glen takes a second drag of the smoke, listening to the advice, and nodding.

"Then what do you do, how do you get past it?" he asks for future reference.

Ken shakes his head. "I try to remember who is it I'm here to help? The patients, or victims, in your case, are what's important. At least, that's what I do."

"Thanks, doc, I think I understand," he says, feeling a little better, and grateful for his kind words.

"Now if you don't mind, constable, I think I will go into town and find a coffee and a sandwich somewhere. It's already been a long day," he says with a smile, knowing there's nothing more he can do here. Ken walks back to his car, leaving the young man to consider his thoughts.

→≫⫸ ⫷≪←

Michael heard the police sirens and all the commotion near the Valiant. He doesn't know what's happening, all he knows for sure is they haven't caught him, yet. He hides the gun from view. It is pointed at the driver's side. He keeps his finger poised on the trigger, whoever it is, he won't go easily.

He hears footsteps approaching the car. He readies the weapon in anticipation of it being the police, however he breathes slightly easier, it's the older man with the beard.

Ken opens the car door, thinking about that coffee and sandwich in town, and nothing else. Settling into the driver's seat, he's about to insert the key when he hears the sound of a hammer being cocked. He looks around in the direction of the noise. A sawn-off shotgun is thrust in his face from the floor of the rear passenger seat.

He sees a bearded, long haired, dishevelled man, covered in blood, staring at him with deadly intent from the floor of the rear passenger seat.

"I'm a doctor, I can help you," Ken says, ignoring the weapon.

"Shut up and drive!" the gunman orders, "No silly stuff, or I'll shoot you."

Ken can't let it go at that; his professional instincts take over.

"Look, you are badly injured, maybe even dying, let me help you before it's too late," Ken argues, focused only on the injured man.

"Maybe you didn't understand me, drive or I will blow your fuckin' head off," he orders, nudging the gun into the back of Ken's head and cocking the second barrel.

Ken gets the point; it would take his entire head off.

"OK, OK, I'll drive, just be cool," he replies in a soothing voice. He starts the car.

There was no opportunity to call for help, not safely anyway. He is alarmed but not scared, having faced a similar situation before. An African warlord once placed a gun against his head, forcing him to treat one of his soldiers who had just killed six people in a village. Ken's instinct then, as it is now, is to treat the patient regardless of who they are or what they have done. It's his job.

The car lurches forward and accelerates slowly away from the accident scene and back onto the highway, "Where to?" Kens asks.

"Just head for Cobar," the fugitive orders, wincing in pain. Ken feels helpless. He wants to give the fellow a chance at life, but he is only intent on escape. Ken needs to be careful. Whoever this fellow is, he's off his head and desperate, and holding a loaded shotgun.

An hour into the ordeal and not a word has been spoken. Ken listens to the fugitive's ramblings as he's drifts in and out of coherence. None of it was directed at him, nor did it make any sense. He just listened.

They're entering the town of Cobar, a mining town in the New South Wales outback, a town noted for its isolation and stunning night skies. This is one place Ken was hoping to stop for a day or two and take advantage of the scenery.

Suddenly, his unwanted passenger is alert, as though on cue to provide further instruction. "Don't slow down," he orders, "just keep going."

"I have to," Ken replies, "we're in the main street of a town and I'm towing a caravan, I can't speed through here, even if I wanted to."

There's a brief silence.

"Just keep moving then, and don't stop," he replies, reaching for a small baggy of heroin and snorting it straight out of the pack.

They pass through the town without incident despite nearly clipping a car and a couple of pedestrians who Ken didn't see until the last minute.

In quick time, they've made it to a few kilometres outside the town where they are alone.

"Stop the car," the fugitive orders.

Ken complies without discussion.

Groaning and cursing, the gunman slowly slithers off the floor and onto the passenger's seat. The floor is saturated in blood and the fellow is almost completely covered in it, '*How is this bloke alive?*' Ken asks himself, amazed he hasn't passed out yet.

Now in the seat, he points the gun once again in Ken's direction, "Drive," he orders.

They travel a few more kilometres along the road when the fugitive issues another instruction without notice.

"Turn here, now!" Somehow Ken manages to make the turn onto what appears to be a dirt road; it was hard for him to see, it's not sealed and worn down. The ride becomes bumpier and, with every bump, the gunman feels it more, groaning louder each time and snorting more drugs.

Ken knows the caravan isn't designed for this kind of terrain, he has to take it as easy as he can to ensure they don't break down out here, wherever here is. Besides, he doesn't fancy being stuck out here for the night with a dead body.

⇒⇒⇛ ⇚⇐⇐

Several hours pass by, as they travel deeper into the desert, into the unknown. Ken's been watching his passenger like a hawk, sitting there with the gun in his lap, head slumped over against the window. He allows his gaze to stray from the road ahead, trying to assess the gunman's condition. The bleeding has slowed but Ken knows it's only a matter of time before death comes for him. He gradually slows the car; he has a chance to escape. He hits a deep pothole which snaps the man back to consciousness.

"What is it?" the gunman yells, unsure of where he is, looking around, briefly panicking, before settling his gaze directly onto Ken. He remembers and raises the gun at Ken's head.

For a split second Ken confronts his own death, not knowing what is in this madman's mind.

"Take the next road on the left?" the man orders.

Ken needs to check his injuries; time is running out. Perhaps, if he gets him talking and is able to lighten things up, then maybe he can save him.

"What's your name?" Ken asks.

No response. The fugitive stares at him blankly with his blood-stained face, barely holding on. "Just drive, he replies sharply.

But Ken doesn't give up, "I told you before I'm a doctor, why don't you let me stop and have a look at your injuries, we're far enough away now. Let me see if I can help?"

He thinks about Ken's offer for a moment, "Got any good drugs?" he asks, laughing at his own joke before erupting into a coughing fit. Blood spurts out as he struggles to get air into his lungs.

It won't be long now, a few hours at most. Ken needs to be patient, when another idea comes to him. This man is going to die a painful and miserable death, perhaps Ken could help ease his pain and assist with his transition to the next life, a form of compassionate service. Ken answers his question, "As a matter of fact, I do have drugs, I have morphine; I can take your pain away."

Even though he's barely compos, the man knows what he's up to. "So you can give me a hot shot and kill me, no thanks, I'm not that stupid, just keep on driving."

Ken thought it was worth a try. A little further down the dirt road, he sees the turn he's been instructed to take as the fellow watches him carefully. According to his best guess, they are heading west, as early evening begins to fall.

"Michael," he says out of the blue, surprising Ken, who looks back at him, "You asked me my name, my name is Michael."

Ken nods. "Pleased to meet you, my name is Ken."

"I'm going to die soon," Michael states with certainty, "then you'll be free."

Ken shakes his head. "Not necessarily, let me look at your injuries."

"Nah...it's too late for me."

"How do you know you're going to die, Michael, are you a doctor as well?" Ken glances at him, a grimace on his face.

"Look at me, a blind man can tell!" He is groaning and squirming as the pain increases; his drugs are wearing off.

Ken's frustration grows. It may well be too late but that doesn't mean he shouldn't try.

"So where are we going, Michael?" he asks, trying to keep him talking and lucid.

Michael shrugs. "I don't know, just out here somewhere. I'll know when."

"Very well," Ken replies calmly, prepared to go along with it for as long as it takes to reach its conclusion.

"He'll tell me when we get there," Michael adds, raising Ken's curiosity as there's only the two of them.

"Who will tell you, Michael?" he asks.

"The bloke sitting next to me!" he replies. "Now, no more talking, just drive."

All Ken can see in the rear vision mirror is the urn, so he instantly dismisses Michael's rambling as drug hallucinations.

꙳⟫⟩⟩⟩ ⟨⟨⟨⟨꙳

They drive on into the night, Ken has no idea how long they've been going, the whole day has become a blur. With only his headlights and a rising moon to guide him, he's struggling to see the bumpy track ahead. Michael continues to drift in and out of consciousness. His breathing is slowing, becoming shallower as death creeps closer. He's been conscious, occasionally shouting random words like "Mum," "Sorry," and "Forgive me," before blacking out again. Sometimes he seems to be having a conversation with someone, muttering unintelligible words, perhaps to his invisible passenger in the back.

This has been a test of Ken's resolve, considering how his own life had been turned upside down in the past few weeks; today is something else. He's grateful for small mercies: that Carol isn't here to go through this with him, otherwise he might have tried to be the hero and probably would have been shot.

Michael suddenly places his blood-stained hand gently on Ken's shoulder, taking him by surprise. "Stop here...please," his voice is weak and can barely be heard. Unsure of what he said, Ken pulls the car over on a flat area in front of him, bringing it to a stop.

Michael collapses onto the seat, dropping the gun on the floor. This is it; this is what Ken has been waiting for. He jumps out and races to the back of the car for his medical kit, running back to Michael. It's a battle against time to save him.

He opens the door and blood seeps out. Michael is covered in it, head to toe, it looks like a slaughter house. It's pitch black and the cabin light is not sufficient illumination. But he has a small flashlight in his medical kit. He shoves the flashlight into his mouth, holding it like a stogie, as he tries to save the man.

Racing the clock, Ken rips Michael's shirt apart, buttons fly off in all directions. For the first time, he can see the full extent of his injuries. Parts of his intestines were dislodged and are protruding from the wound; major veins have been nicked and stomach muscles ripped apart. Ken has no idea how the man lasted this long, it's impossible!

He knows there isn't anything he can do for him, it's too late now. All he can do is make him comfortable in his final few moments. He briefly considers using some his powerful painkillers to put Michael out of his misery, it would be the humane thing to do to end his suffering, but it's too late. Death is imminent.

"Doctor," Michael croaks out, "Are you there?"

"Yes mate, I'm here," Ken replies in a soothing tone, leaning over him compassionately, as all good healers do.

"It's gone dark, I can't see anything," Michael says, panicking, even though his eyes are wide open and staring blankly into the car's headliner. Ken takes his hand.

"The pain will soon stop," he replies, as he grabs a blanket from the back seat, wrapping it over the dying man.

"I'm not scared doc, I don't feel any pain," he says, "I'm just sad, how I wasted my life...how I treated Mum," he whispers, crying, as he coughs up more blood. Ken can hear the sincerity in his voice.

Suddenly, Michael gets a spurt of energy, and rears up, looking Ken directly in the eye, "Do you see it?" he asks, "The lights! It's beautiful, the colours, it's coming towards me...do you see it?" Ken doesn't see a thing, but at a time like this, he tells him what he wants to hear.

"Yes, Michael, I see the lights."

"They're right in front of me," he says, trying to reach out to touch something with his hands. "There's someone there, in the light, coming towards me," he says excitedly, extending his hand, "Hello," trying to touch what he sees in front of him. Ken monitors his pulse, it's slowing even more, any moment now.

"Are you Jesus?" Michael asks, crying out, his rapid eye movement suggest he is experiencing something very real, even if it's in his mind.

"Please, forgive me, I'm sorry," he exclaims, slumping back on the seat. He looks at Ken once more.

"He's coming to see you," Michael says, tightening his grip on Ken's hand.

"Who's coming, Michael?" Ken asks, going along with him.

"Jesus," the dying man states excitedly, "Jesus is coming to see you."

Ken finds the answer completely bizarre and somewhat awkward. "I'm sure Jesus would have better things to do than to come and see me," he says dismissively.

Michael smiles back at him with conviction, "You asked him to, on the beach."

That wipes the smile off his face. No one knew about that. There's no way anyone could have known.

Michael begins to heave, gasping for air. Ken tries to calm him, while processing his strange comment.

"Just relax, Michael, try to breathe...it's OK," he urges, trying to keep him calm as his body shuts down. Without warning, Michael touches his face, he can feel the tenderness in his touch.

"I have been forgiven!" he exclaims. His body heaves once more, before Ken hears the final exhale, just as he heard Carol's. The loud gurgling noise of oxygen exiting from his lungs mixed with blood signals the end, and just like that, the flame of Michael Stewart's life is extinguished. Ken checks his vitals, using his stethoscope to confirm what he knows. He looks at his watch, mentally noting the time of death, an old habit.

He breathes a sigh of relief; the ordeal is over. He looks at Michael's lifeless body and closes his eyes, wiping the blood away from his bottom lip. Michael's beard is soaked in blood. His eyes are sunken, surrounded by the darkness of hard living. Michael Stewart is dead, and Ken can't help but feel saddened by the waste of life.

Ken places his hand on Michael's chest,

"If there is a God and a heaven, Michael, I hope you find them," his voice is solemn. He needs to say something nice about this poor fellow.

The desert freezes at night. The small aluminium flashlight he has in his mouth is like a popsicle. His body is shivering but he has to do some things before he can take shelter. He wraps Michael's body in the blood-stained blanket and secures it with packing tape. He has no choice but to leave the remains outside for the night, the ice-cold temperature of the desert will help slow the effects of decomposition. Besides, he can't leave it in the car or worse, in the caravan with him.

The wind is picking up, turbulent cold air hits him in the face, he can taste a little dirt in his mouth, a dust storm is coming. He needs to get inside the caravan, quickly. Gently he pushes Michael's wrapped body under the car, it's a tight fit between the chassis and the ground but it is secure. At least he can rest easier knowing the body is protected from any potential predators; he wouldn't want to wake to a mess like that in the morning. He's done all he can do and walks his exhausted frame towards the caravan, looking forward to some rest. He'll figure the rest out in the morning.

Before entering, he surveys the area, looking upwards at the near full moon. He can see the landscape, expanding in every direction; it's like staring into another world. He closes his eyes and imagines that this is what it's like being up on the moon. Perhaps this is how the first astronauts felt when they left Earth, alone, isolated, and far from help. He has no clue as to where he is and how far he is from civilisation. All he knows is that his worst fear is realised: he's stuck out here with a corpse.

CHAPTER FIVE

T he wild winds outside thud against the caravan; it sounds as though someone is banging on the walls. Each powerful gust rocks the van from side to side like a large sail catching the wind. The noise wakes Ken from his sleep. He looks at his watch, it's 11 a.m., "Blast!" he exclaims, he can't believe he slept so long.

His thoughts turn to Michael's body. Even though it's the cooler months, the days are still hot around here and his body began decomposing the moment he died. The return trip with a stinking body is not something he's looking forward to; it'll be windows down all the way back. He needs to get Michael's body positioned and to leave quickly. He finds a rag near the bed, wrapping it around his face as a makeshift mask in anticipation of the smell which has been fermenting since sunrise.

He opens the caravan door and is stunned by the majesty of the wide-open barren landscape, complemented by a big powder blue sky. He takes in the scenery which is as dangerous as it is beautiful.

Ken had never been so deep into the outback before and has a feeling of insignificance when looking at the vast country before him. He cautiously steps out onto the ground like Neil Armstrong stepping out onto the lunar surface for the first time. Ken also feels as though he is stepping on alien ground.

He surveys the area, the caravan and Landcruiser are covered in a thick layer of red dirt that swirls around in the wind. He wants to make sure he can follow his tracks back to town, checking behind the caravan to make sure they're still there. He feels his stomach tighten, he's worried and rightly so. Yesterday's tracks have vanished!

"How will I get back?" he mutters, panic rising in his body. However, he reminds himself that he's well prepared, he has maps and a compass, plenty of fuel and is well provisioned, "We'll be fine." he tells himself, pushing his concerns aside for the moment. He has to focus on Michael.

He walks to where he left the body, wondering why he can't smell it before it occurs to him, the wind, of course, it suppresses the smell. He crouches low to retrieve the body from under the chassis. He stops and stares, his panic returns. It's gone! Michael's body is gone!

Ken jumps up and walks around to the other side of the vehicle to check from a different angle. No, it's not there. He begins a desperate search of the immediate area. "How could a dead man just walk away?" he yells at himself, frustrated that yet another inexplicable incident has happened. After a cursory exploration of the area, he finds no signs of animals or other vehicles and no Michael, nothing.

He continues looking, more thoroughly this time, hunting for any sign of activity that may give him a clue to what has happened to the body. He begins to doubt himself, whether his exhaustion from the events of yesterday led him into making a mistake, and Michael wasn't dead? He thinks about it for a moment or two, replaying it in his head, '*Impossible!*' he concludes, reaffirming there was no mistake and the man was dead. However, with no obvious signs of third-party interference with the body, he has no evidence to support his story.

He carries on and, over the next hour or so, he inspects every nook and cranny in the area, but there are no clues. He looks at his vehicle, some distance away, he could just turn around and head back to town, forget the whole thing and no one would blame him, and importantly, no one would know. But those damn medical ethics get in the way. In good conscience, he can't leave an injured man out here to die, he has to find him. Finally, he notices something a few metres ahead of him, down the track in the soft sand.

He meanders over to inspect the find, "Boot prints," he says, noticing they're relatively fresh and go on for quite a while. "Heading west...where are you taking me?" he ponders, deciding to follow them. He returns to his vehicle. There isn't a moment to lose, just in case this man is still alive, however he's expecting to find Michael face down in a ditch somewhere. Slowly, the Landcruiser lurches forward, pulling the caravan in the direction of the footprints.

For fifteen painstaking minutes, he's following the prints along the sandy dirt road. He's only travelled two and a half kilometres when he spots something on the ground. As he approaches, it becomes clear what it is, "the blanket." he says. He stops to investigate, picking it up, holding it out in front of him. It is covered in dry, crusty blood. "Where are you, Michael?" he says, bewildered, shaking his head. He scans the landscape in every direction, none of it is making any sense.

He discards the blanket and returns to the Landcruiser, deciding to continue to follow the path laid out for him. He cannot believe he's made such an error. Thirty plus years of clinical practice including a decade of field work in some of the world's most dangerous places tells him he was right. He's dead, he witnessed Michael taking his last breath. But the evidence says otherwise.

He doesn't drive far before he spots another object in the distance. It looks like someone walking in the middle of the road. His heart rate jumps as he accelerates. As he draws closer, he can tell it's a man, 'It has to be him but how?' His mind is at war with itself, it cannot be true. Trepidation builds within him, not knowing what reception he'll receive.

The Landcruiser and caravan rattle over the corrugated road like some great land-train, thundering along, throwing dust clouds high into the air behind it. He's close enough to see the man, he's slightly built, 6ft or so tall, with long dark, slightly curly hair. He's wearing the same type of denim shirt, jeans and boots as Michael.

He overtakes the man on the road; as he drives past, they lock eyes, giving each other a strange look. It's Michael but he looks totally different. He stops and hops out of the Landcruiser. The man also stops walking. As the red dust swirls around them, they stare at each other in silence. Ken can't believe what he's seeing: his clothes are clean, his pale skin is now a deep olive, much darker in complexion than before, his beard is full as opposed to a wispy thin goatee, and even the deep dark rings around his eyes are gone. He looks healthy and almost completely different.

"This can't be real," Ken says, stumbling over the words.

"Why not?" the man asks.

"Because you died last night, or at least, I think you died, if you are Michael?"

The man nods and replies, "I'm not Michael, but you're right, he did die last night and don't worry, you did everything right." Ken doesn't even recognize the voice he's hearing. It's not an Australian accent, but rather this man is speaking with a slight accent of some other kind, one he doesn't recognise.

"How would you know if I was thinking that?" Ken asks him.

The man breaks into a lopsided grin, "I know everything about you...Ken," he says in a friendly tone.

"You know me?" he asks, his anxiety levels rising higher, "because if so, you have me at a disadvantage, sir?"

"I know everything about everyone," he replies calmly, walking a few steps closer to Ken who edges back towards his vehicle.

"You don't need to be afraid."

"Why would I be afraid?" Ken responds, as a gust of hot wind roars off the desert floor, hitting him in the face and triggering a memory within him. This is familiar, and it strikes him, "My God!" he exclaims, "This is it; this is the dream I've been having and you're the one in my dreams."

A radiating black hole obscures his vision, he is dizzy and feels himself about to faint.

Ken reaches out for the open door of the Landcruiser and grabs hold of it. He closes his eyes and hangs on to steady himself. This location, the wind increasing, it's all playing out exactly as it did in his dreams. He doesn't understand it, "How can this be?" he asks, confused by the *"de-ja-vu."*

"Just try to stay calm," the man says but Ken can't hear him above the screaming wind. He can see his mouth moving but can't hear a thing, just like in the dream. He panics, reaching across for Michael's shotgun. He lifts it up, pointing it directly at the man, cocking the right barrel, ready to fire.

"What the hell is going on here?" Ken shouts, taking aim. Now he is afraid.

Immediately, the man lifts both his hands in the air as a sign of surrender, staying calm, "I can explain," he replies but before he can say another word, Ken cuts him off.

"Lift up the front of your shirt!" he orders the man, shaking the gun, seeking nothing other than compliance.

"Ken, please let me explain -"

"Lift your shirt up!" Ken yells, his eyes bulging and his face red and contorted by fear. With little choice, the man begins to unbutton his shirt. "Slowly," Ken orders as the wind dies down as quickly as it rose, "just in case you have another weapon in there, Michael."

"I'm not armed," the man replies, chuckling, finding something funny, "you know, for a man who wanted to die, you sure seem scared of dying."

"I don't know what you're talking about," Ken retorts with false bravado, knowing full well what he's talking about. The question is how does this man know?

"Sure, you do, but don't worry, I'm not here to hurt you, I'm here to help you, Ken," he says, lifting up the shirt to reveal a perfectly clean, smooth stomach with an impressive six-pack. There are no injuries of any kind. No wounds, not a drop of blood anywhere to be seen.

Ken staggers, trying to keep his balance and not fall. He saw the massive injuries; he pronounced him dead. It's too much for him; he can't make sense of it.

"What are you playing at?" he yells. The man slowly and carefully walks closer to Ken who is struggling to retain any semblance of control over himself. Somehow Ken keeps the weapon trained on him.

"There's no trickery," he says calmly, "let me explain..."

Ken cuts him off again, "You are dead! This is not real!" he screams, his panic is evident.

"You're right, Ken," the man replies, "Michael did die..."

"Then who the hell are you?" He shouts at the man, again not letting him answer the question completely.

"You know who I am, Michael told you last night I was coming." Ken searches his memory and remembers the dying man's ramblings.

"What, you're Jesus Christ?" he asks, laughing and choking, hysteria building, not able to believe his ears.

"That's right, I am Jesus, Yeshua, the Son of God," the man replies with a steely look, "and we have a lot work to do." He walks directly towards Ken in a purposeful stride.

"Don't come any closer!" Ken barks,

Jesus shakes his head, "You can't hurt me, Ken."

"I'm warning you, not another inch!" But Jesus shows no sign of halting his advance. Ken pulls the trigger, intent on showing his resolve to protect himself by firing a warning shot above the man's head but when the right hammer falls, nothing happens; no discharge, no bang, just a click.

Ken tries the left barrel, squeezing the trigger but there's nothing but a click. Jesus reaches him and takes the gun from his hands, throwing it onto the ground. Ken stands still, frozen with fear. He gently places both his hands on Ken's shoulders and he feels instantly lightheaded, as a strange sensation sweeps over him. His anxiety and panic subside; his heart rate is slowing. Jesus looks deeply into his eyes with affection.

"What's happening to me?" Ken asks in a shocked whisper. He's terrified, yet exhilarated.

Jesus stares into his eyes, as though he's looking inside his soul. "I am Jesus, Yeshua, the Son of God, and we have work to do." He repeats, placing his left hand over Ken's eyes which causes him to lose consciousness. He falls but Jesus catches him, laying him gently on the ground, commanding him to rest.

⟫⟫ ⟪⟪

Ken's eyes fling open and he finds himself on his bed inside the caravan. For a brief moment, he'd forgotten why was he sleeping, but that's short-lived as he remembers the events of the day. A part of him believes it was just a dream, but the logical part of him knows that it happened.

He smells smoke wafting into the van. The pleasant aroma of natural wood burning eases him and makes him think of home. Slowly, he sits up and sees a glow outside the window which filters through the curtains into the darkened van. Another day has passed in the blink of an eye.

Why did he pass out? Probably the stress and exhaustion of the last few weeks caught up with him. However, he knows that whatever the reason, he can't let it happen again, otherwise he would be leaving himself vulnerable and at this man's mercy. That's something he's not comfortable with.

He cautiously peeks through the curtains to see 'Jesus,' as he now calls himself, outside sitting there by the fire. A sense of shame comes over him, he cannot believe he pointed a weapon at another human being; warning shot or not, there's no excuse. He recalls the sensations which he had never experienced before. For lack of a better term, it was an out-of-his-body experience. It was as though he was watching it from a distance.

Ken has to assume that this 'Michael' come 'Jesus' still has the shotgun. He sighs heavily, knowing if he is to ensure his own safety, he will need to break his own rule again. The thought sickens him. He recalls what the man said to him earlier, *"That he is scared of dying."* Well, he's right, he is scared, scared he won't see his daughter again. If he is to die prematurely, then it will be on his own terms and not someone else's. Nothing is going to stop him from seeing Gemma again.

He was searching the cupboards for the brown leather case which Ken was certain he'd packed before leaving home. After a few worrisome moments, he finds it and takes out the 38 mm pistol, wedging it down the back of his trousers.

It's time to find out what's going on, he needs some kind of explanation as to how this man managed to resurrect himself, what trick he used, because he isn't buying the 'Jesus' thing. No, he's a criminal and a con man, that is clear. He just has to remain calm, be patient, otherwise this misadventure will end badly for him.

The sun is almost set and he can feel the desert chill of night creeping in. He opens the door and steps onto the ground. Ken approaches the man, who appears to be meditating. He stands there in silence, staring at him, thinking how perfectly he matches the figure in his dreams. He still looks a lot like Michael, but, at the same time, he doesn't, like two sides of a coin, different but part of the one.

He doesn't know what to do or say next, maybe he should take his weapon out and get it over and done with, or should he wait? In the end, he just stands there, watching the man closely.

"Hello Ken," Jesus says, breaking the silence, his eyes remaining closed, "did you have a good rest?"

"I did...thank you," he replies, not seeing the gun and feeling safe to approach the fire with due caution.

"Are you able to have a proper discussion with me, about what happened? Will you give me the chance to explain?" the man asks, hoping to clear the air.

"Well, that depends," Ken asks in reply, "am I your prisoner?"

Jesus opens his eyes and makes direct eye contact with him, giving him a serious look with his shining brown eyes, before breaking out into a wide smile.

"What makes you think you're my prisoner, you're the one with the gun?"

"What makes you think I have a gun?" Ken asks, dismissing the suggestion, completely surprised by the comment.

Jesus realises he has to give a little in order to move this situation along.

"The gun you took from the leather bag and have now shoved down your pants?"

Ken has been caught with his hand in the cookie jar. He looks back in the direction of the van to see if anyone could have seen what he was doing but there is no possible way, the curtains are tightly drawn, and its pitch-black inside - not a chance.

"You have to admit from my perspective, this is overwhelming," Ken says, quickly changing the subject.

Jesus nods, "I can, you're only human." he replies smiling.

"And so are you." Ken adds, letting the man know he isn't buying his story in the slightest.

Jesus sighs, trying to find the best way to explain it to a man who doesn't want to listen.

"This body you see here is Michael's body. He died and I restored it. I'm using his body for the work we have to do."

Ken looks sceptically at him, showing no emotion

He continues, "In order to live in this universe created by my Father, a person needs to be born into it. Michael's soul left as I entered, it was an agreement he and I made. When we are finished, I will return to the Father and Michael's body will be commended back to the earth."

"Then why do you still look human? Where's the halo and the beaming brilliant white light that's supposed to surround you? Where are the angels and the cherubs?" Ken bombards him.

Jesus chuckles, "Like many others, you have bought into centuries of creative licence, as you call it. What you are seeing is an amalgam of Michael's body and my spirit."

Ken takes a seat on the ground, on the opposite side of the campfire, finding it fascinating from a clinical perspective, but impossible on a personal level.

"It's difficult to accept what you are saying. Nearly twenty-four hours ago, you were dead, half your intestines were falling out, mangled. There is no doubt about it, but to look at you now, nearly a totally different person, completely healed and no sign of your injuries."

"What does that tell you?"

"It tells me, I need to figure out how have you achieved this miracle."

"How do think?" Jesus asks smiling, Ken once again scoffs.

"You expect me to believe you are the real Jesus Christ, sent from heaven above just to see me? Pull the other one, will you, it plays jingle bells."

"Is that so hard to believe?" Jesus follows up, "You have the proof before you."

"You're asking me to believe in something I know to be impossible."

Jesus cuts him off, "Why is it impossible, do you distrust even your own eyes, do you not know the truth when you hear it?"

"I know bullshit when I hear it, especially from a man who wants to avoid jail for nearly killing a young girl and her mother." He can't argue with the doctor, he's right.

"I agree that's how it may seem to you, and yes, Michael did some terrible things when he had his time on Earth. He is now getting the help he needs, but I am not he, I am me, I am who I say I am."

This man seems intent on sticking to his story and it's driving Ken beyond frustration. He can't possibly consider his claims, not without tangible proof. He rubs his head, it hurts, another anxiety overload isn't far away.

"I will admit, I am at a loss to explain your apparent resurrection, your return to health and complete change of appearance which doesn't mean I won't figure it out."

"I'm sure you'll get the answers you need. We will have plenty of time to discuss these things and more," Jesus says, as he throws more branches onto the fire.

"I'll ask again, am I your prisoner?"

Jesus shakes his head. "Of course, not," he replies, "no more than I am yours."

"So, I could just drive off and leave you here, if I want to, is that right?"

"Well, you can try, but your vehicle won't work," Jesus says.

"Why, what have you done to it?" Ken, defensive, concerned that his car has been tampered with.

"I have done nothing to your vehicle."

"Then why do you say it won't work?" Ken asks, becoming more alarmed.

"Because my father won't allow it, not until we've spoken properly about the work we need to do, until you agree to see what he wants to show you."

"And what would that be?"

"You will see, when the time is right," Jesus replies, "and by the way, don't be concerned about that weapon, it's right here." he says, pointing to the fire. Ken can see the shape of the gun's stock burning and being turned into charcoal.

He looks at the stranger with bemusement, he can't figure him out. "What do you want from me?" he asks, feeling the overload is imminent.

"The question is, what do you want from yourself?" Jesus asks.

Ken drops his guard slightly in the moment. "How can I answer that, when I don't know myself? Now, if you don't mind, I will take my leave of you for the evening...would you like me to set up a bed for you out here?" he asks. At least he can make sure his 'guest' is comfortable; he must try to be civil.

"That's kind of you but I'll be fine right here. One more thing, Ken," Jesus' adds, "I want to show you something." He throws several of the shotgun shells in Ken's direction, landing at his feet.

"What do you want me to do with these?"

"Break them open," Jesus requests, "It will make things much clearer for you."

Ken inspects the shells; he can see they are new and haven't been tampered with. Reluctant to play games, he decides to comply anyway and snaps one of the shells in his hands, breaking it like an egg. As he does so, its contents spill out onto the desert.

"Sand?" he gasps, to which Jesus nods.

"Now, do you understand me?"

Without another word, Ken scurries away to the safety of the caravan, immediately locking the door behind him. He stumbles in the darkness back to his bed, leaving Jesus - or whoever is out there - to their own devices. His heart rate is through the roof, his breathing is shallow and erratic. He needs to calm himself; he reaches beside the bed, feeling for his flask – got it! At this point, his mind is numb, he can't think, or perhaps he's thinking too much; either way, a fogginess fills his head. He can't even begin to reconcile the plausibility of the man's claims. What he's proposing is beyond Ken's reasoning. He takes a sip from the flask, where the calming effects are almost instant.

Feeling a little less frantic, he takes off his clothes, dressing down to a T-shirt and underwear, despite the outside cold. He wants to be comfortable as he lies down on the bed, ready for sleep, but his brain keeps ticking over. He places the gun under his pillow, for protection; at least the door is locked.

He looks towards the urn, illuminated by the glow of the fire, "What's happening, Carol?" he asks, "Any ideas, love?" He's alone and isolated with either a crazy man or a cunning criminal, either way, he is powerless.

In his mind, the only way he can get to the bottom of this situation is to follow his training, to follow the clues and physical evidence. Unfortunately, the physical evidence falls on his visitor's side at the moment and he absolutely cannot accept it., There must be a more logical, 'earthly' answer. He presses his head into the pillow, not wanting to think any more tonight. He doesn't want to dream; he just wants to sleep.

CHAPTER SIX

Another day has arrived. Ken is dreaming of something pleasant, judging by the smile on his face. Jesus sits on the side of the bed, watching him, so peaceful in slumber. He doesn't want to disturb him but he must. They have things to do today and there is little time remaining. Jesus is on a deadline.

"Ken," he calls to him in a gentle tone, with no response. Jesus calls him again, this time more forcefully.

"Ken, wake up!" he commands as Ken begins to stir. He opens his eyes to find Jesus sitting on the side of his bed, with a smile on his face.

Instantly, Ken flies into a rage, startled and upset to see this man inside his van.

"What the bloody hell are you doing here?" he yells, throwing himself to the far end of the bed, away from the intruder, "How did you get in anyway?"

Jesus smiles, as Ken huffs and puffs.

"I just walked through the door," Jesus states calmly, shrugging his shoulders.

"Rubbish, that door was locked, you tampered with it!" he insists, as his mind clears from his rude awakening.

"No Ken, I mean, I really just walked 'through' the door." he says casually, using his hands to demonstrate the motion.

"Rubbish!" Ken exclaims. "Well, seeing as you helped yourself inside, what do you want?" he demands, a sheet covering the lower half of his body.

"We have to get going, we have a long way to go."

"Go, go where? The only place we're going is back to town, to sort all of this out with the police."

Jesus shakes his head. "There's no time for that. There is somewhere we need to be."

"Really?" Ken chuckles, "Well, unless you're pointing a gun at me, it's not happening." He pauses, "Do you think I'm fool enough to assist you to escape the law?"

"No, of course not. I understand your scepticism, but there is something important happening, and you need to be there for it," Jesus adds, emphasising the importance of his request.

Ken feels very uneasy about it. He can read his body language: this man does have somewhere to be, but his motivation will be to get away from what he's done.

"And why do I need to be there?" Ken asks.

"My Father wants you to see something," Jesus replies.

"And what would that be?"

"As I said, you will have to come with me and see for yourself."

"Of course I do...Well, here's an idea, why don't you just pop yourself where you need to go, you know, being the Son of God, surely that's within your power, and I'll meet you there, how's that?" Ken's words drip with sarcasm. He is unwilling to go anywhere other than back to Cobar, but Jesus is intent on gaining his co-operation.

"Someone needs your help, and I need you to take me to him."

"Again, why don't you pop over there yourself, heal the person, and then return to wherever it is you go. Isn't that what Gods do, blow in and out when it suits them?" He senses this 'Jesus' is getting tired of his recalcitrance. If he pushes him a little bit more, he's convinced he can get him to break character and return to the criminal he was yesterday.

"Ken, I need your help, it's important!"

"And as I said, Jesus, unless you have me at gunpoint, the only place I'm heading is back to Cobar."

The two men share an awkward gaze, neither willing to change their position; it's going around in circles.

"I'll wait for you in your car," Jesus says, deciding to break the deadlock, leaving the caravan without further discussion. Ken scoffs at the temerity of the man to make such demands of him, *"Who does he think he is?"* Ken knows he has one final card to play to end this game, unfortunately, it doesn't seem like he has any other choice.

After taking a few minutes to get ready for the day, Ken, reaches for the gun from under the pillow. He quickly wedges it in the right-hand side pocket of his pants for quick access, readying himself to take this man in to face justice. As he exits the van, he pushes the door forward but it won't budge, it's locked! "Odd, it should be unlocked?" he mutters, assuming it was open from when Jesus forced his way in. He unlocks the door, dismissing it from his mind as he steps out.

He approaches the driver's side of the car and sees Jesus sitting in the front passenger's seat, with a big smile on his face like a kid going to the shops to buy a secret bag of lollies.

Ken gets into the car, wondering if this man really does have some mental issues.

"I've never been in a car before," Jesus states.

"Really, I find that hard to believe," Ken replies dryly, rolling his eyes.

"Well, of course Michael had, but I haven't, it's quite exciting."

"Do you mind if we don't talk," Ken requests, not wanting to listen to another word out the man's mouth. He's had enough of this charade and is going to force the issue.

The skies are clear, the bluest shade of blue you have ever seen – it's a big sky, the full 360-degree view is stunning.

"Beautiful, isn't it?" Jesus asks, receiving a grunt in return. "Let this be my first lesson to you: whilst the destination is ultimately important, equally so is the journey itself."

"And let me guess, life is the journey?" Ken asks condescendingly.

"Yes, that's right, the journey prepares you for the destination," Jesus replies enthusiastically.

Ken engages first gear, and the juggernaut lurches forward, however instead of continuing straight ahead into the unknown, Ken immediately does a U-turn in the direction from where they came.

"What are you doing?" Jesus' asks, concerned by the turn.

"You can you read my mind, can't you, Jesus?" Ken asks.

"No!" he states categorically, "We don't interfere with free will."

"Well, that's good to know," Ken says, "because we're heading back to town to sort this out." Jesus becomes frustrated.

"I told you, we have somewhere we need to be and it's the other direction. Please, turn the car around."

"I am afraid you are going to be very late," Ken says, as they head towards Cobar, an unknown number of hours away.

"Ken, please, we don't have time for this," Jesus says in a sterner tone. He reaches out and touches the dashboard. When his hand makes contact, the car instantly loses power and comes to a slow stop.

Ken looks at him in dismay, wondering how he did that with a simple touch. "What did you do to my car?" he exclaims.

Jesus smiles, "This vehicle is not damaged, however, it will not start again until you agree to take me where we need to go."

"Rubbish!" Ken insists, "you did something to the car while I was asleep, like a kill switch or something, I'm sure it's something simple." He hops out of the Landcruiser, strides to the front, lifts the hood, and starts tinkering around.

He checks all of the cables and connections; everything appears to be in order. He can't see anything out of the ordinary to support his theory about some kind of manipulation of the car's systems.

He returns to the driver's seat and tries to re-start it, but no dash lights come on, no static from the radio, nothing.

Ken is a handy backyard mechanic when it comes to cars, its failure to start contradicts his examination, this only leaves him with one conclusion.

"Well, that's that, the battery's dead, and I don't have another one," he says, frustrated this has happened a million miles from anywhere. Jesus smiles like a Cheshire cat and shakes his head.

"No, Ken, there is nothing wrong with your vehicle. I told you, we need to go that way and unless you agree, the car will not start again...ever." This man is pushing things, just as Ken had: it's so ridiculous as far as he's concerned.

"Are you suggesting that unless you obtain my complete compliance you will not allow this car to start?"

"Yes," Jesus replies calmly, "that's exactly what I am saying."

Ken lets out a sceptical bellow.

Jesus gently touches the dash one more time, ever so lightly, with the very tip of his finger and the car instantly starts. Ken's laughter immediately stops.

"I didn't expect the Son of God would revert to blackmail, this is some kind of trick, isn't it?" He reaches over and starts banging the same part of the dash Jesus had touched, but nothing happens, the car keeps running. Jesus touches the same spot once more and the car instantly stops.

"A trick, is it?" Jesus asks.

"You've done something to my car."

"Ken, you just tried it yourself and it didn't work for you, how do you explain it?"

"As in the other matters you have presented me with, I can't, at least not yet," he replies defiantly.

"Your ears are dull of hearing and your eyes are closed," Jesus replies.

Ken retorts, "Beware of false prophets who come to you in sheep's clothing."

Jesus nods, knowing the conversation is going around in circles again, unless they can arrive at some accommodation.

"How about this, Ken, turn the car around and take me where we need to be, and at the end, if you're not satisfied, I will go to the police with you, willingly? Jesus offers.

"What's wrong with right now?" Ken reaches for his weapon, intending to break their deadlock.

Jesus waves his hand in front of both of them as if to swipe a fly. "Don't bother with the gun, Ken, it's gone!"

He reaches into his pocket for the gun. "Impossible!" he shouts, desperately feeling his trousers. He had it when he entered the car, he felt it press against his leg when he sat down. He jumps out of the car again, frantically searching the area around the vehicle in case he dropped it.

Jesus looks calmly on.

After several minutes of searching, Ken is satisfied the gun is nowhere to be found, it's vanished. Dispirited, he looks at his passenger, knowing he's lost his leverage; he doesn't seem to have many options.

He returns to his driver's seat; he can't stand to think this weird character has got the better of him, even if it's just momentarily.

"What do think, Ken?" Jesus asks, "Will you help me do what I have to do and then, if you don't believe me, I will turn myself in?"

"It doesn't seem I have much of a choice now, does it?" Ken replies, feeling more vulnerable than he's ever been. He nods his head, signalling an agreement, surrendering for the moment, just to see where this goes. "Very well...Jesus," Ken says, "I will hold you to your word."

"Agreed," Jesus replies, smiling, the deadlock is over and he's won this one, "I told you that you would do this willingly," he says gleefully.

Ken huffs, "I thought you said you don't interfere in free will?"

"I don't," Jesus replies, "but my Father, he has a plan for everyone."

"Well, where I come from, there's a word for this, it's called coercion. I'm hardly doing this willingly."

Again, Jesus touches the dash, restarting the car. Ken engages the first gear, moving the car forward, completing another U-turn before slowly proceeding down the track into the unknown.

Chapter Seven

The track is rugged, yet despite the dips and bumps Jesus has somehow managed to get some rest over the last few hours. He wakes, and Ken notices how rested he looks; obviously, he employs some kind of meditation technique.

"Enjoy your sleep?" Ken enquires.

Jesus nods, "I wasn't asleep, but I do feel rested, thank you."

Ken's curiosity gets the better of him, "What where you doing then, meditating?"

"Something like that...besides, you don't want to hear the answer, given you doubt who I am?"

"I would like to hear it, that is, if you don't mind telling me," he asks, wondering what this charlatan will come up with next.

"Alright, I was talking to my Father."

Ken smirks, not taking the answer seriously, "What, you were talking to God?"

"Yes."

"And how is he, and what did he have to say?" Jesus detects the sarcasm and won't take the bait.

"I'll tell you when you're ready to hear it."

Ken had never forgotten the teachings of his father that were 'thumped' into him as a young boy. Regardless, he remembers them well enough to expose this fellow as a fraud. He is hoping by challenging the man, making his deception obvious, frustrating him, that he'll revert to who he truly is.

"Can I ask you a question?"

"Yes, if I can answer it, I will."

"What's heaven like?"

Jesus beams with excitement. "It's more beautiful than you can imagine, colours so bright and vibrant, deeper and richer than anything on Earth," he explains, shaking his head. "The language of man can't do my description justice, it's something you really have to experience for yourself."

"Experience?" Ken asks, "I don't know if that will be for me."

"All souls are created in heaven, Ken; you've already been there; you just don't remember it."

"And why is that, why can't I remember any of it?"

Jesus chuckles once more.

"Do you remember anything that your mother told you when you were a one-year-old?"

"No, of course not, I was a mere baby."

"Then it's the same answer." Jesus replies, smiling. It makes Ken stop and think for moment. He needs a better question.

"So, does everyone go to heaven?" he asks, convinced this will be the one to get him.

"Almost," Jesus replies.

"What, even sinners, they get to go to heaven?" Ken asks, surprised by the statement.

Jesus turns towards him, focusing, taking the question seriously. "Let me ask you a question: would you turn your back on your child, even if they had broken the law?"

Ken doesn't even need to think about the answer.

"No, of course not, I don't know how any parent could."

"And, as a parent, don't you always try to steer your child into the right direction, towards a better path in life. To be good and just?"

"Of course, again, what decent parent doesn't?" he replies.

"And you would try everything you could, to save them from themselves, even if they refuse to listen to you?"

A serious expression comes over Ken's face. "I could never turn my back on my child, even if she did break the law. Yes, she would have to face the consequences of her actions, but I would support her through it. If she rejected my help, then I would like to think she would find her way back to me when she's ready. But to answer your question, I could never give up on my child, **never**. "

Jesus smiles broadly. "Amen, Ken. Now you have your second answer."

Again, the simplicity of Jesus's remarks has given him pause - he expected a more fabricated reply, not one that makes sense.

"So, you're saying, in essence, the things I want for my child are the same things God wants for each of us, and as such, he won't turn his back on us, is that correct?"

Jesus gives a nod in confirmation. "If you keep your heart open to him, yes!"

"That's not what I was taught. I was taught that if we sin we go to hell regardless, that's it. I've always assumed that's where I'll end up."

"Why would you say that?" Jesus asks.

"Because I've sinned."

"According to who, God?"

"No, because the dogma says so, and that's what I was taught growing up."

"And there's the problem with some of these 'religions,' that were created in my name. They try to control everything and everyone, but that's not what I taught. I taught love and compassion for your neighbour, to care for each other, to love the Father as he loves you, not to fear him."

Ken wishes that last statement was true. If only it did work like that, however his experiences lead him to a different conclusion. According to his father, Ken has a VIP reservation in hell for rejecting the Word of

God, and for his reverence of earthly teachings and material things, such as science and women.

He goes to ask his next question but Jesus interjects,

"That's a bigger answer than you're ready to hear at the moment."

"What is?" Ken asks.

"You're going to ask me, why does God allow bad things to happen to good people?" Ken is stunned, that's exactly what he was going to ask.

"I thought you said you wouldn't read my mind?"

"I didn't, it's a common question," Jesus replies.

"I see. Well try me, I think I can handle it?"

Jesus thinks for a moment and shakes his head, "No, I don't think you are ready."

Ken tries to bait him. "I thought you wouldn't have an answer for me, probably too complicated for you to explain."

Jesus knows what he's doing,. "Very well, remember, this is what you wanted?"

Ken nods, doubtful this chap will have anything of substance to tell him.

"People break the laws of man and the laws of God, and as you said, they must face the consequences of their actions."

Ken interjects, "I understand that, but why are innocent people the ones who have to suffer for it?"

"There are no bystanders, everyone in this world is an active participant. Do you know why my father created this place?"

Ken shakes his head.

"So that your soul can grow. So, it can learn what it's like to experience, not only a physical life, but my father's love in his creations. A soul cannot grow if it does not know pain from happiness, or victory from defeat, or even life from death. When you have a child, that joy you have, that's what the father feels when a new soul is created. The love you feel when you look at your baby, it's the same for him. You even feel the same pain he feels when they ignore you and turn away. He wants you to feel what he feels, that's why he created this place."

Ken can relate to the statement, especially the part about your kids, but Jesus still hasn't answered the question as far as he's concerned.

"But how does that relate to those who die from sickness through no fault of their own?"

"You mean like your wife?" Jesus asks, stopping Ken mid-rant.

"How do you know about that?" Ken asks, perplexed.

"I told you; I know everything about you," Jesus replies, before continuing, "But to answer your question, if someone dies of a sickness, then it's a sickness born of this world, not of God. He does not hand out disease as a punishment. There are laws of man and laws of God, so too there are laws of nature."

"So, it's just bad luck?" Ken asks sharply, infuriated by his answer. It is just the type of rubbish he'd been expecting; the imposter couldn't keep it up.

He wants to knock his block off for bringing his wife into it, 'How dare he?' However, as someone who abhors violence, he has to let it go. Breathing deeply, he allows his anger to subside, before it escalates into conflict which would be a waste of time. He reminds himself he's dealing with a conman, and so his anger turns to laughter.

"You almost had me there. I almost forgot you're not the real Jesus Christ."

"And, as I told you, you weren't ready to hear the answer," Jesus replies, closing his eyes, ending the conversation.

⇉⇉⇉ ⇇⇇⇇

Several more hours have passed since silence fell upon them. Ken has been stewing on his passenger's comments. He's calmer now, but still angry that he's been forced to drive out to nowhere. What's even worse is the heat. He looks at his watch, it's almost midday. He's amazed at how hot it is at this time of year. There are no beaches or sea breezes to cool things down out here.

He's refusing to use the car's air-conditioner. He's convinced it uses too much fuel. It's probably an old wives-tale, but he isn't going to take the chance. No, for now he's happy to get some relief when the air blows through the window as he picks up speed. His companion, on the other hand, looks as fresh as a daisy, despite wearing denim. For whatever reason, he is not feeling the heat at all.

Again, Jesus's eyes flick open as though some internal alarm brought him back to the here and now. He sits forward, his vision is fixed on the road ahead. He points to something in the distance that escapes Ken's ability to see.

"We need to take the next left," Jesus says, "There will be a sign."

"What kind of sign?" Ken is fed up with the lack of details.

"You will know when you see it."

They continue down the track for a few hundred metres. As they round the next bend, Ken can see a large mound of rocks, but that's not all. There are two thick, wooden branches in the shape of a cross mounted at its top, exactly as it was in his dream. *"How?"* he asks himself, dumbfounded, with no way to explain it. Instantly, he feels that band tightening around his head again.

"This is it," Jesus says, staring at his driver, as though he expects him to make some remark about the sign, but Ken keeps quiet. The vehicle creaks while slowing to take the turn.

Shortly thereafter, they travel over a small hill where an old, weather-beaten shack sits in the middle of nowhere. An old rusted truck sits out front, again exactly as he had dreamt.

"We're here." Jesus says.

Ken only nods, as he brings the little convoy to a halt. He feels hollowed out and weak. He could never have conceived of the things which have occurred. If he believed in such things, he had a premonition of these scenes in his persistent dreams. He rubs his forehead, puzzled, and cannot settle on what to believe.

Perhaps it was pure coincidence? However, he knows the mathematical odds are beyond astronomical.

"What are we doing here?" Ken asks, wary of getting out of the car, wishing he had his gun.

"Seeing a friend," Jesus replies, aware of Ken's discomfort.

"You've been here before then?" Jesus shakes his head,

"Never."

"Then how did you know how to get here?"

"I had some good instructions but you know this place as well, don't you?"

Ken is grasping for answers and remains silent, trying to focus on what they are doing here.

They can see the door is wide open, swaying slightly in the hot wind. Both men slowly alight and gaze about them, surveying the area, as Jesus heads straight for the front door.

"Can you please bring your medical kit? Henry's going to need your help," Jesus asks kindly.

"Who is Henry?" Ken asks, wondering what he's walking into.

"A friend who needs a doctor." This comment puts him into work mode where he doesn't question what's going on. Someone needs him, that's all that matters. He opens the back door of the car and retrieves his medical kit, before walking to the door where he follows Jesus into the shack.

A strong odour of urine assaults them; it's a musky stale stench made more potent by the heat. The house is a basic two-room cabin. The first room they enter has a rickety table, two chairs, and a stove, together with something that looks like an old cool box.

A wave of dust circulates through the room, pushing up through the cracks in the floor. Each puff of the breeze reveals strands of light seeping through the cracked roof and shining across the room. The floor is a rotten mess which creaks with each step, 'Am I going to fall through it?' Ken thinks.

Another door leading to the second room is partially open. A man is lying on the bed with a lightweight sheet covering his abdomen.. He is coughing and spluttering like an old lawn mower. Blood-soaked rags are scattered on the floor around the bed.

Jesus takes the lead, "Let me enter alone, please Ken, I'll call you."

"As you wish," Ken replies, happy to defer to his judgment, as he looks for a place to sit.

Jesus opens the door fully; it swings freely to reveal an old Aboriginal man, with a flowing grey beard on the bed. Both men stare at each other and smile as Jesus closes the door behind him.

The old man begins to speak in his traditional language which Ken isn't familiar with, but can hear clearly as the old wooden walls don't allow much privacy. To Ken's surprise, Jesus responds to the old man in the same language. They have what seems to be a nice chat, given the old man's poor condition.

Although he can't understand what's being said, Ken gleans the two men know each other well. They speak as if there's a great deal of affection between them.

After a few minutes, the door gently re-opens.

"Please come in, Ken, this is Henry," Jesus gestures to him. Henry tries to lift his head but can only manage to wave a greeting. Jesus looks at Henry with brotherly love in his eyes and says "We are old friends."

"Hello, Henry," Ken says in his doctor's tone, "pleased to meet you."

"He's a doctor, Henry, he's going to help, and see if he can make you more comfortable," Jesus explains. This time the old man nods.

"Please see what you can do for him, Ken, I'll be outside," Jesus leaves the room as Ken takes one of the chairs from the kitchen and places it next to Henry's bed. It is rather wobbly so he sits down cautiously.

Ken unpacks his medical kit, taking out his stethoscope, placing in the customary position around his neck. Next, he pulls out the bladder for measuring blood pressure, wrapping it firmly around Henry's arm.

"So, are ya a good doctor?" Henry croaks.

"I like to think so," Ken replies, pumping the bladder, measuring the old man's vitals, mentally noting the numbers. When he's finished, he expels the air and has a concerned expression on his face. His patient's blood pressure is dangerously low.

"It's OK, doc, I know I'm dyin'," Henry says, not wanting the doctor to fuss too much.

"Why don't you let me be the judge of that," Ken replies with a smile.

He takes the stethoscope, placing it on Henry's chest,

"Just breathe normally for me, please," not asking him to sit up as he's too weak. He listens intently.

As the old man breathes in and out, Ken hears obstruction after obstruction in his lungs. His situation is dire.

After a few more checks, he knows his patient is suffering end-stage lung cancer. An X-ray would confirm it, but regardless, he knows the poor fellow is in his final days of life, perhaps even his final few hours.

"Henry, when we walked in here, the other man spoke to you in your own language, what did he say, if you don't mind me asking?"

The old man smiles back.

"He said you would ask me that."

"Did he?"

"Yeah, he said you would ask me and I told him, I would tell you if you did."

"Do you mind if I ask you what you two talked about?"

"He asked me if I knew who he was, I said 'Yes.' He told me he'd come to keep his promise to take me home."

"And when did he tell you this?" Ken asks, trying to find some evidence it is the next step in a con, despite the fact that the old man's illness is very real.

"He visited me in my dreams and told me everything will be OK."

This information prompts him to think about his own dreams, but his were different, and he isn't dying.

He pushes for one more question, then he'll let him rest.

"You said he'd come to take you home, so where's home for you?"

His patient looks bemused, "You know."

Ken shakes his head; he has no idea what he's talking about.

"To heaven son, home to heaven."

Ken concludes the examination as fast as he can, desperate to get out of the room so he can think and breathe.

"I'll let you rest," Ken says, "I'll be back a little later."

His patient settles back in his bed, exhausted by the 5-minute consultation.

Ken's confusion grows, now more than ever. He can't deny his dreams or visions or ignore that Jesus knew of his dreams. A new emotion begins to take root within him: confliction.

He hurries out of the shack to find Jesus, staring out into the vast, desolate landscape.

As he approaches, Jesus speaks, "Can I ask you a question, Ken?"

"Of course."

"When you first met Michael, when he was in this body, did he look familiar to you?" Ken thinks about the question for a moment,

"It didn't really occur to me, but on reflection, I suppose so, a little."

"And what about now, do I look like the man in your dream?"

Ken doesn't want to give him any kind of emotional leverage by admitting it but he can't deny it.

"Yes," he answers, "you are exactly the man I saw in my dreams."

"My spirit healed this broken body when I entered it, I have demonstrated dominion over your man-made transportation device, I have made your destructive weapons vanish from sight. And now, we are here, in the company of a man whom I have never met. Not only was he expecting me, but he also accepts the truth of who I am and welcomes me.

I told you in your dreams I was coming. Whilst he was dying, Michael also tried to tell you, but yet you deny me, why?"

"Because, you're not the real Jesus," Ken replies bluntly, not holding back.

"And why do you say that? he asks, stunned by the frankness.

"Because God doesn't exist, and if he doesn't exist, how can Jesus?"

"What do you mean God doesn't exist, the evidence is everywhere around you, seek and you shall find?" Jesus challenges him.

Ken isn't letting him off the hook. "You had a shotgun to my head just 24 hours ago and now you want me to believe you are the son of God. How can I?"

"So you are judging me?"

"No, I am making a determination on the available evidence, and if you really want to get into it, how can a loving God exist in a world where evil is allowed to prosper, where innocent people suffer immeasurably and..."

He stops himself short, he's doesn't want to lose perspective, but his blood is beginning to boil.

Jesus wants him to finish what he was going to say; he wants Ken to free himself of his emotional shackles.

"And what, Ken? You wanted to speak your mind to God, here's your chance. Talk now, instead of screaming at him on a beach, drunk, in the middle of the night, finish the sentence," Jesus says sternly, calling him out.

Ken just stands there, shaking his head in disbelief. "I can't do this with you anymore," he says, intending to walk off,

"Do what?" Jesus replies, stepping in front of him, trying to force the issue.

"This...shit!" he yells, unable to contain himself, "I don't know how you know the things you do about me, but it's too much, you hear me, too much. I can't do it anymore!"

Jesus holds his hands up, expressing peace and calmness. "Listen to me, Ken, I know all these things are hard to accept, but I am who I say I am. You talk of 'available evidence,' fine, let's talk about it."

"No! God and Jesus cannot exist. If they did, they would not have allowed my wife to die, taking her away from me. She spent her life serving others and praising God, and for what? To die a slow and painful death? Tears fill his eyes as he thinks about Carol, unlocking the chest of feelings he thought he had buried.

Jesus understands his companion's grief, but he also knows he's taken the first step to becoming truly healed, to accepting the truth of things that have happened, whatever that might be. He places his hand on Ken's shoulder as Ken continues to sob.

Jesus smiles gently, "I think we're getting somewhere."

He then bends down and plucks a piece of grass, separating the seeds into his hand. "If you created a seed, and allowed it to grow in your garden, in time it would grow into a plant that would produce more seeds, and those offspring would produce seeds of their own, and this cycle will continue over and over." Jesus says, showing Ken the thirty or so seeds of grass in his hand. "Occasionally, a plant will die, or a damaged seed will not sprout, or...."

Ken interrupts him, he's not in the mood for a lecture. "What's your point?" he snaps.

Jesus is visibly frustrated. "The point is, Ken, the father created the original seed but how they turn out is up to nature. It isn't anyone's fault, sometimes seeds fail."

Ken looks at him blankly, "So you're saying people who get sick and die, it's just nature taking its course?"

"As I said to you before, it's the laws of nature. Some seeds are damaged by the conditions, sometimes it's passed down from an ancestor, maybe decades or hundreds of years before, and this was the person and the time it manifested," he replies calmly.

"You're talking about genetics; every bloody doctor knows that!" Ken retorts, "I don't know what I expected from you, I shouldn't have expected anything, given who you are."

"What do you want me to say?" Jesus asks gruffly.

"There's nothing you can say. You've given me an answer that God created the original creatures to live here, on some sort of set-and-forget basis, to see how we pan out. You make us sound like we're some kind of experiment he won't interfere with, that he'll observe, watching and judging who is suitable to join him in heaven," Ken replies.

"Free will is about non-interference, letting people choose their own path, right or wrong, good or bad."

"Or until a situation suits him," Ken adds, scoffing at the comment.

"He has a plan for everyone, Ken, even you," Jesus replies.

"Well, there goes free will if that's the case."

"It's hard to see how everything connects when you're in the moment. For humans, only hindsight can do that. As I explained, the journey prepares you for the destination."

"You're suggesting there is no such thing as coincidence, or random happenstance, that it is all some orchestrated pantomime?"

"Oh, it's more than that, much more," Jesus says assuring him he's wrong.

Ken has had enough, he has a patient who needs his attention. "I'll take your word for it," he says, walking off towards the caravan.

"One more thing, Ken," Jesus calls out, "When will he be able to travel?"

"Travel, travel where? This man has, maybe, hours left to live, he isn't able to travel anywhere."

Jesus shakes his head, "We need to take him with us," he says, "it's one of the reasons why I needed you."

As a doctor, he could never consider placing a patient at so much risk, not without a damn good reason. "Why risk it, why not just let him pass here?"

"Because I promised him I would take him home, back to his country, so he can join his ancestors."

"Yes, he thinks you're taking him to heaven," Ken remarks bitterly, suspecting he's led a dying man up the garden path.

"And I will, but first, I promised to take him back his land, and that's what we must do for him."

"You know, I have travelled the world, caring for people, I am sensitive to cultural beliefs but he may not even make it through the next hour, let alone a trip of who knows how far."

"I made a promise Ken, will you help me or not?" Jesus asks, desperate not to let the old man down.

Ken knows how important connection to their land is for an Aboriginal person; it means everything.

"Very well. I will help, but for him, not you! I will need at least 12 hours to try and stabilize him which means we will have to spend the night here."

"Thank you, Ken, I can't do this without you." Jesus replies, appreciative of his cooperation.

Ken steps in closer, looking directly into his eyes, and asks "Why don't you just repair him, like you did to this body."

"I can't," Jesus replies.

"Why not? Unless you are not who you say you are?"

"Do not tempt the Lord thy God, Ken," Jesus warns sternly.

"I'm not, I'm asking you to heal him, and not to let him die the way my wife did," Ken says sharply,

"Only my Father has that power and any power I have is through him. It is Henry's time to come home, as it was Carol's."

"I need to get back to Henry," Ken says tersely, leaving the conversation there, and heading to the caravan for medical supplies. Jesus whispers something to the seeds he has in his hands, before throwing them into the wind that will carry them to places in the desert.

⇝⇝⇝ ⇜⇜⇜

Ken trudges into the caravan, and sits down, thinking about the conversation, angry that he has again allowed this man to get under his skin. It's only mid-afternoon, and he's already exhausted, this whole episode is draining but he has a patient who needs him and that's more important. He grabs a small bottle of Glenfiddich from one of the drawers and takes a decent sip, just one though, enough to calm him. He puts the bottle back where he found it and turns his focus towards Henry, gathering the medical supplies he's going to need. He isn't convinced they'll be taking him anywhere, he's in such bad shape, but he will stay with him until the end.

His desire to be prepared to the point of being overprepared has so far served him well. Before he left Sydney, something told him he may need it, call it a gut feeling, or was it? So far, he has come across car accident victims and a man with end-stage cancer, what will be next? He leaves the caravan with packs of fluids which will help Henry as he's very dehydrated. Ken returns to the room where he finds Henry still asleep. Undeterred, he starts the treatment.

He finds a place on his patient's leathery arm to insert a drip. He uses a piece of old wire he found on the floor to secure the bag up high, letting gravity do the work. Ken measures his pulse, to make sure his patient is still alive, it's there - just - the fluids will help.

Using a syringe, he adds some liquid glucose into the solution to try and spark his patient. He has no idea how long it's been since Henry has eaten or if he could eat at all. When he wakes, he'll try him on some baby food he brought, and see if he can keep it down.

He continues to sit with his patient throughout the night, monitoring him carefully, catching some sleep here and there, regularly checking his vitals. His patient is comfortable and the coughing has abated a little.

When Ken dozed off, despite being slumped on the old chair, he dreamt of Carol and Gemma, and their simpler, happier times.

CHAPTER EIGHT

I t's dawn, the morning chorus reverberates throughout the windless desert. Ken wakes to the birdsong, extending his limbs, and letting out a subdued yawn. For a moment or two, he's back home in Sydney. Henry's snoring is part of the chorus; it's a good sign, he survived the night. He tends to his patient, taking his pulse and blood pressure which are stronger than they were last night, another good sign. He needs another saline bag; the old timer's body is terribly dehydrated and has taken a few bags since yesterday. Ken has fifteen bags left, hopefully it will be enough.

After changing the drip, he walks to the door to take in the morning. He sees Jesus, sitting cross legged on the ground, meditating; but he's not alone. Several of the desert's marsupials sit calmly around him as if they were tame pets waiting to be fed. Kangaroos, wallabies, dingoes, and even birds of prey sit peacefully with other animals that normally would have become their breakfast by now.

Whatever's happening here, these animals feel secure with this man, they know they can trust him. Ken has never seen anything like it outside of Taronga Zoo, *'Could this man really be 'The Christ?'* he asks himself, allowing his intellect to seriously entertain the possibility. Jesus lifts his arms high into the sky, exhaling, ending his meditation. At that moment, the animals take off in all directions.

Jesus looks relaxed, despite how cold the night must have been for him out there with no fire.

"You must have been freezing last night?" Ken enquires.

"My Father's warmth sustains me, he's all I need," Jesus replies. "How's our patient this morning?"

"Better," Ken replies, "he seems a little stronger, rehydration seems to be helping. He might be strong enough to take a trip after all, the next few hours will tell the story."

Jesus nods his approval, "Thanks to you, he may get his wish after all."

"Well, that would still be a miracle and is yet to come."

Jesus laughs, "That's the spirit, Ken."

For the first time since this ordeal began, he allows himself a laugh, briefly forgetting the insanity of the situation. It's been days since he'd eaten properly, if at all. In fact, he can't remember the last time he ate and his stomach growls like a bear.

"I need some food, surely you must be hungry as well?" Ken asks, to which Jesus nods in confirmation, "Right...well, I'll get us some breakfast, then I'll try feeding my patient."

Jesus stops him as he goes to leave.

"How do you feel this morning, I mean about our conversation yesterday?"

Ken thinks for a moment, before answering. "Truthfully...I've been so busy with Henry, I haven't had time to think about it," he replies, trying to dodge the conversation, especially at this time of the morning, he needs coffee, "Now if you don't mind, breakfast waits for no man."

>>>> <<<<

Jesus is praying over Henry, while Ken potters around the caravan preparing the food. Baked beans on toast with orange juice and a pot of hot coffee for the pair of them, and a tin of baby food for Henry if he can manage it. With no power available, he has to make toast and warm the baby food the old-fashioned way, by fire. Once ready, he loads everything onto a large tray and takes it into the house where he unloads his cache of food onto the table. He can hear Jesus praying in a soft gentle voice. He can hear the warmth and sincerity in his words; after a minute or so, the prayer comes to an end, Henry wakes and begins to speak, in English this time.

"How was that?" Jesus asks the old man who smiles back despite the pain.

"Jesus, what's heaven like?" he asks, "What am I gunna see?"

With a reassuring look, Jesus lays his hand gently on Henry's head, "Brother, it's beautiful, a wonderous place, it's a different state of being, there's nothing to fear, you will love it," he assures the old man who knows his end draws close.

"And what about, you know, the other one?"

"Sssh," Jesus says, "Do not worry, they are there as well."

"Thank you, Jesus," Henry replies, taking comfort in his words, "What will I do there?"

Jesus reassures the worried man. "Whatever you would like," he says simply, "however, I have something in mind for you, but we'll talk about that later."

Listening carefully, Ken clears his throat, loud enough to be heard.

"Breakfast is here," he declares, walking into the bedroom where his patient looks brighter.

"How are you feeling today, up to trying some food?"

Henry nods, "Yeah, I think so, doc."

"Good, it's puree of granny smith apples," Ken says, trying to make it sound inviting.

Jesus gets in on the act as well. "Sounds delicious," he says, standing up to walk outside,

Ken takes his place on the chair and leans over to feed his patient.

"You know doc, I can feed myself, I'm not a child, you know," Henry says, reaching for the can and spoon. Ken realizes he has accidently belittled the proud man. He doesn't want to rob him of his remaining dignity.

"Of course, I just didn't want you to overdo it, sorry," Ken says, embarrassed, handing over the can and spoon, "I'll leave you to it."

He joins Jesus at the table where he begins praying over the food. He waits for the prayer to finish before digging in.

"Giving thanks?" Ken asks as he reaches for the coffee.

"Always," he replies.

Ken pours a cup of coffee first, sipping it, and feeling that overdue caffeine hit. His enjoyment isn't lost on Jesus.

"Does it taste better than the bottle?" he asks, momentarily silencing the doctor who isn't going to question how he knows these things anymore; he just knows.

"In fact, yes, it does," Ken replies, glossing over the question, taking another gulp.

"I want to ask you a question this time," Jesus says, "why do you do it to yourself?"

Ken draws a blank, shrugging his shoulders. "Do what?"

"Torment yourself with guilt, over and over again. You hate yourself for not being there for Carol and Gemma. You seem rather content in your misery, feeling sorry for yourself."

"And what would you know about it?" Ken snaps back, pretending the comment slid off his back as he continues to eat.

"Everything! You can't change the past but continuing to torment yourself about it only leads to one place."

"And where would that be?" Ken chuckles.

"To the darkness."

On some level Ken knows he's right which is why he isn't erupting in anger. He knows he went to a pretty dark place before this trip, and he is not sure he's completely out of it.

"What would you suggest then, ask God to forgive me for squandering my marriage, my daughter?" he asks with a mouthful of food.

"Try forgiving yourself first. God's forgiveness is guaranteed!"

Ken stops what he's doing and thinks about those words.

"I'm not sure I can...I don't know how."

"Try one day at a time," Jesus says, as Ken nods, taking the advice on board.

⤞⤝

They finish their breakfast without another word being spoken. Ken has a lot to think about. He returns the remnants of breakfast to the caravan, cleaning them, before attending to Henry with some painkillers and a fresh bag of fluids. Jesus has vanished again, but Ken knows wherever he is, he won't be far away. He wants to ask him about Carol, but is afraid to. He's afraid that if he asks, he'll be sending a message that he believes his story, validating it, and he is far from sold.

He returns to the house with the fresh supplies and enters the bedroom to find Henry awake and alert, trying to change his body position.

"How's your pain?" Ken asks, as Henry grimaces as he moves.

"Alright I guess, doc," he replies, finding it harder to breathe. With every breath, the wheezing from his obstructed airways becomes louder. Ken places his stethoscope on his patient's back and listens. If only he could get him to a hospital, and gain a clearer picture of what's going on.

"We'll be leaving soon, to take you home to your country," Ken says.

"I know, doc. The nice lady told me you'll do your best, that I'm in good hands."

"Oh really, and what lady was that?"

"The pretty white lady I was dreaming about, she spoke to me."

"And she mentioned me, did she?" Ken asks, as he swaps out the bag of fluids.

"Yeah, she did."

"Tell me about her, the lady that is?"

110

"Well, she is tall, brown hair, likely about 50."

Ken allows himself a smirk, "Sounds like my type," he quips, "what else?"

"She had on brown trousers and a white top, a brown jumper over her shoulders, like a fashion model you see in them magazines, you know the ones?"

Ken nods, pretending to be interested in what he's describing, he's no fashionista.

"She has this red brooch thing...like, ah, like ah, you know, a horse's head, yeah, like a horse head."

A cold shiver runs down Ken's spine and his skin begins to tingle, now he is paying attention. It was the exact gift he had given to his wife on their last Christmas together. There is no way Henry could have known about it.

He finishes his work and goes to walk out the door, wanting to get out of there and collect his thoughts.

However, Henry has more to tell, "She gave me a message to give yar...did ya want to....."

Ken stands frozen in anticipation. his back towards his patient, "Yes," he utters. If there is the slightest chance the message is really from his wife, he wants to hear it.

"She said she feels like some cobblers," Henry speaks softly in a sing-song voice, "she said you would know what it means."

"Of course, she does," he says, leaving the room and rushing out of the shack, making a beeline for the safety of the caravan. He slams the door behind him.

Jesus appears out of nowhere, hot on his heels. He enters the van to find Ken, busying himself in an effort to suppress his feelings.

"I'm getting us ready to leave, I'll prepare the car for Henry shortly," he says, throwing things around in frustration, avoiding eye-contact.

"What's wrong?" Jesus asks in a caring voice.

"You're the Son of God, you tell me?" Ken snaps, "I'm sorry, but there is a man in there, dying, who claims to have had a conversation with my dead wife. He gave me a message, allegedly from her."

"Oh," Jesus replies, "I'm sorry if it upset you."

"Upset me?" Ken pauses, trying to keep himself in check, "What upsets me is that he was 100% right in what he said, and it's impossible!"

"I see," Jesus replies, "All I can say is that you should accept it for the rare gift it is."

Ken bites his tongue, choosing his words before continuing. "I've said many times, I don't believe that you, or any of this, can be happening. How many times do I need to say it?"

Jesus calmly replies, "But it is happening Ken."

"What do you mean?"

"On the beach, you asked God to 'show you he is real,' I am here, with you."

Ken's body is shaking uncontrollably.

Jesus finds his reaction understandable, given his human limitations. "It would help you a great deal if you were to surrender yourself to what's happening, surrender yourself to God instead of fighting what your heart is telling you is real."

But he can't surrender, not yet. "My mind controls my heart."

"When your heart and mind become one, in you, there is nothing you cannot do," Jesus replies.

"How can I trust you are who you say you are?" Ken whispers, his voice breaking. He is desperate to be convinced so his head will stop splitting apart.

"Trust what you see and what you hear, trust your heart," Jesus says, "If you cannot trust those, what else is there?"

"I don't know," he replies, wishing for a solution to his despair.

Ken sits on the bed, trying to calm his emotions and contemplating Jesus's advice. He stares at Carol's urn on the bench top. If she was here, this wouldn't be happening.

"When I was a child, I was made to study your book, the Bible, day in, day out, by my father who was a brute of a man at times, and your book never brought me as much comfort as a science book did."

"When you grew up and moved away, your father also tormented himself with guilt and anger," Jesus replies, surprising Ken who puts his hand up to stop him from continuing.

"Please, let's not go there at the moment. My point is, I need to be able to rationalise things in my head, I need evidence that makes sense, not leaps of fantasy."

Jesus decides a break is in order. "Perhaps you're right, we should be leaving soon, we have a long way to go."

"Good idea," Ken replies, wanting to be left alone.

"And by the way, it isn't my book, I didn't write it." Jesus says, walking out of the caravan, dropping a bombshell that distracts the doctor, who follows closely behind. There's no way he can let that comment go.

"What do you mean it isn't your book?" Ken asks, as they walk towards the Landcruiser.

"It isn't my book, I didn't write it, others wrote it, some long after I had left this world. Let me ask you, does a person write their own biography?"

"Not unless it's an autobiography." Ken replies dryly.

"Exactly." Jesus says, "The Bible isn't an autobiography, it's a collection of works, stories and teachings from when I was last here on Earth. Some consider it a guide to life, and I like that, because it contains many good things, but others treat it as though it is my biography, and it isn't. But it is something to take comfort in unlike the bottle."

Ken isn't going to get into it and ignores the comment as if it was never made, he has more pressing concerns.

"On a different note, I've been thinking, I'm going to need some help on this trip, with Henry."

"What do you mean help, can I do it?" Jesus asks in reply.

"I need medical help, as in another trained professional to monitor him while we travel, given his condition is precarious."

"I understand, I have friend close by who could help."

"Great! Until then, what would really help is if you could drive for a while so I can monitor Henry constantly, until help arrives."

"Drive?" Jesus asks in surprised tone, "You want me to drive your car?"

"Yes, would you mind?" Ken asks.

"Ah, well...I can't drive. Actually, I don't know how," Jesus says, plainly embarrassed.

A stunned look comes over Ken's face. "What do you mean, you can't drive a car?"

"Well, they weren't invented when I was last on Earth so I don't know how."

"Do you expect me to believe Jesus Christ, the all-knowing and omnipotent 'Son of God,' cannot drive a simple human motor vehicle?"

"It's a matter of man, not of heaven," Jesus replies, "If I was expected to do such a thing, I would know how, but I don't."

"You see Jesus, it's because of rubbish answers like that, I don't believe who you say you are. If you don't want to drive, just say no, instead of coming up with...bullshit!" he blows up and walks off back to the caravan, muttering and swearing.

Chapter Nine

An hour later, Ken has worked off his anger and frustration and is calm, ready to transport his patient. He empties the last of his fuel into the tank, hoping it will be enough until they can resupply. He doesn't know what their destination is, or how far they must travel to reach it. He's worried. Only Jesus knows that information, and he's not sharing it.

In preparation for the trip with Carol, Ken had custom work carried out on the rear bench seat of the Landcruiser. He had metal fabricators split the solid metal seat into two so one could be up and the other down, in case this type of situation arose. Now he can lay Henry down and care for him.

He calls out to Jesus who is wandering around the property. He signals for him to come over to him.

"Yes Ken, what is it?"

"We're ready to go, we'll place Henry on the longer side, I have cut up a spare foam mattress to make him as comfortable as I can, everything else is ready."

"That's great, I knew you could do it," Jesus says.

"Shall we bring him out and start the journey?"

The two men carry the patient to the car, with Jesus taking his upper torso and Ken his legs, while a saline bag sits on his chest.

With great care they place him into the car, almost exactly where Ken wanted him. He jumps into the backseat, to pull the dying man closer, head first. After some adjustments, his patient is finally situated, as Ken resets his fluids and places pillows all around him, to make Henry as comfortable as possible. He turns the air-conditioning on.

It's 9 a.m., the sun is already blazing, the heat is rising off the desert. Jesus is about to get into the passenger's side of the car when Ken stops him, saying "Where are you going?"

"Getting in the car."

Ken shakes his head. "Remember, I asked you to drive?"

Jesus remembers perfectly. "Yes, and I told you I can't drive."

Ken smiles, there's no escaping what he has in mind for Jesus, even though he's sure he's faking the *I don't know how to drive'* thing.

"I am going to teach you," he says sternly, "There's no traffic, no other cars, nothing to hit, just listen to my instructions and we'll be fine, OK?"

"Very well, I'll try, I'm a quick learner," Jesus replies, determined to prove his worth. Both men get in the car, Jesus on the driver's side and Ken in the rear passenger's seat, next to his patient.

"Now, given we are in the middle of nowhere, I will forgo the usual things, such as checking mirrors and indicators, we'll just concentrate on the basics."

Jesus nods confidently as Ken continues "Now, this is what is called a manual car, these gears go into order from one, two, three and four, the fifth one is reverse, and you move them in order to get the car moving."

"Yes, I have seen how you do that when you have been driving."

"Very good. The pedal on the left is the clutch, you depress that to move the gears, and release it slowly, whilst pressing the pedal on the right, the accelerator, which gives the car fuel and the power to move forward. Think of driving as a dance between the two."

Ken spends the next 10 minutes instructing his student on the nuances and mechanics of driving a manual car. They are on dirt roads, so they won't be going fast, they just need to stay on the road.

Jesus goes through all of the instructions, he's confident he can do it, it's time to drive.

"Are you ready?"

Jesus nods, "Yes, I am."

"Good, let's go."

As instructed, Jesus starts the car and lets it run before engaging the clutch and first gear, hearing the rev of the engine as he presses down on the accelerator,

"Just a little bit more power," Ken instructs, to which his student responds. The engine revs increase, "Now let the clutch out slowly," Jesus does so. Bit by bit, the car edges forward.

"What do I do now?" an excited Jesus exclaims.

"Keep accelerating until you hear the top of the revs and engage the clutch, pulling the stick down to second gear." Again, the revs build up, just about at the top of the change, "Clutch in, pull the stick to the second position now!" Ken yells which his student does flawlessly.

"What now?" Jesus calls out.

"Same process, we repeat the process over until we get to the speed we want to travel at," Ken replies, "nice and gentle." The top of the revs come and again, Jesus executes another perfect change, and so onto the fourth gear, moving at 50 kilometres an hour.

"Which way do I go?" Jesus asks. "Turn the wheel in the direction you want the car to go and follow the road to where you are taking us. Slow down for the corners, we don't want to tip over," Ken advises.

"How do I slow down?"

Ken can hear the enjoyment in his voice.

"We will do the same process in reverse, using our gears to slow us down and also using the brakes, remember, gently tap the middle pedal to slow down, I'll tell you when it's time. For now, just keep your eyes on the road."

"I am driving!" Jesus yells, genuinely ecstatic at his achievement, smiling like a Cheshire cat, "I am driving!"

"Yes, you are, you're driving, well done," Ken replies, both men sharing a laugh as their moving hospital thunders down the track.

>>>>>> <<<<<<

Jesus has been driving for a solid three hours while Ken has been keeping a close watch on his patient; they have chalked up some good miles. He continues to instruct his student, showing him how to slow down and take corners and he's impressed. Jesus wasn't joking when he said he was a quick study, that's if he really couldn't drive, of which Ken remains highly sceptical.

He would be happier if he knew where he was going and when this so-called 'help' was going to show up? As a student of cartography, he's studied the maps of these inland routes closely, but as far as he can tell, they aren't on any of them. They have to be somewhere near the South Australian and Western Australian border, if not near the Gunbarrel Highway, or perhaps near the Great Central Road; he's just guessing and it's frustrating the hell out of him. All he really knows is they are in the middle of Australia, with dwindling fuel supplies. His anxiety is rising.

An object appears in the distance, just off the side of the road. As they draw closer, he can see it's an old rusted-out car, a Morris Minor, maybe an early to mid-50's model by the looks of it. Not that old by 1979 standards, but like the rusted truck at Henry's place, it's an old wreck after sitting in these conditions for so long.

Ken looks at it with some sadness, 'Poor old car, what was it doing out here?' he asks himself, before turning his attention towards Henry who is resting comfortably. Clearly, the after-market air conditioning was worth the expense after all.

He had his doubts that Henry would last the trip without some kind of intervention. The minimal care Ken has provided with only basic resources has worked so far, but that could change at any moment. Henry's breathing is worsening.

His mind moves to his personal issues which he has been able to block temporarily but now they flood back. He still has no answers other than the ones Jesus himself is putting forward, that he is 'The Christ.' He still doesn't know what to think, even after what he's experienced, he needs more proof. Perhaps Jesus is right, perhaps he doesn't want to believe, perhaps he's happy within his misery.

He turns his thoughts to his driver, wondering if now would be a good time to throw him a few questions while he's occupied. Maybe he would slip up, even though he hasn't thus far.

"You said before, things that happen, good or bad are as a result of man's actions, right?"

"Yes," Jesus replies knowingly, "Man must be accountable for his actions, hence when things happen, good or bad, it's a direct result of those actions."

"You mean karma?" Ken asks.

"No, I mean consequences," Jesus replies. "Karma, or whatever name you wish to call it, comes about by how you act or treat people and it comes from a higher plane within the universe. Consequences are the results of those actions or decisions you make; reap what you shall sow."

"You almost make it sound as though karma comes from a spiritual place, and consequences from an earthly one?"

"There is no escaping judgement, Ken, in this world or my Father's."

"Then what about the young kids, children, why do they have to suffer the brunt of adult's actions?"

Jesus thinks for a moment, he wants to be as clear as he can be, in order for his answer to be understood.

"As I said to you already, all souls are here only for a finite amount of time, not only to experience a physical realm, but also to do one, or many things, in order for their souls to take the next step in their path."

"Path?"

"Yes, path. We rejoice in our sufferings, knowing that suffering pro-duces endurance, and endurance produces character, and character produces hope, and hope does not put us to shame because God's love has been poured into each one of us." Ken knows that chapter, his father used to quote it often when punishing him, as a way to try and make him understand why.

"Suffering builds character?" he asks.

"Yes," Jesus says, "man is soul and spirit wrapped in flesh; his character is shaped by the sum of his experiences. You are still those things, regardless of how long you are on this earth, and my Father choses when that time is, not you. There is a long way for you to go, more for you to learn."

"What do you mean?" Ken is puzzled and curious.

"You know what I mean."

Then it clicks, it wasn't Ken's proudest moment, but again, the comment makes him defensive.

"Meaning?"

"Meaning, I know you tried to kill yourself and the gun wouldn't work. Who do you think put sand in those bullets? Why do you think I showed you that on our first night together?" Jesus asks with a smile, revealing he was the one who thwarted Ken's plans.

"And if you were the one who did that, why would you?"

"I was trying to get your attention: the dreams, the photo frame...even the tree, do you want me to go on?" he asks, as Ken concedes his failings.

"So why couldn't I hear you in my dreams?"

"People are entangled in the moment and their emotions stop them being aware of other things going on around them. It consumes them, which is part of being human. You were so caught up in your grief and guilt, you couldn't hear or see anything."

This conversation creates a shift in his mind. He has to stop constantly repeating that one statement, *"How could he have known?"* It's driving him to the limits of his sanity. All he understands is for this Jesus to know what he knows he had to have been there, it's the only answer that makes sense, but now Ken has a bigger problem. He has to consider exactly who or what is in the car with him.

Over the next few kilometres, he's silent and preoccupied, contemplating the possibilities. His head is racing in a near neurotic fashion as he mind-games various scenarios. So many 'what ifs.' Meanwhile, Jesus is enjoying his job of driving.

They both spot another object in the distance, a welcome distraction. Ken can't quite make it out due to the diffusion of heat coming off the track, but it's there, a hundred metres or so away.

"Is that a person?" he asks,

Jesus nods. "Looks like it," he replies, accelerating the car towards the object.

"What's someone doing out here, it must be 37 degrees outside, we better stop to make sure they are OK," Ken says. They edge closer to see a female form take shape, a lone woman, walking along the track.

Jesus slows the car down, pulling alongside her. Her presence instantly raises Ken's suspicions. She is immaculately dressed and there are no settlements nearby, strange to say the least.

She's a young, indigenous woman in her early twenties, wearing a dark blue dress with white polka-dots. She is wearing white gloves and blue shoes and is holding a blue and white handbag. She's perfectly dressed for a summer's day, if it was 1955.

The Landcruiser stops next to her and she looks directly towards Ken whose face occupies the rear passenger seat.

He winds down the window.

"Do you need some help?" he asks, "This is an awful place to be stuck."

"Thank you, I do," she says, "my car broke down a while back and I was walking to find some help."

"A car?" Ken asks, confused, looking at Jesus before looking back at the woman, "We didn't see any car back there, other than an old wreck, but that couldn't be it."

Jesus cuts him off. "We would love to offer you a lift," he says, without consulting the car's owner but he knows it won't be a problem.

"Yes, of course, we would," Ken adds, feeling bad he didn't offer it straight away.

"Thank you both, that would be great." she replies, as both men get out of the car, Ken holding the door open for her.

"I'm Doctor Ken Burton and you are?" She smiles the broadest smile he has ever seen.

"My name is Maisy Gibson, I'm a trainee nurse from Wiluna, pleased to meet you, doctor," she says bashfully, extending her hand to shake his, as if she is meeting a rock star.

"A nurse, you don't say, what a surprise. I was just saying to my friend how we need a nurse, God himself must be looking out for us today," Ken says ironically, giving Jesus a sly look who simply smiles back. "Could I prevail upon you, Maisy, to sit with our friend in the back and monitor his vitals for me, he's very sick."

"Of course, doctor," she responds, excited to be called into service, "May I ask what's wrong with him?"

"It's cancer, I'm afraid he doesn't have long left."

"Well, I'll do my best," she replies, understanding the care required.

She hops inside, taking off her wide-brimmed hat, looking tenderly at her new patient, the doctor was right, he doesn't look great. Henry can't stop staring at her, he's looking at her as though he has seen the most wonderous vision.

"Hello Uncle," she says, "What have you done to yourself today?"

"I know you, you're...her, but how?" he asks, waving his finger.

Maisy smiles. "It'll be our secret, hey, Uncle?"

The old man smiles back, closing his eyes to sleep.

"You just rest now, it's my turn to take you home," she gently whispers, stroking Henry's flowing white hair.

Ken re-takes the driver's seat, relegating Jesus to the role of passenger.

"Did I do something wrong?" he asks.

"No, not at all, I just feel like driving, you did a great job."

"Thank you," Jesus says proudly.

As Ken settles into the driver's seat, a concerned look comes over his face: the fuel situation is low, much lower than he expected it to be.

"We need to get off the road and make camp, get Henry out of the car, he needs a decent sleep."

"Yes, he does," Jesus replies, nodding in agreement,

"How much further do we have to go before we reach our destination?"

"Another day, why do you ask?" Jesus replies.

"We're very low on fuel, we're using it too fast and I don't have any more."

Jesus raises his hand in a calming gesture.

"Don't worry, we'll be fine," he says, trying to allay Ken's concerns.

"Doctor, there's a place a few miles away that would make a good camping spot," Maisy chimes in.

"Sounds good, we'll head for it and worry about fuel tomorrow."

⤜⤜⤜ ⤛⤛⤛

They wind their way through another five kilometres of rocky roads in the harsh landscape. Ken spots two large boulders that mark the entry of their camping spot for the night. The rocks are enormous, the size of houses, and act like sentries guarding the gates to this place. He wonders how these rocks got here in the first place, remnants of an ancient geological event perhaps?

"Is this the place, Maisy?" Ken asks.

"Yes doctor, this is it, just follow the road down around the bend and you'll see a clearing."

He follows her instructions, continuing to bump and scape along the track, occasionally bottoming out in deep ruts. He sees a large flat area, protected by a rocky ridge that reminds him of a quarry.

"This will do nicely," he says, guiding the car and van into the middle of the space. He is relieved another day of travel has ended; he needs the rest too. He glances at Jesus who looks unsettled as if he's displeased.

"Are you alright?" Ken asks, concerned by how anxious Jesus looks. But he doesn't answer, rather he gives Ken one of his stern looks before exiting the car. Something is wrong.

They work together, setting up the camp, transferring an unconscious Henry into the caravan so he can sleep more comfortably. Ken finds two extra oxygen bottles he had forgotten about, stashed in one of the storage bins. They are smaller than the ones hospitals use, but they will be useful. He gives them a quick test by squirting some oxygen out, sniffing it, making sure it's good to use. They're still within the date stamped on the tags, and now Henry will reap the benefit of his preparedness.

"These will come in handy, Maisy," he says, connecting a resuscitation mask, "they'll help him sleep better."

"He sure will, doctor," she replies, focused on her job, as if she were back in a hospital. He looks at them both with affection, wondering if there is more, he can do.

"He hasn't got much time left, the poor bugger; all we can do is to make him as comfortable as possible."

"And we will doctor, I'll see to it." He passes her the nasal mask and she loops it around Henry's head and up under his nose

They reset the drip and administer another dose of glucose into the fluids, the last one worked well and Ken hopes another one will have the same effect. Earlier, Ken had set up a second bed for Maisy, he needs to make sure she is comfortable as well.

"I've made a bed for you, just outside the door, where you can sleep, if you like. It'll be warm and I can watch Henry while you take a break."

"Thank you doctor, that's very kind but I'll stay with Uncle tonight and keep an eye on him, if that's alright."

Ken nods, "As you wish, I will relieve you later," he says, feeling slightly useless as she has everything well in hand.

He feels the change in the weather, the temperature has really dropped off as the sun moves behind the ridgeline. It's getting late in the day and soon it will be dark.

Jesus sits on a nearby boulder, his eyes are closed and deep in thought. Ken approaches him, wanting to know what rattled him earlier.

"Are you OK?" Ken asks, "It's a little strange seeing you like this."

"Like what?" Jesus asks without breaking his concentration.

"Preoccupied and anxious."

"I am not anxious, maybe a little preoccupied."

"With what?"

"We not alone out here," he replies in a voice that is clipped and icy.

Ken finds the coldness in his voice ominous. "What do you mean, are we in danger?"

"For I am the Good Shepherd; I will keep watch over my flock."

Ken watches him and tries to figure out what he means by quoting that biblical passage. He gets the feeling that pushing for an answer is pointless, besides he has things to do before they run out of daylight.

"OK! I'm going to try and find some firewood for tonight; it's going to be cold," he says, walking off to scout the area.

"Get as much as you can," Jesus calls out, "we are going to need a big fire."

⫸⫸⫷⫷

The afternoon rapidly rolls into evening and all is quiet. Henry's sleeping more comfortably, thanks to the oxygen and Maisy's care. It's another full moon and Jesus has been sitting next to the fire, constantly glaring out into the emptiness of the night. Only the light of the moon permits them to see deeper into the nightscape which would otherwise be a black void.

Ken is snoring his head off, exhausted from lugging firewood for over an hour. He didn't get any help from Jesus, who spent the afternoon

125

perched on top of the largest boulder as if he was communing with someone, occasionally yelling "More!" each time Ken brought another piece of firewood back to camp.

Just after 3 a.m., Jesus becomes aware of a new presence approaching, something menacing. The rocky ridgeline provides 180 degrees of protection, shielding them from the elements but it leaves the front of the camp wide open.

The brilliant light of the fire extends well out into the darkness, Jesus stands there, leaning on a large stick, waiting for whatever is coming.

Suddenly, the winds intensify and swirl up, engulfing the camp and trying to blow the fire out.

The eerie howling of dingoes and wild dogs fills the air. Their growls, whimpering and whining, barks and howls draw closer as if some kind of frenzy is about to begin.

Jesus stands on the edge of the campfire light, putting himself between the darkness and his friends who sleep. The sounds of human cries for help, moans, and screams, join the chorus.

Ken is woken by the noise, ripped from his dreams, having no idea as to what's happening. Bleary eyed, he hears the hellish noises and is afraid.

"What's going on?" he calls out, trying to focus his vision, but there is no reply to his question.

Ken can see Jesus standing there, looking out, with the stick in one hand and his fists clenched with the other. He gets up from his bed and walks towards him which instantly draws a reaction.

"Stay there!" Jesus barks in caution, stopping him in his tracks, "this is not a matter for you, stay out of sight!" Ken ignores the request and keeps coming towards him before Jesus loses some of his composure.

"Stay out of sight and stay behind the fire!" he commands, which Ken is compelled to obey. He sits back down on his bed.

The fierce sounds of fighting, ripping and tearing echo off the rocks rise to ear-splitting levels, matched by the woeful cries of men, women, and children begging for forgiveness. He covers his ears as the unbearable sounds pass through him like an electrical charge, penetrating every part of his body.

Maisy opens the door and stands at the entrance of the caravan, also with clenched fists. She and Jesus exchange eye contact.

"Stay with him!" he yells, meaning Henry. She immediately closes the door, locking them both inside. Keeping low, Ken peers over the fire, just enough see the creatures' eyes shining, hundreds if not thousands of pairs of eyes emerging from the darkness. They are surrounded.

They begin to file in, in front of Jesus, careful not to fall into the light, hugging the darkness. Suddenly the wind stops, the sounds of the animals cease, and the cries of the dammed are subdued to barely a whisper. Something bigger is coming.

The flames of the fire freeze in mid-air as time and space have been suspended. Not a sound can be heard, no movements can be made. Ken is frozen, immobile, yet he is aware of what's going on around him and can see and hear everything. This experience feels familiar to him, something similar happened the night Carol died; he thought it was just him, but now he's not so sure.

Jesus is not frozen, he's standing out there, pacing, as though he is about to confront a schoolyard bully. The silence is deafening, Ken can hear his own heart pounding, every beat like a drum, pumping adrenalin; he's terrified.

Suddenly, a deep, gravelly voice, booms out from the dark.

"I've come for the old man, give him to me, now!" the powerful voice demands, Jesus is unphased and remains calm.

"He is not for you, unclean spirit, he belongs to the Father!" Jesus replies with equal power.

"He broke the first rule, that means he is mine, give him to me, or I will take him." Jesus remains steadfast.

"No!" He yells back, "The Father has forgiven him, he belongs to the Father."

A few moments of dead silence follow, before the voice speaks again. "Who are you to deny me?" it demands.

"I am the Son," Jesus replies calmly.

"No!" the voice is enraged, "The Son is in the other place."

"Yet I am here! Come forward into my light, unclean spirit, see for yourself that I am he who commands you in the name of the Father."

Using the large stick, Jesus draws a line in the sand in front of him, it instantly erupts in a brilliant blue–white flame of such intensity that Ken cannot look in that direction.

One by one, the rows of shining eyes move aside as something large passes between them, parting them, as the proverbial Red Sea parted for Moses.

Slowly, the most hideous creature a human has ever seen appears from the void of night. It resembles a giant dog, or hound of sorts, almost as big as his car. Unafraid, it walks up to the line of fire Jesus has created, bearing its giant canines as saliva oozes from its open mouth and the stench of death fills the camp.

The creature looks Jesus up and down, being careful not to enter the line of light which continues burning brightly. It sits on its hind, licking its giant jaws as it makes itself comfortable before it speaks.

"So, it is you, the Son," the beast says, satisfied with Jesus's claims, "It doesn't change anything, the old man is still mine by right, and I will take him tonight."

Jesus shakes his head yet again.

"I've told you no! He belongs to the Father and that is where he is going, now be gone from my sight!" Jesus orders, but the hideous creature dismisses his reply, changing the subject.

"Why are you here?" it asks inquisitively, "What could be so important for the Son himself to come and visit these lower life-forms?"

"That's not your concern, heed my words and do as I command in the name of the Father, or you will feel his wrath upon you." Jesus orders.

"On your way, your sight offends me!" Jesus raises his arm high and points at the ghastly cur.

The beast bursts out with a long, sinister laugh which stops as quickly as it started; something else has caught its attention.

It lifts up its massive head, sniffing the air as it catches a new scent. It looks at Jesus, giving him a contemptuous smile.

"I know what your secret is!" it says, singing the line like a nursery rhyme. It takes another big whiff of the air,

"What is that beautiful smell? Oh wait, I know! The smell of innocence, a fresh soul, ripe for the taking. Give it to me instead of the old man and I will leave!"

Again, Jesus shakes his head. "That one isn't for you either, he also belongs to the Father," Jesus says, denying the beast, who erupts in anger.

"Belongs to the Father, belongs to the Father!" it screams in a distorted voice, like a child throwing a tantrum.

"That is the order of things, now leave as I have commanded you, before I cast you and your kind back into the void!" Jesus orders, beginning to lose patience. The beast is silent as it contemplates its next move.

It sniffs the air deeply one more time.

"Such a beautiful scent, I'll be watching and waiting for this one," the beast issues its warning with a deadly seriousness.

Ken knows the creature is talking about him. Despite being in shock at what he's witnessing, his instinct is to run but he is petrified and still can't move. He begins praying, reciting a 'Hail Mary.'

The creature laughs again, even more loudly this time.

"Pray all you want; our paths will cross again soon!" the beast yells, determined to be heard. It looks down towards Jesus and scoffs in arrogance, as it retreats into the darkness, looking straight at the human which sends shivers down Ken's spine.

The flames of the fire begin to flicker once more in the wind, as the night sounds of crickets and insects return to the camp. Whatever had him suspended is over and Ken can now move. He is beside himself, the realisation of everything he denied was true; this man is Jesus Christ.

He runs over to his companion, they look at each other, Ken doesn't know what to say or do. "You are real! I feel so ashamed I doubted you," he cries out, "Can you forgive me for denying you?"

Jesus looks at him, weeping on his knees. He bends down, takes him by his arms and pulls him up.

"Look at me, Ken," Jesus says.

Ken doesn't dare to make eye contact with Jesus.

"Look at me," Jesus reiterates.

"How can I?" Ken replies, "I've denied you; I've insulted you; I've argued with you; I dare not look at you. I am a disgrace."

Jesus smiles reassuringly and says, "You are none of those things. Look at me now."

Ken finally lifts his head slowly, his eyes are red and watery, his hands tremble at the realisation he is in the presence of the Son of God.

Jesus gives him a beaming smile; Ken can feel his compassion and love, as he struggles for something fitting to say. "I guess Carol was right all along," Ken says, with a nervous chuckle, still avoiding looking directly at Jesus.

"Yes, she was," Jesus replies, "Now come, sit with me," Jesus guides him to a place next to the fire. They sit close together, as Jesus holds his hand, gently patting it, a reassuring and soothing presence.

Ken can feel the warmth flowing through to him. His mind is racing, so many questions, let alone what just happened in front of his eyes. '*Where do I start?*' Ken asks himself, how does one proceed with an omnipotent entity you have spent your life avoiding or dismissing. However, first, he needs to know what just transpired.

"Jesus, what just happened, was that the...?" Ken asks, trying to remain calm as the adrenalin dissipates through his body.

"Yes, it was," Jesus interjects, before continuing, "they were unclean spirits, they're gone now, no need to worry."

"I assume it was after Henry, but why?"

Jesus sighs, "It felt it had a claim to him, however my father's claim takes precedence above all others."

"Why did it think it had a claim? It said he broke the first rule, *'Thou shall not kill,'* is that right?"

"Yes, that is right, but as I said, my father cannot turn his back on any of his children, especially if they ask for forgiveness."

Ken no longer doubts anything. After what he saw, felt and experienced, how could he? The realisation he has been with the real 'Christ' for the past few days hits him.

"Jesus," Ken says in a subtle tone, "I have been a fool for not believing you when you told me who you were. How can you forgive me?"

"You have nothing to be ashamed of and nothing to apologise for," Jesus replies, instilling a feeling of love and compassion through his words.

"But I doubted you, you tested me and I failed," Ken replies, overwhelmed by the magnitude of the revelation.

"No, Ken, I tested you and you passed with ease."

"What do you mean? I rejected you," he asks, confused once again by Jesus's answer.

"I asked you to have an open mind, to give me an opportunity to show you who I am. You did that. I asked you to help me, you did that as well, and now, you no longer doubt me. More importantly, you no longer doubt yourself."

Ken shakes his head. "But..."

Jesus cuts in, "I told you this was a time of trial for you and so it has been. Have you disappointed me? Of course not, you honour me."

Ken wipes the tears from his eyes. Jesus is right, he can believe in himself, he wasn't going mad after all. God does exist, heaven is real and Carol is still alive, somewhere. He feels as if a gigantic weight has been lifted off him.

"Find peace in the knowledge that I am always with you, whether you see me or not, I will never leave you," Jesus says, pulling him close, hugging him as a father hugs a lost son.

Jesus rises to his feet and walks over to the caravan, knocking on the door. Maisy opens it, she too was on high alert.

"Is everything alright in there?" Jesus asks

"Yes, it is," Maisy replies.

"Bless you, child."

Jesus looks at Ken, reminding him, "We don't have much time left; we have to get moving as soon as it's light if we're going to make our destination in time."

Ken understands the urgency and nods, "Of course, I'll pack us up as soon as its light enough."

"Good, try to get some sleep before we leave, we have a big day ahead."

Chapter Ten

K en wakes to the sounds of bangs and clangs around the camp-site. The sun hits his face, forcing him to lift his head from the pillow and join the world. Maisy and Jesus have been busy packing up the camp, not that there was much to do: collapse a table, an awning and his bunk, and that's it. He can't believe he managed to sleep after the events of last night which are like a nightmare that begins to fade once you wake. His companions obviously knew he needed the rest, so he can scrub packing up off the list.

Jesus and Maisy are inside the caravan, spending some time with Henry, praying. Regardless of what her connection to Jesus is, she is a wonderful nurse, whether it's in this life or a previous one. Ken is certain he's figured out Maisy's true identity but only time will tell if he's correct.

Right now, he has to get on with things, there isn't any time to lose if they want to get Henry home in time. He enters the cabin, trying not to interrupt them while he checks his supplies. He can hear Jesus and Maisy praying in a unfamiliar language. For Jesus and Henry, praying or talking to God is a private matter, but Henry is still out cold.

He continues with his quick inventory, and as he thought, he's running low on fluids. He takes a quick look at the gauge on the oxygen tank, he'll have to switch that out as well, one left. He isn't sure how long it will last, maybe a day which, according to Jesus, is how far they have left to travel.

When the prayers are eventually finished, Ken goes to Henry and measures his vitals. His heart rate is dangerously slow and his blood pressure keeps dropping. This will be Henry's last day.

Once preparations are made, all three of them work together to get their patient loaded in the car. After some fussing about, everyone is finally ready to go. Ken jumps in the driver's seat and turns the key, expecting to hear the diesel engine kick over. The vehicle won't start. He tries again, as the engine groans over and over. He looks down and sees that fuel light is on and the tank is empty.

"Blast!" he exclaims, drawing Jesus's attention.

"What's wrong?"

"I'm not sure, I need to check something, give me a minute."

He jumps out of the car and heads straight for the rear of the vehicle. He has a hunch, but he won't be certain until he checks it out.

At the rear of the vehicle, he sees a damp spot underneath the fuel tank. He climbs under for a closer look and smells the fumes in the sand, it's as he suspected. "Shit!" he yells, "bloody rocks!" He crawls out from under the car where Jesus has joined him.

"Well, that's just bloody great!" He is cranky, the lack of sleep is making his fuse a bit shorter.

"What's is it?" Jesus is concerned but calm.

"We have a hole in the fuel tank, and what's worse we have lost all our fuel." Ken replies, "Must have been a rock yesterday which explains why the fuel went down so fast."

"Can you fix it?" Jesus asks.

"Yes, I can fix the hole, I have the things I need, but that's not the problem."

"Then what is the problem?"

Ken takes a deep breath, trying to keep a lid on his temper, he just said the problem and repeats, "We have no fuel, we have none left, we're not going anywhere! It's one thing after another on this trip, never bloody ending!"

"I understand," Jesus is confident and serene, "Fix the tank, I have a solution for your fuel."

Ken shakes his head; he has no idea how they are going to get out of this situation, they're in big trouble.

The tank repair is a relatively, straightforward, quick fix. He uses new metal putty that sets like concrete making the job easier, but they must wait for it to cure; the heat from the desert floor should make it cure faster.

Jesus had been walking around the old river bed and now approaches him.

Ken informs him, "The hole is repaired; we just have to wait for it to cure." Now he's calmed down, Ken is yet again ashamed of himself, "I want to apologize for being grumpy earlier, I didn't mean to."

"I understand, this trip has been difficult for you, don't be discouraged, it's nearly over."

"It is?" Ken asks, "When?"

"Soon," Jesus replies, "now, please tell me, how much fuel do we need?"

"I don't know, but if we could fill those two jerry cans, that should do for a while, at least until we can get to a petrol station."

Jesus shakes his head. "There are no petrol stations where we are going. What are those two canisters in the back of the car?"

"That's our emergency water supply, why do you ask?"

"Can you spare one of them?"

"Yes, why?" he asks suspiciously.

"You will see. Please get one, and place it in front of me."

"Sure." Ken replies, without further questioning, but wonders how water is going to fix their problem.

He places one of the canisters at his feet. Jesus lays both his hands on it. For the first time Ken sees some odd markings on his hands, more like scars that have been long healed. It is odd he hadn't noticed them before, then it occurs to him they're stigmata, the wounds of the crucifixion Jesus suffered at the hands of the Romans.

Jesus begins to pray, again in that language he hadn't heard before today, softly and quietly, whispering, repeating one short prayer, over and over. He looks skywards, almost as though he's asking permission, explaining what he needs and why. The ritual continues for another minute or so before he abruptly finishes and lowers his head.

"It is done."

"What is?" Ken asks, unsure what has happened.

"Use what is in this vessel to power your vehicle, we won't need more." he says, walking back towards the front of the car without further comment and taking his seat in the passenger's side.

Ken opens the lid and takes a deep sniff: it's diesel! He's flabbergasted by what can only be a miracle.

He may have accepted this man as Jesus Christ but this miracle boggles his mind. Growing up, reading the Bible, Ken thought the stories of miraculous feats such as the loaves and fishes, Lazarus rising from the dead, and the resurrection, were just that, stories; never in a million years did he ever expect to be in one of them!

"How?" he yells out to Jesus, who senses his shock.

"I asked my Father to give us what we need, that's how his power works through me." he replies nonchalantly,

"And what if we run out again?"

"We won't," he replies confidently, "now, we must leave."

He reaches into the caravan's utility box, grabs a funnel and begins to fuel the Landcruiser, hoping this works and he hasn't destroyed his engine.

Ken returns to the driver's seat, nervously holding the keys out in front of him, "Moment of truth!" he says, trying to be funny, while they all watch on.

He inserts the key into the ignition and turns it to the on position. The dash lights come on, diesel indicator light is on before going off as it should, the fuel gauge reads full. He turns the key a fraction further and the car fires instantly. He lets out a huge sigh of relief.

Jesus shoots him a glance. "It's alright, Ken," he says with a smile, "you can apologize to me later."

Two hours into the day's driving and Ken has been watching the fuel gauge like a hawk. The car's been running beautifully and they're making good time. The gauge still shows as full, it's incredible and he's having a hard time believing all of it is real.

"Unbelievable," he mutters to himself but loud enough to get Jesus's attention.

"What is?"

Ken has a sheepish look at his face as he says, "The fact we have holy diesel, I can't believe it, again, I'm sorry I doubted you."

Jesus nods, acknowledging the apology.

"I seem to be apologising to you a lot in the last twelve hours, don't I?"

"That's alright, I know it is a lot to take in."

"You know we haven't had a chance to speak since last night, I have more questions."

Jesus nods. "I know you do, but I can't answer all of them."

"I expected as much," Ken replies, "I don't know what is stranger, the fact I'm sitting here talking with Jesus Christ. or that you are real, and not some fictional character."

"This isn't the first time I've returned, and you're not the first person I've appeared to and helped, and you won't be the last."

"I'm grateful for your presence, I am, very, only I haven't quite figured out how you're helping me when I don't even know what help I need?"

"That's the quandary isn't it, Ken? As I've said to you, it's hard to see the problem when you're in the midst of it. Sometimes you need an objective set of eyes to steer you toward a solution."

"Is that what you're doing, helping to steer me towards a solution?"

"Yes. I am steering you towards what my Father has planned for you," replies Jesus, stroking his beard and looking out the window.

"But if the path the Father has planned for me was always intended, wouldn't it happen anyway?"

Jesus shakes his head. "Not always, people often don't hear the call to their path. They resist it for more earthly pursuits or pleasures, distracted by things like greed, temptation, and selfishness. Not every life is fulfilled as my Father would want it, that's why it's such a precious thing."

"You mean life?" Ken enquires.

"Yes," Jesus nods, "it's the most precious gift that was ever created, equally so is free will; it truly is up to you as to how you live that life."

Ken understands what he means, but the time has come for him to ask the big question, the one that's been burning inside of him ever since they met.

"What about Carol: is she in heaven?"

Jesus senses his friend's desperation, making it hard to disappoint him, "I'm not going to answer that question yet, but I promise, by the time this is over, I will."

His answer isn't to Ken's satisfaction and he objects, "Why not, why can't you tell me about my wife?" He wonders why this question is such a big deal, why can't Jesus answer it for him right away?

"When the time is right, I will," Jesus replies, "until then, I need you to be patient." His response only serves to irritate Ken further but he decides to move on, it's not as though he's going to argue with the Son of God.

"Well, can you at least tell me what we encountered last night?"

Jesus quickly replies without breaking his gaze. "It was Satan. He and his unclean spirits wander the earth, in the shadows, existing only to tempt and torment man, to cause pain and heartache, to create and sow chaos and discord."

Throughout his life, Ken has struggled to believe in God and Jesus and, by extension, Satan. To find out that Satan is also real opens up a whole raft of new questions.

"So, there is a hell?"

"My father casts the unclean spirits into the void, there, in that place, they will remain until judgment."

"Who is there, what kind of people?" Ken asks, fascinated by his answer.

"Those who have allowed themselves to be seduced by the unclean, others choose that path," Jesus answers, "my Father will judge them and He will decide whether they are to be saved or not. Until then, they will remain in that place."

Just as Ken thought, not everyone wants to be saved. After what he experienced last night, however, the thought of spending an eternity with those things, in that place, is a fate worse than anything his mind can conjure. The sounds of those souls screaming for help will never leave him.

"You know, if people on Earth could see what I saw last night, the world would be a different place."

"Perhaps, but fear is no way to rule," Jesus says, "look at all the human empires based on fear, how long did they last? Ruling by fear and control doesn't work, which is why people who follow the path my Father has laid out must do so willingly. He can only show us the way, it's up to each person if they want to follow it."

Jesus looks tired, the trip wears on him as well.

"I need to rest, please stay on this road until you see a large rock with a small tree in front of it, turn there, that is our last destination."

"Certainly." Ken nods, confirming the instruction as Jesus gets comfortable in the passenger's seat.

He closes his eyes and almost immediately seems to drift into a deep relaxed state, his body becomes motionless, as though the power was suddenly turned off and only a shell remained.

⤞⤞⤞ ⤝⤝⤝

Ken drives throughout the hot day and into the afternoon, periodically stopping to check on Henry who is continuing to fade. As the day has pushed on, the terrain has changed. Whilst still largely arid, there's is more greenery now. They must be getting close to water of some kind and the end of the trip. Jesus still hasn't moved or made a sound of any kind, he has stayed in that same position, not moving a muscle for hours. Finally, after a full day of solid driving, he spots the landmark Jesus spoke of, a large boulder and with a small tree in front.

Ken slows to make the turn, powering the vehicle through the dust as the track gets rougher. They proceed along the bumpy road before coming to a large sign which reads 'Lake Carnegie,' an ephemeral lake, that has been filled thanks to the heavy summer rains. Some 100 kilometres at its longest point and 30 kilometres at its widest, this is Martu Country, Henry has come home.

At once, Jesus's eyes open and he looks refreshed. The sun is beginning to set as the cover of night creeps over the land from the east, Ken is utterly exhausted and can't wait to stretch his legs.

Jesus smiles proudly at the job Ken has done without complaint. He knows he's still brooding over their earlier conversation and pats him on the shoulder as a sign of appreciation. "Just a bit further, brother."

Ken tries to smile back, but he can barely keep his eyes open.

They drive over the beaten track lined with thick bush on either side as they head around to the northern end of the lake. Jesus spots a giant gum tree hanging over a flat space with only a short walk to the shoreline, it would make a perfect camp.

"That's the place," he says, pointing to a spot under the giant tree. Ken stops the Landcruiser there. He gazes at the fuel gauge one more time, incredibly, it's still showing as full.

'Unbelievable,' he whispers again to himself, looking at Jesus before breaking into rapturous laughter. Jesus starts laughing as well, so too does Maisy, but they have no idea what they are laughing at.

"What's so funny?" Jesus asks, laughing along until Ken can compose himself enough to talk.

"The fuel gauge," he says, pointing to it, "It's still reading as full."

His laughter intensifies and escalates to hysteria. Jesus senses something is wrong and takes his friend's hand, comforting him as his laughter turns into tears.

For Ken, the stress and exhaustion of the last few weeks has taken their toll and have finally come to a head now that they have reached the end. He erupts, spilling emotion out of his body like a volcano, into the ether, breaking free of his personal prison.

Jesus holds his friend in the warmest of embraces for a long time, whispering private words into his ear only meant for them. Maisy watches on with affection, gently rubbing Ken's back, doing her part to soothe the doctor's distress.

He slowly comes out of it; his eyes are red and swollen. Jesus looks at him with love and compassion, and Ken returns his gaze.

"Amen." Jesus whispers, indicating Ken is now free of all of the emotional bindings which held him captive and unable to embrace the beauty of life.

They all sit for a few more minutes without speaking, everyone's aware of the transformation that has occurred. Having gathered himself, he sees the world with new eyes, as the three of them finally alight from the Landcruiser.

"Will we need another big fire tonight?" Ken asks his friends, wondering if those creatures have followed them here or not.

"Only if you're cold," Jesus replies, chuckling at his own joke.

"Good, I don't think I could handle another night like that."
Both men are in agreement.
"Get some rest, we have a big day tomorrow," Jesus says.
"With what, I thought we were finished travelling?" Ken asks,
"We are, but there's still more to do."

⟫⟫⟩ ⟨⟨⟨⟨

The rough beauty of this location is a sight to behold, even at night.
The stars reflect off the lake's surface creating a wonderous, cosmic
blanket. Ken can see why Henry wanted to come home, to spend his
final few hours here, it's a magical place. After setting up the camp, he
checks on his patient to perform his final observations before heading
off for some sleep. To his surprise, Henry is awake, having slept all day.
The trip has taken an enormous toll on him. He's so weak and frail
that, if not for Maisy's care, he would surely have perished by now.

"You're looking fighting fit, Henry, ready to go a few rounds?"
But Henry can only smile. Ken takes his pulse and blood pressure
and shoots Maisy a concerned look, shaking his head. Henry motions
for Ken to come closer, he can barely speak, and wants to tell him
something, without delay. Ken lowers his ear to the old man's mouth.

"Outside...let me sleep under the stars, one last time, hey doc?"
he whispers. Ken can't deny him this favour; it won't make any
difference now.

He leaves the caravan and grabs the spare bunk, setting it up near
the fire he started earlier. Jesus wandered off shortly after they arrived
and now reappears and has company with him.

"Ken, these are Henry's people." Jesus says, as an older,
clean-shaven man sporting a large cowboy hat steps forward to greet
them.

"We've come to pay our respects to uncle, and to see that he gets
home to the ancestors," he speaks with a deep indigenous accent.

"Of course," Ken replies, "I'm his doctor, but we need to hurry, we don't have long."

"Thank you for bringing him home to us," the man says.

Ken nods to acknowledge his words of gratitude. His heart swells with pride to have played his part in this trip, despite his initial opposition. Being back in his country has given Henry immeasurable peace of mind and contentment, a chance to complete his journey.

"He's asked to spend the night outside, under the stars..."

"Yeah, that's good, we'll bring him out," the spokesman for the group says as they walk over and go into the van to retrieve their kinsman.

From his vantage point, Ken can hear them talking to Henry who is doing his best to join in.

Although he has no idea what they're saying to each other, he can hear the excitement in the old man's voice to be surrounded by his people once more.

Jesus looks at Ken whose face is glowing, "Didn't I tell you it would be worth it?"

"Yes, you did," he replies, "I'm glad you made me listen."

Jesus puts his arm over Ken's shoulder. "As I said, it's hard to connect things when you're in the moment."

They stand together, watching, as the men bring Henry out of the caravan, they're singing and gently rest their brother on the bunk next to the fire.

"Feels good, doesn't it, to do something for someone else, something important?" Jesus says quietly.

Ken nods, realising the significance of this moment.

Henry's mouth and eyes are smiling as he gets comfortable on the bunk. He never thought he would be with his people again. At this moment he is happy.

He lies there, breathing in the smells of the area that trigger his childhood memories of running around with his brothers and sisters, chasing each other through the scrub.

He looks up at the millions of twinkling stars spanning the heavens. As he stares into the night sky, taking in the majesty of the cosmos, shooting stars burst across the vastness, thrilling him with their brilliance.

"This is heaven," he whispers as he closes his eyes, recalling more memories of his younger days.

The elders sit around him and sing their sacred songs with their hand-made instruments. Their voices flood out across the lake, echoing off the surrounding hills. Their voices and instruments carry across the land and are heard by all within earshot. Jesus, Maisy and Ken sit quietly and listen to the songs, as they would have done more than 60,000 years ago.

Ken lays his head down, feeling the vibrations of the didgeridoo pass through him, the sounds it makes of the dingoes, the kookaburras and other characters that shape the culture of the people. He slowly drifts off, allowing his consciousness to float across the land with each note, a part of the song.

>>>>> <<<<<

Ken jerks awake. He didn't realise he had fallen asleep, albeit for a short time. He looks at his watch, 11 p.m.. He hopes he didn't appear disrespectful.

The songs have continued unabated as Jesus approaches Henry whose eyes never reopened. He bends down towards the old man and whispers into his ear. As he does so and without prompting, the singing and music stops.

He can hear the laboured breathing and wheezing from Henry's chest and goes to render aid but Jesus puts his hand up, waving him away. Suddenly, he hears the final exhale, as the air rushes out of Henry's body, signifying his time on Earth has come to an end.

A purple glow with a dash of pink is seen surrounding Henry's body, like a gas hovering over the bunk, before it takes the shape of a small ball. It rises up in the air, to meet Jesus at eye-level, and he smiles at it.

"Go and see your ancestors, brother, then I will take you home." he says, as though giving a child permission to go out and play with his friends.

The colourful orb flies off, buzzing around the camp, weaving in and out of trees, like a bird let loose after captivity. It races around the shoreline before shooting off across the body of water at great speed, and disappearing from view.

Everyone looks on in amazement at what they have witnessed.

Ken has never seen a soul leave the body before. "There is life after death!" he exclaims, gazing out into the lake in wonder, witnessing a different state of being.

The elders approach him, led by the man with the cowboy hat. "Excuse me, doctor, if it's alright with you, we would like to take Uncle with us and give him a traditional burial."

Jesus nods in approval.

"Of course," Ken replies, knowing this ceremony is not for his eyes,

"I am going with them, I'll be back later," Jesus says, "Maisy, will you come with us?" She nods and rushes over to join them, "We'll see you soon Ken, get some rest."

The men lift Henry's body off the bunk and casually wander off into the darkness, singing their songs as they go.

For Ken, the satisfaction of being able to grant a dying man his final wish will never leave him. Jesus was right, what a reward!

CHAPTER ELEVEN

It's the seventh day of the trip. Once again, the sun is breaking from the east and the sounds of the morning chorus are in full swing. Ken could never tire of waking up to this elixir. This morning, the sounds are richer and the colours are brighter and he can feel each molecule of the gentle breeze touching his face. His senses are more acute than they have ever been before. Today, he sees the world differently.

He rises from the bunk, feeling fresh and rested, it's the best he's slept in a long time. Straightaway, he can see Jesus and Maisy meditating by the water's edge. He's pleased to see them back in camp, he's missed them and can't wait to see what the day brings, now the mission is over.

He is sad knowing this experience is at its end, he has no idea what that will mean or what he will do with himself when it is. Right now, those big decisions can wait, he needs breakfast.

He throws some small logs on the fire, blowing on it, exciting the coals in the pit, getting the fire going again. He places the kettle on the ashes, waiting patiently for it to whistle. Jesus and Maisy end their meditation and walk towards him with purpose. Ken can tell by the look on Jesus's face that he is cooking up something for him to do, he just has that look.

"How do you feel today, Ken?" Jesus asks, as he walks towards him.

"Great, thank you, breakfast anyone?" he asks, but they both politely decline his offer.

"No, we're fine, thank you," Maisy replies.

The kettle comes to a boil and Ken quickly makes his coffee and sits back to enjoy it, sipping it slowly. Jesus takes a position next to him. Like a cat who ate a plump pigeon, he has something to ask.

"We might get some visitors today," Jesus says, easing into his news.

"Oh really, that's good, who?" Ken asks, continuing to sip his coffee.

"We ran into some people last night, a few of them hadn't seen a doctor in over a year and well, some of them really need your help."

"So, you mean I may get some patients today?"

"Yes," Jesus replies, "it shouldn't be a problem to treat a few people, should it?"

"How many are we talking about?"

"Oh, I don't know, just a few."

Ken knows by the tone in his voice that's not totally accurate.

"They should be here soon."

"I see," Ken says suspiciously, "Tell me, how many are we really talking about?"

"Maybe twenty or thirty."

Ken almost chokes on his coffee.

"Twenty or thirty??" he exclaims.

"Is that a problem?"

"No, not at all," Ken replies, "it took me by surprise. My only concern is that treating Henry took a lot of my supplies, I may not have enough for everyone and I wouldn't want people to miss out on treatment. I don't have much in the way of penicillin and pain relief or any other medications they are likely to require."

"I understand," Jesus replies, thinking for a moment before walking into the caravan, returning with Ken's black medical bag.

"This is your doctor's bag?" he asks.

Ken nods.

"Yes, why?" Jesus sits down next to him and places his hands on either side of the bag and commences praying. Again, he finds himself staring at Jesus's hands bearing the scars of the crucifixion.

He finishes his prayer and sees Ken staring at the scars.

"I made a pact with myself that I wouldn't ask you any more stupid questions, but I need to know. Even though you are in a different body, do those scars still hurt?"

Jesus shakes his head. "No, but they remain with me by divine will, so that people who see me, like you, do not forget the Father sent his only Son to pay for the sins of man."

"The guarantee that because you have paid for our sins, we will have eternal life?" Ken asks.

"Yes." Jesus replies. He holds up the bag. "For today, whatever you need to help people, you will find in this bag. Just think of what you need, and it will be there."

"I'll be interested to see how this turns out," Ken says, knowing he shouldn't be sceptical, not after everything he's witnessed.

He gets up from his seat, mentally preparing for a day of doctoring. "I need some food, a change of clothes and perhaps a bath in the lake before I do anything."

"That's a good idea," Jesus replies, "you are beginning to smell."

⟫⟫⟫ ⟪⟪⟪

An hour later, after an invigorating swim, some fresh clean clothes and a full belly, Ken is feeling revitalised. Maisy had cleaned the caravan, changing the sheets for him, the smell of sweat and stale air has been replaced with a faint but pleasant smell of roses, which is odd as he didn't bring any air freshener with him.

He doesn't question anything anymore, there's no need, it is what it is!

He rattles around the cupboards, looking for his glasses and finds the bottle of bourbon that provided him with comfort. It's a crutch he no longer needs and no longer has a place for. He opens it, tipping it down the sink without even taking a sniff. A new chapter has begun.

He steps out of the van ready for the day. Jesus has arranged the awning, fold-up tables and chairs to create a makeshift triage and treatment area. He looks at the area with affection; it reminds him of his days overseas. He is feeling like a doctor again, no longer weighed down. He is truly free and optimistic. He takes his seat, placing the stethoscope round his neck, making sure his blood pressure measuring device is on the table and ready to use.

Jesus walks over to him, radiating goodwill with every step, "All ready?" he asks, "It's going to be a good day!"

"Yes, I am," Ken replies in equally high spirits, "Are the people coming?"

Jesus looks confident. "Yes, they should be here any minute," he replies, "Remember what I told you, think of what you need before you reach into the bag and it will be there."

"Got it," Ken replies.

The beep of a car horn can be heard coming up the road. They look in that direction to see a Ford station wagon coming around the corner, followed by another car, and another, and another, all filled to the brim with would-be patients.

Word had travelled quickly. In no time at all, a line of at least thirty people, indigenous and non-indigenous, had formed.

After she organised the arrivals in order of first come, first served, Maisy calls the first patient. An older woman stands and waddles her way over to Ken's table. She's over 50 and looks a little worse for wear.

"Please take a seat," he says to her, extending his arm warmly, inviting her to sit next to him.

"So, what can I do for you today?" he asks.

"Hello doctor, I have a bit of a sore throat and a bit of a fever. I've had it off and on for a few weeks."

"Weeks?" he asks, surprised by her delay in seeking help, "we better have a look then." He begins his examination, and asks her to open her mouth where he can see a raging infection.

"Yes, I can see you have a pretty bad infection, some penicillin, pain relief and some rest for a few days should fix you up," Ken says in a matter-of-fact way.

"I'm sorry doctor, but we can't pay you, we don't have any money,"

Ken smiles. "You don't need to worry, let's get you well, hey?"

The lady smiles in return, grateful for the care. He does what Jesus said and thinks about what he needs before dipping his hand into his bag.

He focuses his thoughts, thinking of penicillin and some painkillers, then, carefully reaching into the bag, he feels two boxed items that were not there before, he removes his hand and to his surprise, he finds the packets of medicine he requires.

"Well, bugger me," he says, astounded at another miracle.

"What was that, doctor?" the patient asks.

"Oh nothing," he replies, smiling, "Now, here is the medicine you need." he says, touching the woman kindly on her arm, "and don't worry about money, my services are and always will be free for the people of this place."

The patient looks so relieved and happy that he thought she was going to cry.

"Just don't forget, two a day of the penicillin with food and two painkillers every four hours, until the pain is under control, OK?" he adds, making sure she understands.

"I will, thank you doctor," the woman replies, as she leaves the table making room for the next person.

Over the next few hours, Ken continues to treat people with all kinds of maladies. He keeps putting his hand in the bag and sure enough, the medicine keeps coming out. It seems as though the more people he treats, the more arrive. He's thrilled, of course, to be practising real medicine again to people who actually need him. He feels he could make a difference here, and the best part is he isn't in a war zone, or dealing with people who just want a day off work. To be in a place where he can make a real impact is incredibly satisfying.

It's time for a break and Maisy has made Ken a well-earned cup of coffee which he gratefully accepts. He walks over to the shoreline, taking in the beauty of the place and notices a large crowd gathering some fifty metres away from the camp. Intrigued, he strolls over to see what's going on.

He sees Jesus, stripped down to his underwear, standing waist deep in the water some ten metres away from him, with a line of people waiting their turn. Ken watches intently as a young man approaches Jesus, stopping in front of him. He smiles at the teenager before placing his hands on his head. It looks like he's praying, then the penny drops.

"Baptisms!" Ken says out loud, "He is doing bloody baptisms."

It may not be the east bank of the river Jordan, but it will do. He can't help but think of John the Baptist and wonders, is this what it was like when Jesus roamed the land, giving sermons and performing miracles? It's surreal.

Two young men approach him as he continues watching the baptisms. Both in their late teens, they are dragging a couple of dead kangaroos by their tails.

"Excuse us, doc," one young man says meekly, not wanting to bother him.

"What have we got here?" he asks in a playful tone,

"Just a bit of tucker, doc, we were wanting to ask if you mind us getting a cook-up going for everyone."

"Sounds like a great idea," Ken replies.

The young men break into wide smiles at his response. They rush off to make the bush oven to cook the marsupials.

Jesus, who had just dunked another one in the waters of the lake, waves, with that cheesy smile he has when he is pleased with himself. He should be, it's a wonderful day. As far as Ken is concerned, this is a near perfect moment, only Carol's presence would complete it.

Ken watches as the young man go about preparing the fire for the kangaroos. Some of the women in the group get up and begin searching the tree line, chattering with each other, they grab a bit foliage from this tree, a bit from that bush, and so on. He can only assume they are looking for some edibles, and other kinds of bush tucker to add to the meal. This activity inspires a couple of other men who walk down to the shoreline, in deep discussion.

"Going to try some fishing?" Ken hears Jesus call out to the men who shake their heads.

"No good for fish here, boss, this place only fills up on rain, no fish," they call back, but Jesus isn't convinced.

"Are you sure?" he calls again, "You should really try down there," pointing to another place, a further fifty metres along the bank.

They shrug their shoulders and after further discussion, one of the men runs to his car, returning with some handlines and a small cast net.

The men walk down to the place that Jesus pointed out and, using stale bread for bait, they cast their lines into the water. To the men's amazement, they are getting bites within seconds, pulling in large tilapia and carp. Before they know it, they have caught plenty of fish for everyone.

Ken looks over to the treatment tent. Maisy is trying to get his attention, waving at him, more people are waiting to see him.

"Oh well, break's over," he says, acknowledging Maisy by waving back and tipping out the remains of his coffee. He takes one final look at this setting, a moment he will never forget.

›››⟩⟩ ⟨⟨⟨⟨‹

After a gruelling six hours, Ken finally sees the last patient and once again, he's exhausted. By his estimate, he's seen over 100 people today and is ready for bed. Maisy on the other hand looks fresh, as she always does. The community elders, including the young men who brought the kangaroos, are laying out the food for all to see. The old women lay out the edibles including what looks like yams, berries and cooked roots of some description, not to mention the fish which have been cooked to perfection.

It surprises Ken that such a feast has been created out of what most Europeans would perceive as a barren landscape. That's the difference thousands upon thousands of years of knowledge and instinct makes. These people don't just survive in this landscape; they thrive as they have done since time began.

He surveys the food being laid out on pieces of bark like a buffet. The kids are eating first, as they should, and Jesus is holding court with the elders, and deep into discussion. It reminds Ken of the last supper story, as Jesus holds court, sitting in the middle of the men, passing food between each other. He's too tired to eat, he just wants to sleep.

A man in his late thirties approaches the medical table. A short, stocky man, wearing only a green singlet and pair of shorts.

"Scuse me, doc," the man asks, "I know you've been going all day but do you have time to see one more?"

"Of course I do." Ken replies, hoping no one else joins a new queue as he ushers the man towards the seat. They sit down and Ken begins by taking the man's blood pressure.

"Can I ask you something, doc?" Ken nods while listening to his pulse, "This fella you're with, the one with the beard, do you think he's the real deal?"

Ken stops and looks at the man.

"What do you mean, the real deal?"

"Well, he seems to think he's Jesus, the real one, 'cause that's who he said he was and my aunty said she saw something strange when she sat next to him."

"What did she see?" Ken asks curiously, as he continues to check the man out.

"She said when she looked at this fella, all she saw was a brilliant white light in the shape of a person, everything was just this light. I don't know what to make of it."

Ken is puzzled. "Which one is your aunty?" he asks the man, looking at the row of elderly women sitting by the fire.

"She's the one in the red shirt," the man says as Ken scans the crowd, seeing an old lady with white hair wearing what appears to be thick sunglasses.

"Why is she wearing sunglasses in the evening?" he asks.

"Well, you see doc, that's the thing, she's been blind since she was ten years old, she can't see anything."

Ken should be stunned, but he isn't. The blind woman could be seeing Jesus as he really is, without the distortions of this world? There is only one answer he can give the man, only one that makes sense.

"I think she is seeing him exactly how she is supposed to," Ken says,

"As for you, however, your blood pressure is fine, your pulse is nice and steady, so what's wrong with you?" he asks, changing the subject.

"Nothin'. I just wanted to come over and thank you for what you did today."

"Thank you for saying so, but it's my pleasure, believe me."

"I also wanted to thank you for taking the trouble to learn our language. Speaking to a doctor in our own words makes things a lot easier."

Ken thinks for a moment, he hasn't learnt the language, he certainly doesn't know how to speak it.

"What are you talking about?" Ken asks the man, puzzled by his extraordinary statement.

"Come on doc, don't muck around, you know you've been speakin' in Mantjiljarra around here all day," the man replies, chuckling to himself, "You're a funny fella doc, thanks again." he says, leaving Ken shaking his head at the wonder of it all.

The remainder of the crowd help themselves to the food, as singing breaks out amongst the people. Suddenly, it's a party and once again music rings out.

Ken sits on the edge of his bunk, lying down, stretching out as the light from the fire dims slightly.

"You're going to miss the party, doctor," Maisy says, as she closes the caravan door,

"No, I'm not," he replies, "I just need to stretch out for a few minutes, that's all."

"Sure." Maisy says cheekily, knowing full well he'll be asleep within a few minutes, and, as predicted, he begins to drift off.

CHAPTER TWELVE

Jesus stands over a fast-asleep Ken; again he needs to wake him as something is afoot. He's been poking and prodding him and keeps it up until the older man stirs. Groaning and muttering, Ken starts to come around, waking once again to find Jesus hovering over him.

"I wish you would stop doing that," he says, startled by the disruption and trying to focus his eyes.

"Sorry, Ken," Jesus says, "but I need you to come with us."

"What time is it?" he asks, barely awake.

"3 a.m., doctor." Maisy replies with a serious tone in her voice.

He stands upright, looking at the pair of them and with them, a young boy around nine years old, a boy he had never seen before.

"I'm sorry about that everyone, I must have dozed off," he says apologetically.

"Please come with us, Ken," Jesus requests a second time, ushering him around the back of the caravan, out of sight of the people who have remained at the camp.

"Who are you?" Ken asks the young boy as they walk.

"It's me doc, Henry, good to see you again," he says, stepping in front of Jesus.

"How can you be Henry, you died and your spirit left, I saw it?"

"It did, but the soul age and human age are two different things. Besides, Jesus said I could thank you for bringing me home before we go."

"Well, it was my pleasure, but what do you mean go, go where?" Ken asks, as the comment panics him. He thought he had more time with his friends, he isn't ready for them to go yet.

Jesus places his hand lovingly on his shoulder. "It's time for us to go home," he says gently, "The journey has come to an end, and we have other work to do, as do you."

"I don't understand, you can't go yet, I have many more questions, there's more to learn!" Ken protests.

"I told you this trip was nearly over and now it is. We have to go."

"Take me with you, Jesus, take me to Carol, please?" he implores the Son of God who can only shake his head.

"It isn't your time yet; you still have so much to do here."

"How can I live in this world, now that I know the truth?" Ken asks.

"By using what you have learnt from me to help those here, to help those who need you now more than ever," Jesus says calmly.

Ken sheds a tear.

"Is that what this is all about, to bring Henry home, to bring a doctor to these people?" Ken sounds scorned, like a brooding teenager.

"In part," Jesus replies, "but it wasn't the main reason why I came back."

"Well, what was that reason then?" Ken asks, feeling excluded.

"Have you not figured it out yet?" he says, "I came to save you."

Ken is taken aback.

"Me, why me?"

Jesus swiftly replies, "Why not you? You're just as important as anyone else." Ken thinks about the significance of that comment for a moment, it's touched him.

"What am I to do now?" he asks, sounding lost.

"Tell me, did it feel good being a doctor again?"

Ken recalls how good it made him feel, "Oh yes," he says as his eyes light up with excitement, "more than good."

"Well aside from living the rest of your life to its fullest, I think these people and other communities like them need a doctor out here, don't you?"

Ken knows what is being asked of him and it's an assignment he will gladly accept, especially if he gets to keep feeling like this.

"Yes, I do." Perhaps, this is what Jesus meant about people being called to their purpose, and he hears the call, louder than ever.

"For as long as you come to these people on this land, the bag will always provide for you, these waters will nourish you and the people will care for you."

"You've brought me back to life," Ken says warmly, extending his hand which Jesus grasps affectionately.

"It's been my pleasure, brother." The men hug tightly, as dear friends do when they part.

"Travel south west, you will find the nearest town in an hour or so, another day from there and you will be with your daughter."

"Will do," he replies, "what say you, Maisy, want a job?"

She has an awkward look on her face.

I'm sorry, doctor." Maisy says apologetically, "I'm going with Jesus, I'm going home as well."

Ken laughs, "I thought as much."

"My time here ended long ago, but we are occasionally allowed to come back to help, like I did with Henry."

"You died all those years ago in that rusty car we drove by, didn't you?"

"Yes," Maisy nods. "Would you do me one favour, doctor?"

"Anything," Ken replies.

"My family still live in Wiluna, would you…"

Ken knows what she is going to ask; she doesn't need to say it. "I'd be happy to," he says.

Maisy smiles again, "Thank you."

It begins. As Ken experienced two days before when they encountered the unclean spirit, everything pauses. Time and space once again stand still.

The cycle repeats, the sounds of the night cease, no crickets, no insects, no wind, nothing. Not even the snoring sounds of his sleeping patients can be heard.

Jesus bends down and extends his index finger, reaching up into the air and drawing an imaginary line which instantly fills with ripples of a brilliant white light, bursting out from what appears to be another place, it's a glimpse into another realm.

The brilliance of the light reflects off Ken's face so strongly that it illuminates the entire area, turning night into day. The three beings stand ready to depart this world. For Ken, it is as if he is farewelling his family. He cannot move, yet tears somehow find a way to trickle down his face.

The ribbon of light hangs in the air like a vine from a tree, it's time to go. First, it's Maisy who walks through without hesitation, followed by young Henry, unsure of what to expect, he cautiously steps through.

Jesus gives him a nod of appreciation. "Just remember, your time of trial is not yet over, and the father never gives more than you can handle. Just know I am always with you."

The brilliant white line wraps itself around Jesus, like a rope, consuming his body to a point where the figure of the man is indistinguishable from the light. The two merge and become one.

The light penetrates Ken's eyelids, seeping into every corpuscle in his body. A final pulse of brilliance erupts before the light vanishes into God's kingdom.

"Goodbye, my friends," he whispers, now being able to move, he wipes the tears away as he stands alone in the dark. He walks over to the edge of the lake where Jesus was baptizing people earlier and sits on the side of the hill, watching the occasional shooting star drop in from the heavens.

He reaffirms in his mind this incredible experience was real, and that it did happen.

He spends the next few hours contemplating what he learned from his time with Jesus, knowing more wonders in his life are possible, that his life didn't end with Carol's passing, and that there is much more for him to do.

His thoughts turn towards his daughter.

'Poor girl, she must be beside herself with worry, not knowing where I've been all week.' He hopes she isn't too angry with him.

⤳⟫⟫ ⟪⟪⟪⤶

Dawn breaks over the horizon and Ken is joined by the elder with the cowboy hat, the first man he met when they arrived. He sits next to Ken and they share the dawn.

They look at each other, knowing they have had their own special encounters with Jesus which has created a bond between them.

"I've realized I have been very rude; I didn't ask your name?" Ken apologises.

The man smiles and extends his hand. "My name is Stanley," he says proudly. The two men shake hands firmly.

"Ken, my name is Ken and I am very pleased to meet you, Stanley."

They watch the morning birds hunt for insects across the water's surface as the sounds of wildlife echo throughout the land.

"They've gone back?" Stanley asks without breaking his gaze.

Ken nods, "Yeah. They've gone back."

"Do you think they really were who they said?" Stanley asks, trying to come to terms with his own experience, that it was not his imagination.

"They sure were," Ken assures him.

"Well, bugger me, hey?"

Ken chuckles, knowing exactly how he's feeling.

"You gonna come back to us, doc?"

160

"Yep, how does the last Sunday of every month sound?" Ken replies, the thought of returning here brings him a sense of peace.

"Great, we need ya!"

"I know," he replies, knowing full well he needs them just as much. "You put on the food, and I'll bring the medicine, OK?" He winks.

"Sounds like a good deal to me."

Ken and Stanley shake hands, confirming their new friendship.

>>>>> <<<<<

Getting on the road again was delayed by long good-byes to his new friends. He wasn't short of helpers in getting everything stowed away. At one point, he wasn't sure they would let him go. He received their genuine appreciation and affection which he had never experienced before.

Eventually, he was back on the road and in around an hour, he hit the town of Wiluna just as Jesus said he would. It was an eerie feeling for him, driving on these roads alone, having become used to the company. He still has Carol though; her urn rides up front with him.

As he enters the town, the fuel light finally comes on. He laughs as he surmises that so long as he was on God's business, the holy-fuel would last. Now he needs an earthly source of fuel, and pulls into the only petrol station in town. He stops right at the pump, eager to find a phone and to call Gemma who must be having kittens by now.

An attendant, wearing long grey overalls and covered from head to toe in grease, approaches his car, eager to help.

"How much would you like, sir?" he asks in a friendly tone.

"Fill it up and the jerry cans as well if you don't mind...do you have a phone box?" he asks the attendant who points to the street.

"Outside the general store, it's the only public phone around."

"Thank you," Ken replies, "I'll be back in a few minutes."

He scurries over the dusty road, dodging a truck in the process. It might be an outback town but it's smack in the middle of the goldfields, and visited by many people hoping to make their fortune.

Ken can see the phone box, He checks his pockets, he has enough coins for the call. He can't get inside the booth fast enough, loading the coins into the slot, impatiently waiting for them go down so he can make the call.

He dials her number, it rings a few times before it's finally answered as the distinctive beeps are heard, letting everyone know it's an out-of-town call.

Gemma's been at her home in Perth for over a week, patiently waiting for her father to ring, and worried sick. She is furious he didn't bother to let her know when he left home or where he was for that matter, and now the police are looking for him.

They visited her a few days ago for a welfare check, at the behest of the New South Wales Police who believed he had been abducted by some criminal, but they weren't sure.

She's been worried sick ever since, not knowing what's happened to her father, but she swears that when she sees him, she'll kill him for making her worry so much.

The phone rings, she races to it, as she has done every other time it has rung over the past week.

Kevin has been doing his best to keep her calm but he has to return to work, and a part of him worries Gemma may have lost her father as well. Losing both her parents would be too much for her to cope with in such a short space of time.

She answers the phone to hear the beeps coming down the line, her heart races in anticipation. Is it her father or the police with bad news?

"Hello," she says cautiously.

"Gem!" A voice yells excitedly on the other end of phone, "Can you hear me?" he asks, as the sounds of a passing car drowns out his voice.

"Dad! Is that you?" she asks frantically, straining to hear him. Kevin looks on, praying it's his father-in-law.

"Gem, it's Dad, can you hear me?"

"Yes Dad, I can hear you, just, where are you?" she yells back down the line.

"I'm in Wiluna, darling, about a day's drive away from you."

"Oh, thank God, I've been worried bloody sick. Are you OK?"

"Yes, I am fine, actually I'm great, I've had quite the adventure, I can't wait to tell you about it," he yells, unaware of the fuss he's created, "I'm going to stay here the night, get a good sleep and drive to your place tomorrow."

Old phone boxes amplify outside noises as another four-wheel drive roars past. Gemma can barely hear him, but she has the gist of what he's saying.

"I'll see you tomorrow," he cheerfully adds, and not knowing whether his daughter was still on the line or not, he hangs up the phone.

Gemma hears the disconnection sound and slowly places the phone back on the receiver. She is stunned, not sure if she's glad he's safe or furious.

Kevin waits patiently for his wife to say something, but he can see the cogs in her brain turning over, thinking about the call.

"Well, what did he say, where's he been?" Kevin asks.

Gemma looks at him blankly, "All he said was he's had an adventure."

"An adventure?" Kevin is confused, "What the hell does that mean?"

Gemma shakes her head, "I have no idea."

"Where is he now, did he say?"

"He's in Wiluna, he's going to spend the night there and come straight here tomorrow."

Kevin isn't as quick to condemn his father-in-law for not staying in touch. After all, it's the outback, and it isn't as though there are phones on every corner.

"I think you'll find he has no idea of the drama he's caused. When you calmly tell him, I'm sure he will be deeply apologetic," Kevin says, trying to give his wife some perspective.

"I'm relieved he is safe and well, Kev, I really am."

Kevin takes his wife's hand, "At least he's alive and we can be grateful for that."

⟫⟫⟫ ⟪⟪⟪

Ken walks inside the general store where he's greeted by the store-keeper, a mature lady in her early forties wearing a yellow flowery dress that is clearly too tight as her chest is barely contained within it. Something tells him she wears it too tight on purpose.

"What ya looking for, luv?" she asks, speaking with a deep, raspy voice. Ken can tell it's from many years of smoking, but it seems to suit her.

"Do you have any flowers?" he enquires, turning around and scanning the store.

"Flowers?" she sounds surprised, "don't get much call for flowers around here. What do you want them for, some lucky lady I suppose?" she asks.

Ken shakes his head and smiles, "No, I promised myself if I ever came to Wiluna, I would put some flowers on a friend's grave."

"Oh," she says, "well, I do have some flowers I keep for special occasions in the fridge, next to the dairy section," she points to the large refrigerator at the back of the store.

Ken goes where he's directed and can see small bunches of pointed flowers through the glass. Brilliant small flowers in all the colours of the rainbow. There are purples, pinks, white with yellow, pretty combinations of all kinds.

"Perfect," he says aloud, opening the door to select a bunch, "What are they?" he asks, "I've never seen them before?"

164

"They're called a starflower; they grow around here, more of a shrub than a flower, but still nice."

"Well, they are beautiful," he remarks, "How much?"

"Ten bucks, luv," she says. Ken is a little shocked by the price but to find fresh flowers out here is almost a miracle in itself. Besides, they are an appropriately-named flower, given who they're intended for.

He hands over a $10 note without hesitation, which she almost snatches from his hand.

"I haven't seen you through here before?" she asks, as she rings up the till. Visitors to the town, outside of the prospectors, she finds a novelty, and she can't help but snoop a little.

"No, this is my first time in your town, I'm from Sydney, on my way through to Perth."

"Well, you're a long way from home,"

Her words hit him. The home he knew is gone, the life he had is over. Gemma lives her own life; nothing remains for him in Sydney. It's time for a new chapter.

"Actually, I don't live there anymore, I'm moving over here but I haven't yet decided exactly where as yet."

"I see, and what do you do?" she asks, continuing her inquisition.

"I'm a doctor," he states. His disclosure seems to pique her curiosity even more as she tidies her hair and presents her cleavage in some vain hope he may find her of interest.

"If you don't mind me asking, is there a Mrs Doctor?"

Ken knows where this is going and is afraid his answer is only going to encourage her. It's not as though she's unattractive; he just isn't interested.

"I'm widowed."

Her eyes light up. "I'm sorry to hear that, doctor. You know Wiluna is a lovely place to live," she says,

Trying to be polite, he says "I'll keep that in mind, thanks for the flowers." He rapidly exits the shop before she can utter another word.

He hurries back over the road to the service station where his car and van have been moved to the side of the building. He sees the attendant who is working on another car.

"Sorry I took so long; I got talking to the storekeeper," Ken says, rolling his eyes.

The man smiles, "You're lucky to have escaped, usually a man by himself doesn't get out of there easily."

"I got that feeling, what do I owe you?"

"Two hundred and twenty-eight-dollars, thanks."

Ken hands over two-fifty. "Keep the change."

"Thank you very much!" the attendant says, excited by the large tip. "Is there anything else I can do for you?"

"I don't suppose you know where the cemetery is around here?"

"The cemetery? Yeah, I know where it is."

"There's an old friend's grave there, I promised myself I would visit it if I ever made it to this town," Ken explains, grateful for any help.

"Well, I do some work there occasionally, volunteer you know, keep the place tidy. Whose grave are you looking for, maybe I know them?"

It didn't occur to him he could be looking for a needle in a haystack. He thought it would be easy to find her in a small country graveyard.

"Maisy Gibson," Ken says, not giving the reply much thought, however the man stops what he's doing.

"How do you know her?" he asks defensively.

Ken picks up on his reaction. "We worked together once, many years ago, I'm a doctor, did you know her?"

He walks over to a chair and sits down, looking as though he'd seen a ghost.

"I haven't thought about her for quite some time, doctor, it's even been a while since I've been there, to see her, you know."

"I know what you mean," Ken says, "are you related to her?"

"Yeah, I'm related to her, I'm her brother."

"I'm sorry," Ken says kindly, "I had no idea."

"Oh, it's OK, it was a long time ago, I was eleven when she went missing. It was hardest for Mum, of course, her and Maisy were very close," he says, recalling the day she failed to return home. "I always believed Mum died of a broken heart. They never found Maisy while Mum was alive; it wasn't until a few years after she passed, we learnt what happened to her."

"And what happened to her, if you don't mind me asking?" Ken says gently, not wanting to upset the man further, but he needs to know.

"I was working here, when one day, this older bloke turns up in this truck, telling us he'd found someone dead on an old back road a few days from here. He brought her here because her licence said she lived in Wiluna. It turned out to be my sister, at least what was left of her."

"What happened to the man?" Ken asks, "Did he tell you how she died?"

"No. He had her wrapped up in a sheet and just dropped her off in a real hurry and left town. Never saw him again."

Ken thinks for a moment, he wonders about the man who found her, it couldn't be who has popped into his head, but then again, it wouldn't surprise him either.

"The old man who brought her home, do you recall his name?"

John thinks about the question for minute, he hasn't had to think about any of this for a long, long time, but he knows the answer.

"His name was Henry; I've never forgotten his name."

Ken nods, now it makes sense to him. As he thought, Henry brought her home and Maisy returns the favour. Even in death, God has a plan for everyone.

"John, I hate to impose on you further, but could you show me where her grave is?"

He nods. "Of course, I'm just glad some of her friends have finally turned up to see her...are those flowers for her grave?"

"They are indeed," Ken replies, "I thought they would be nice."

John smiles, "Starflowers, they're her favourite."

⇝⇝⇝ ⇜⇜⇜

The two men travel to the cemetery in John's shop truck as he reminisces about his younger years with his big sister. The cemetery itself is unremarkable; you would miss it if you didn't know where to turn off the highway. The only indication it's a cemetery is two small brick fences forming an entry statement. A quiet and lonely place. As the vehicle stops, John points to his sister's resting place, a short walk from the car.

They both approach the spot; this is another surreal moment for Ken, he only saw her a few hours ago, and as far as he or anyone else could tell, in the flesh.

He wishes he could tell her brother she is OK and doing God's work. It would give him peace of mind, but Ken knows the man wouldn't believe him.

He looks at the neatly maintained grave, surrounded in rocks and deposits of old dried out starflowers from previous visits.

"I come out here from time to time, you know, birthdays, Christmas, the big ones, other than that, there isn't a lot of reason to visit," he says. "it's strange sometimes, you know, when I'm out here alone. There are times I could swear I've seen her, other times, like now, I swear I can feel her presence, watching me."

"Sounds perfectly wonderful to me," Ken says, knowing it is her and he's not imagining it; he feels her presence too.

"I'll give you some time, doctor," he says, slowly walking towards the car. Ken bends down and collects the dried flowers, throwing them to the side and putting the fresh ones in their place. He clears other little bits of debris such as sticks and leaves.

"Thank you, Maisy," Ken says out loud, "I see why you led me here to meet your brother; he's a nice fellow who misses his sister."

Ken stands, fixated, knowing her remains, the physical Maisy, is there, deep below the ground, but Maisy the person, well, she's somewhere else.

"Rest well, my favourite nurse." he says, blowing a kiss towards her grave. As he turns to leave, he feels as though someone is standing to his left, out of the corner of his eye, in his peripheral. He looks in that direction to see Maisy, standing there, next to a lone tree, some thirty metres away, wearing that dress and smiling. He returns her smile as her image fades away.

Ken returns to the car where John is sitting on the bonnet, having a smoke, thinking of his sister.

"Thank you for bringing me out here, John," Ken says graciously,

"Can I ask you a question?" John asks.

"Sure."

"I know doctors are people of science, but do you think there is a heaven, and do you think my sister is there with Mum?"

Ken recognizes the angst; John's been carrying the loss with him for years. Just a few days ago, he was asking the same question, not knowing the answer which is hard to live with. At least he can give her brother an answer he knows is true.

"I promise you, John, she's there alright, doing God's work," he replies confidently, wishing he could say more.

"I hope so, doctor," he says forlornly, dropping his cigarette on the ground, and stomping on it, "Come on, I'll get you back to town."

Ken spends the next few hours getting to know him a little better, sharing a beer or two, gaining a better insight into his sister and her life, how selfless she was, he isn't surprised by what he hears.

John invites Ken to keep his caravan parked next to the petrol station and spend the night there.

He enters the caravan and lays on his bed, thinking of Carol and of course, Gemma. His thoughts travel back to his daughter's grief and how selfish he was. He didn't know any better then, things will be different now.

He wonders how Gemma will respond to his fantastic tale. There is one small thing that's niggling at him. When Jesus left, he said Ken's *'time of trail was not over.'* What did he mean? What's going to happen next?

Chapter Thirteen

G emma woke early to drop her husband off at the airport for his flight back to the mines. On her return home, she finally has some time to herself. She sits down to a quiet breakfast of toast, plum jam and a hot cup of tea. She hasn't slept much since speaking with her father yesterday, she's still worried. She was so angry he didn't let her know when he was leaving, and terribly frightened something had happened to him when the police contacted her. It sent her panic into overdrive. Perhaps Kevin is right, her father has no idea of the fuss he accidentally created.

When she was a teenager and her father would go on his trips to Africa, it could be weeks before he would check in, so this isn't anything new. At first, he would call every few days, but as time went on and the trips became more frequent, Gemma and her mother would hear from him less which only made them worry more - she had hated him for it.

When he came home, all he would do was work, six days a week, evening house calls, he would do whatever he could to avoid being at home. If Carol hadn't taken the practice manager's job, she would never have seen him. It was like he didn't want to be there. Little did they know that his work addiction was how he fought his demons.

She always wondered if it was possible to love and hate someone at the same time. Was it wrong to feel that way? As she got older, the feelings passed and she began to understand a little more of his battles and what he had gone through.

As she sits down with her tea and toast, she is startled by a thunderous knocking at the front door. According to the kitchen clock, it's 7 a.m.

'Who the bloody hell could it be at this time?' she asks herself, surprised someone would have the audacity to knock on her door this early.

She gets up from the table and storms down the hallway, ready to give whoever it is a piece of her mind. She swings the door open, ready to spit fire, when she is pleasantly surprised by her visitor.

"Dad!" she exclaims, jumping on to the front landing, hugging her father, "What are you doing here this early? I thought you weren't arriving until this evening?"

Ken smiles. "Hello darling," he says, looking dishevelled, with his overnight bag in his hand, his wife's urn in the other. "I couldn't sleep and drove through the night. I have so much to tell you, I couldn't wait."

"I'm so glad you're here, please, come in." she says, excited to see him safe and well. She gives her father another big hug as he enters the house, "Oh my God, Dad you absolutely stink." she exclaims.

"Sorry, I haven't had a shower for a day or so."

"Well, before you sit yourself on any of my furniture, it's into the shower, mister," she orders.

"Yes mam," he replies with a broad smile.

⇒⇒⇒ ⇐⇐⇐

He walks out of the bedroom to join his daughter at the kitchen table. Fresh clothes and properly showered, he feels like a new man. He may have had a dip at the lake and changed his clothes, but it's hardly the same thing as a hot shower.

"Feel better, Dad?"

"I cannot begin to tell you how good it feels," he replies, pulling out a chair next to her. She slides the fresh coffee over to him which he eagerly accepts in both hands.

"You read my mind," he says, diving into the mug of hot coffee.

"So, Dad, where have you been for ten days?" she asks firmly, getting straight to the point; Ken knows by her tone he's in a bit of trouble.

"Eight days," he replies calmly, which throws Gemma off balance. "What?"

"Eight days, that's how long my trip took, well technically nine days if you include today," he corrects her with a cheeky grin, unaware of how much stress she's been under.

Gemma isn't seeing the funny side. "Dad, this isn't a joke, I was bloody worried stupid for eight days,' and then the police contacted me, telling me that some criminal may or may not have been holding you against your will. I have been worried sick."

"Police?" Ken asks.

"Yes, the police, they came here to do a welfare check, to see if you had made it back. So, if you don't mind, just tell me where you have been?"

Ken puts the coffee down, not sure if he should tell her the whole truth or some other version she may find more palatable. She is more like him than either of them is prepared to admit, but he has to be true to himself about his experience.

He takes a big breath, followed by a big gulp of coffee, preparing himself to tell her a story that defies logic, that defies science and that defied his understanding of everything. He isn't sure how Gemma will receive his story of extraordinary happenings. It's now or never, he takes the plunge.

"When I left Sydney, I tried calling you a couple of times but the phone kept ringing out, and I needed to get going, so I left. To be honest, I couldn't wait to get out of there," he explains.

"On the second day, I came across a very bad car accident, it had happened just before I arrived. A young girl and her mother were critically injured and I was desperately trying to save them until help arrived."

"That's terrible, Dad." she responds, feeling guilty for being cross with him.

"Yes, it was," he says, buttering his toast. It's at that moment he decides to tell her everything, as it happened.

"Go on Dad, what happened then?"

"Once the ambulance had left, I went to check on the driver of the other car who caused the accident. Police at the scene thought he was already dead. When I went to check, his body was gone. Clearly, he was not dead."

"Where did he go?" Gemma asks impatiently, captivated by the story.

"When I went to my car to leave, I found the man sitting on the floor in the back; he was pointing a shotgun at my head."

"What!" she yells, covering her mouth in shock, "He had a gun to your head, why didn't you call for help?"

Ken gives her a look, "Gem, please, the man had a gun on me, I didn't get a chance to call out. He forced me to drive him into the desert for hours and hours. I didn't know if I was going to live or die. He was off his head on drugs, he would have killed me in a second if I didn't comply."

Gemma apologizes.

"I'm sorry Dad, of course you're right, you've been through an ordeal, I had no idea, I was angry, thinking you had gone off on one your treks, I'm sorry."

Ken places his hand lightly on hers, letting her know it's OK.

"We all get consumed by emotions from time to time, it's easy to do, I should know, right?" quietly admitting his faults to his daughter which wasn't lost on her.

"Now, I have a great deal more to tell you," he continues, "The man, whose name I learnt was Michael, was severely injured and was fading in and out of consciousness. I knew from the blood loss it would only be a matter of time before he passed out or died. So, I had to bide my time and wait."

Gemma nods, understanding her father's strategy, "Makes sense."

"I thought so as well, but it didn't quite work out that way."

Over the next three hours, Gemma sits silently, listening intently to her father as he tells his tale of supernatural entanglement and the rebirth of his soul. The look on her face never changed, as she sat there, silent, listening, as he unpacked his story.

As she tries to make sense of it, Gemma is thinking that his mind created this adventure fantasy to mitigate his grief. Little did she know that he also had the same thoughts, and was using that exact same rationale, until finally he could no longer deny the events as he experienced them. What is clear, however, is that her father believes his story to be true.

Exhausted from the retelling, Ken stands to stretch his legs. He helps himself to a glass of water from the kitchen sink. He is exhausted and needs to sleep.

Gemma is trying to find something supportive to say, but all she can do is look at him as if he was from another world.

He walks back over to the table, sitting back down, exhaling heavily as he waits for his daughter to speak.

"I promise you, Gem, everything I've told is the absolute truth," he said, looking into her eyes and speaking with the utmost seriousness. He waits for the barrage to begin.

"I don't know what you want me to say," she replies. "Do you understand how fantastic it all sounds?"

"I do, I wanted to be completely honest with you, after all, you're all I have left and you deserve the truth, regardless of how it sounds."

Gemma can't believe he expects her to buy into this fairy tale. She did, after all, inherit his views on hard factual evidence but in the same breath, she also respected her mother's beliefs. Still, it is as big a leap for her as it was for him.

"Can you hear the words coming out of your mouth, Dad?" firing her first salvo. "Can you hear how ridiculous it sounds?"

Ken nods. "Believe me I do, but I cannot deny what I saw with my own eyes."

"Yet you expect me to believe you have been in the outback for nearly ten days with a man who abducted you at gunpoint, died, and then resurrected himself as Jesus Christ...it had to have been some kind of elaborate deception. Dad, he played you!"

Ken is frustrated with her response, but what else did he expect?

"Again, I said the same thing myself for the first few days, but there was no scientific or rational explanation for what I experienced, none."

"You yourself once told me that everything we don't understand has an answer somewhere in science. Now you expect me to abandon that view?"

"No, I don't. But all I can say is I was wrong, very wrong. There is a higher power at work in this world, regardless of how many years I insisted there wasn't. I saw a man die and come back to life, with his injuries healed. I saw a man turn water into fuel, I can go on, but unless you were there, it's impossible to comprehend."

"Dad," she says, focusing on her words, "I believe you experienced something out there; I really do, I don't know what, but something did happen, I can hear it in your voice. However, at the moment, I can only go so far."

He understands how she feels, it was a big ask. He stands up from the table, so weary he can't think. He must sleep.

"If it's alright with you, I'm going to rest, I'm pretty buggered, thanks for listening, my love," he says, giving her a fake smile, disappointed she didn't share his excitement.

"Do not tell that story to the police tomorrow, they may not be so understanding."

"No, I don't suppose they would," he replies, leaving the kitchen for his room.

CHAPTER FOURTEEN

Gemma tossed and turned most of the night, trying to understand her father's story from a clinical perspective. Knowing the man he was, recounting this incredible story to her, it's as though he's a different person. Even the way he looked at her was different. Nothing is ever easy with her family; she's working tonight, and what she wouldn't give for a little normalcy after the last few months.

The front door of the house rattles loudly again with the sound of forceful knocking.

"Oh, they're early," she says under her breath, "best get it out of the way."

She stops setting the table for breakfast and walks purposely to the front of the house, taking a moment to gather herself, ensuring she gives a suitable welcome.

She can see two blue uniforms through the screen. Putting on her best smile, Gemma opens the door.

"Good morning Mrs. Reece, I'm Senior Sergeant Johnson and this is Constable Stevens of Western Australian (WA) Police, we're here to talk with your father, Doctor Ken Burton."

"Yes gentlemen, we've been expecting you, won't you please come in?"

She welcomes them, hoping this will only take 15 or 20 minutes.

"Thank you, Mrs. Reece," the senior sergeant says, as they take off their uniform hats and step inside the house.

"Gentlemen, if you'll follow me, please," she instructs them, putting on her best 'Lady of the House' routine as they walk down the hallway towards the main dining room. The kitchen table is set for breakfast but as they are guests, the dining room table is a more fitting place.

"If you wouldn't mind taking a seat, I'll go and tell my father you're here?" she says, ushering them to the table.

The men take a seat and get their note pads out.

Ken sits on the bed, putting on his shoes after a good night's sleep. He didn't dream of anything in particular, even though he thought that perhaps, Jesus may come to him in his dreams again, as he did in the beginning, or perhaps Carol might have dropped in, but alas, no such luck.

He feels relatively at peace when he thinks of her now, knowing she is with Jesus. He hears a gentle knock on his bedroom door.

Gemma peeks around the door, "Dad, are you decent?" she chirps.

"I've always been decent, darling, but if you're wanting to know if I'm fully dressed, the answer is, yes, I am," he chuckles to himself.

"The police are here to talk to you."

Ken looks at his watch, it's only 10 a.m.

"Very well, I'll be there shortly," he replies, as Gemma retreats behind the door. He wonders what they'll ask him, and more importantly, what will he tell them? Certainly not the truth, that's for sure; Gemma is right, they'll lock him up if he does.

He needs to keep it simple, surely the police don't want to do a lot of paperwork to close this matter out. After all, they are simply following up for the New South Wales police to make sure he's safe.

He confidently strides to the dining room, ready to get this over with. He has a lot to do, including closing his old life and starting his new one.

He enters the room to see a tall, older policeman, around 45, with a handlebar moustache, sitting patiently at the table. With him is a younger, shorter man, obviously the junior of the two, sporting the most egregious mutton chop sideburns he has ever seen.

"Gentlemen." he says, acting as if he's happy to see them, "Ken Burton, pleased to meet you," extending his hand to the fficer who stands to greet him. As they shake hands, he is aware of a coldness in the older man's hands. It makes him pause and think how peculiar it was and how clammy his touch was but he dismisses his response as lingering tiredness.

"Senior Sergeant Tom Johnson, this is Constable Stevens, Western Australia Police," he replies.

"Please, gentlemen, sit down," Ken urges them.

"Can we get you gentlemen a cup of coffee or tea?" Gemma asks.

"No thank you, Mrs. Recce," the senior officer replies, "this shouldn't take long."

"Well, I would like one, I can't function without a cup in the morning," Ken tells the officers with a smile, trying to be jovial, but the two stony-faced policemen sit there with blank faces, all business.

The sergeant turns to the matter at hand.

"Well, it's good to see you're alive and well, doctor. By all accounts, you are a very lucky man."

"In what way?" Ken asks.

"Well, the report we are following up is that you were possibly abducted by a man responsible for a car accident which nearly claimed the lives of a young girl and her mother in New South Wales. As you may be aware, we are here at the behest of NSW Police to follow up this report and make sure you're safe."

"Yes, my daughter told me when I arrived yesterday but, as you can see, I am alive and well; thank you for stopping by," Ken replies, standing to see them out.

The senior sergeant carries on, he's not finished, "NSW Police were pretty certain you were in some kind of distress. They have witness reports of your vehicle driving through the town of Cobar at a quick pace. In the same report, a man fitting the description of the fugitive was seen in your car with you. Is that correct, doctor?"

Ken pauses before answering, he still hasn't decided what to tell them, the truth will not fly. He'll have to provide another version of it.

"Yes, Senior Sergeant, that's true."

"And you didn't think it was important enough to mention?"

"No, I didn't," he replies, realising a can of worms has been opened.

"If you wouldn't mind running through the events as they happened that day to provide clarity for our colleagues in New South Wales," the junior officer chimes in, earning a stern glance from his superior for speaking out of turn.

"Very well. I left Dubbo, drove for a few hours and I came across the accident outside of the town of Nyngan, a horrific crash. I saw one car wrapped around a tree and another car in a ditch some distance away. There was debris everywhere so I parked near the car in the ditch. I ran over to the officer, identified myself and asked where I could help. He directed me to the car with the mother and daughter," he tells the officers as Gemma brings out his coffee, and he takes a quick sip.

"And what happened then, doctor?" the junior officer asks, writing furiously, as the senior sergeant listens with folded arms.

"There I found a female teenager and her mother in the front seats, both with massive head injuries. They were still alive, just."

Ken takes another sip. "Is there any word on them, did they survive?" Senior looks in his folder.

"NSW Police advise the mother is alive, she's in hospital and her recovery could take many months. The daughter, however, suffered far more serious injuries and is in an induced coma, it's unclear what her prognosis is."

Ken nods. "I figured as much; her injuries were extensive."

"So, what about the occupant of the second car, did you treat him?" Senior asks.

Ken shakes his head. "No," he replies, putting his cup down, "when I arrived on the scene, the officer told me the driver of the second car was dead, however, he had also told me the occupants of the first car were dead. I dare say it was that young officer's first major incident of that nature."

"Why do you say that?" the junior asks.

"It was obvious he was in shock; the carnage would have been overwhelming for a young man to confront," he replies.

"Please continue, doctor," the senior sergeant prods.

"With the officer's help, we stabilized both patients and waited until the ambulance arrived before moving onto the second car. When I got there, I found the car empty. I called out to the police and by this time other officers had arrived and they were searching for the occupant. There was nothing for me to do so I left."

Just then, a voice enters the Senior Sergeant's mind, interrupting his concentration. It's a voice no one else can hear, only him. It's not his conscience or intuition speaking to him, but rather a clear, concise second entity which resides deep within him.

"This is the one, this one is next," it tells him in a covetous tone.

"I know, you've told me already," he replies, mentally acknowledging the instruction he was given before he arrived at the house.

Senior takes out a large A4 colour photo and places it in front of Ken who looks at it, recognizing the face instantly.

"Doctor, this is Michael Stewart, the man wanted over the crash. Did he abduct you?"

"Yes," Ken replies, "sort of." Both officers looked surprised.

"Is there something wrong?" Ken asks, noticing the look on their faces.

"Doctor, the man who abducted you is a career criminal who not only caused that accident but also is wanted in connection with the murder of a known drug dealer. The fact you're sitting here, alive and well, is, to be frank, a surprise. NSW Police are still trying to find Michael Stewart, as we speak. Are you able to shed any light as to his whereabouts?" Senior asks.

"I had no idea this was such a fuss. But to answer your question, yes, I can. He's dead," Ken states bluntly.

"Dead?" the police look at each other, this story has taken an unexpected turn.

"I buried him in the desert."

"Please elaborate, doctor?" the junior constable asks, writing feverishly.

"When I returned to the car, he, um Mr Stewart, was sitting on the floor with a shotgun pointed directly at my head; he ordered me to get in and start driving, otherwise he would shoot me. I had no choice but to do it."

"And where did he take you?" Senior asks.

"I don't know, out into the desert somewhere. He got me to drive for hours and hours, out into the middle of nowhere, along dirt tracks, I had no idea where we were going. After we drove to a certain point, he told me to pull over, which I did and then he...just died."

"And what did he die from?" the junior officer asks.

"In the accident, the steering wheel punctured his stomach wall, causing massive internal injuries and blood loss, eventually the blood loss was too great and Mr. Stewart died in the desert," Ken replies, knowing what he has told them is technically true.

"Biscuits anyone?" Gemma asks, walking in with a plate of treats, deciding to break things up a little. The two police officers decline her offer, and even appear slightly annoyed at the interruption. Ken happily reaches for one.

"Another coffee, Dad?"

He nods in confirmation.

"Thank you, darling, that would be great."

"So, he dies, what happens next?" the junior officer prompts.

"I wrapped him in a blanket and left him under the caravan, as it was evening when he passed and with no idea of where I was, I decided to stay there for the night. I had every intention of returning to Cobar in the morning."

"So why didn't you?" Senior cuts in with a hint of disbelief.

"Well, to be honest, a dust storm hit overnight, covering my tracks from the day before and, it's embarrassing to admit it, but I was lost."

"So, when you woke, what did you do with him?"

"I buried him in the desert and continued on before returning yesterday."

The voice inside the officer's head returns, "He's lying, he killed him," placing doubt in the policeman's mind.

"Well, this all sounds very...convenient."

"I beg your pardon?" Ken asks, a little agitated at his tone.

"Well, look at it from where we sit. A man takes you at gunpoint into the desert, you claim he succumbs to injuries sustained in the crash. Instead of returning with the body, you bury it out there with no one the wiser. Is that clear enough for you, doctor?"

"I see what you are saying, I was going to report his demise today, actually." Ken replies, not liking the police officer's suggestion.

"Of course, you were. Do you own a gun, doctor?" he asks sharply.

"Yes, I do," Ken replies, "What has that got to do with anything?"

"And where's your gun now?"

"I don't know, at my home in Sydney I guess, why?"

"Would you consent to a search of your home for the weapon, doctor?"

"What are you suggesting?"

Gemma comes into the room, standing by her father's side. "Dad," she says softly, "have your coffee hey, it's OK." They both sense something is going on.

Ken has a sick feeling in his stomach and bowels. He looks sternly at the senior sergeant and senses a cold and negative energy, like when he shook his hand. He isn't about to let this man intimidate him, not in his daughter's house.

"Sadly, Gemma, it isn't OK. You see, darling, the good sergeant has something on his mind. I suggest he speaks up and comes out with it."

The senior officer is smirking; it's cards on the table time. "By all means, doctor, did you kill Michael Stewart?"

"How dare you!" Ken snaps back, enraged and offended, "I'm a doctor, not a murderer."

The senior sergeant cuts him off again. "You should know, doctor; NSW Police conducted a search of the area they believe you were located."

The senior sergeant once again produces a photo, placing it in front of him. "This blanket was found in an area near the New South Wales–South Australian border, on a dirt track far off established roads. Would this be the blanket that you, by your own admission, wrapped Mr Stewart's body in?"

Ken instantly recognizes it and nods.

"New South Wales Police are testing it against blood found at the scene of the car accident, they expect it to match. All we need is to locate your gun and the location of Mr. Stewart's body."

"I'm not a killer," Ken says, knowing that was not entirely true. He recalled Africa and the people whose pain he'd helped to ease. He never thought of it as killing; they were going to die anyway; he just didn't want them to suffer.

"I think, doctor, you killed him as payback for nearly killing the mother and daughter. To be honest, given the circumstances, it would be somewhat understandable, given the recent death of your wife."

Gemma cuts in. "That is enough!" her voice is loud and shrill. She is furious with them and their disgusting questions. "You told me this was nothing more than a welfare check, not a murder investigation. The fact you are accusing my father of such an act is unforgivable - get out of my house!"

Both policemen stand and quickly gather their things, they know when they have worn out their welcome. They also know this will not be the last time they speak to Dr Burton.

"As you wish, Mrs. Reece."

Gemma escorts both officers to the front door.

"A word to the wise, doctor, don't go anywhere, we'll be wanting to speak to you again very soon," Senior adds, satisfied he's ruffled their feathers enough for now.

"From this point on, it will be best if you can contact my solicitor, Mr. Harry Turner of Turner & Company Solicitors, George Street, Sydney," Ken says, indicating that unless they make it official, he has very little else to say to them.

The officers exit the house, as Gemma slams the insect screen behind them.

"Piss off!" she yells, as the door crashes into its frame.

Ken looks at her in surprise. He hasn't seen her so worked up since she was a teenager.

"What, Dad?" she snaps, still fired up.

"Not a thing." he replies, almost afraid to speak.

"The bloody nerve of those bastards, Dad, suggesting you killed that bloke but you should have told them something else, something like he didn't hop in your car, or he passed out and was gone when you woke up."

"Don't worry, this will sort itself out," he replies, trying to keep calm, if for no other reason than his daughter's sake; she's upset enough for both of them,

"Will it? There was a time when you would have jumped across the table and belted him, police officer or not," she remarks.

"I know Gem, but that was then and this is now. I know the truth of what happened and I have faith that justice will prevail. Besides, I get the feeling he wanted me to lose my temper, and I wasn't about to give him that satisfaction."

CHAPTER FIFTEEN

The following day, Ken left the house early to run some errands in preparation for the next phase of his life. He didn't sleep well; the police were on his mind. Gemma was right, perhaps he should have given them a different explanation, he hopes it doesn't become a problem. He spoke to his solicitor before bed, and explained the situation; of course, he didn't tell him everything, but at least he's on standby.

After running around Perth for several hours, he walks to the car with a trolley full of shopping. His trusty Landcruiser is a sight to behold, thickly covered in the red dust of the outback. 'Time for a wash,' he tells himself.

He wants to get home; he's cooking dinner for Gemma tonight. She returned to work last night, and he wants her to be able to relax.

As he loads the groceries, he notices something in his periphery, a dark blue XD Ford Falcon parked about thirty metres away.

Two figures are sitting inside, looking very official and somewhat dubious, both wearing sunglasses and sporting bad moustaches. It's the police.

He looks directly at them but they don't seem bothered that they have been spotted. They sit there, staring back at him. Aware he's being followed, he proceeds with his final few stops, visiting several other places, including the car wash.

At every turn, the blue Ford sticks to him like glue, making no bones about their intentions. Even at the car wash, one of the detectives stepped out of the car for a smoke, fixing his gaze upon him. It's clear they want him to be uncomfortable.

'This is ridiculous,' he tells himself, laughing at the absurdity of it.

He exits the car wash with water still dripping off his vehicle.

He forgoes the vacuum, he's tired and its only 11.30 a.m., with dinner still to cook. Also he wouldn't mind sneaking in an early afternoon nap.

He's five minutes out from the house when the blue Ford overtakes and speeds off, leaving him in their exhaust. Ken is surprised they've ended their surveillance so soon. He enters Gemma's street, and his attention is drawn towards several police cars, a tow truck and the blue Ford in front of her house. As he gets closer, he sees his daughter, standing there, remonstrating with that senior sergeant on the footpath, giving him a good mouthful by the look of it.

He can see people going in and out of his caravan.

"What the bloody hell is going on?" he exclaims, as he presses down on the accelerator to hasten his arrival. As curious as he is, his only thought is to get to Gemma.

He comes to a fast stop, screeching his tyres, which gets their attention. He jumps out of the vehicle to race to his daughter but officers quickly move to cut him off.

"Gem!" he yells, jostling with them, trying to get to her.

"Dad!" She also is rushing towards him until a female police officer intercepts her, keeping them apart.

"What in God's name is happening?" he asks, hoping someone has a good reason for these actions.

"They turned up with a search warrant for your car and caravan, Dad, I had just arrived home," she says, as if she is somehow responsible for letting them do it.

"It's alright, honey," he calls back, 'there was nothing you could do."

He looks towards the senior sergeant who is standing close, his mouth lopsided in a gloating smirk.

"Senior Sergeant, what's the meaning of this intrusion?" he yells, outraged. The officer walks over and hands him official-looking paperwork.

"Doctor Burton, this is a search warrant, issued by the Western Australian Magistrates Court. We're seizing your caravan and car for forensic analysis," he says with a tinge of glee, obviously enjoying exercising his power and authority. .

"And what is it you are expecting to find, Senior Sergeant?" he asks, as he scans the warrant.

"Evidence."

"Evidence of what?" he retorts.

"Of murder." They stare fixedly at each other, and it's in that moment Ken knows what's going to happen.

"I had nothing to do with that man's death, and you know it."

"No doctor, I don't know it," the Senior Sergeant says coldly, looking at the Landcruiser, "Rather convenient you washed it today, wasn't it?"

"It was filthy, it needed it."

"I'm sure it was, but it's also a good way of getting rid of evidence."

He directs two of his officers to search the car while he waves off those holding Ken and his daughter, allowing them to finally reach each other.

"Don't worry, Gem, I'll sort this out," he assures her, ushering her closer to the house so they can talk privately, "I want you to go inside, and call Harry, my solicitor, his details are in my notebook, next to my bed. Let him know what's happening, tell him I'm going to need his help."

"What do you think will happen. Dad?" she asks, looking worried.

"They're going to arrest me, but don't worry, I have faith everything will be OK, calm heads hey?"

"Yes Dad, calm heads," she replies, it's the phrase her mother would say to her when she was upset as a teenager.

It doesn't take long for one of constables to emerge with a black bag. "Senior!" He calls out with urgency, raising the bag in the air. The superior officer quickly walks to the car, takes the bag, and uses the vehicle's bonnet as a table to examine its contents.

"Shit!" Ken exclaims quietly, immediately realizing how this is going to look.

"What is it, Dad?" Gemma asks, "Is that your bag?"

Ken shakes his head.

"No, it was Michael's, he had it when he was hiding in the car. I completely forgot about it."

"Well, what's in it?" she asks, as they both watch the police take out a couple of bags of white powder and a large amount of cash.

"Drugs," he replies. The police have a brief discussion, huddling close together, with lots of head nodding and staring. Suddenly the huddle breaks and several of the officers approach him, as one of the policemen takes his handcuffs off his utility belt.

"What can you tell me about this, doctor?" the Senior Sergeant asks, presenting the illegal contents from the bag.

"It was Michael Stewart's, he had with him when he got in my car, I completely forgot it was there," Ken explains.

"Well, it was well hidden, pushed way under the seat, perhaps someone intended to spend the money later?" Senior suggests, "Do you know what this looks like, doctor?"

"What?" he asks, shaking his head.

"Motive."

The sergeant nods to his constable, who steps forward, taking Ken by the arm, roughly securing his hands with the cuffs. He doesn't resist, despite how much he wants to. He told Gemma, "Calm heads," and that's exactly what he will do.

"Ken Burton, you are under arrest for possession of a trafficable amount of heroin with intent to distribute. You do not have to say anything, but anything you do say may be written down and used as evidence. Do you understand what I have said to you?"

"This is crap!" Gemma yells, rushing towards her father as another constable blocks her path.

"It's all right, we'll sort this out, just do what I asked, call Harry," her father yells, as he's marched by two officers towards the waiting police car. Gemma stands, helpless, watching on as her father is whisked away.

Without delay, the caravan and car are loaded onto the flatbed trucks. Gemma races inside the house, straight to her father's room, and finds his notebook exactly where he said it would be. She flicks through the pages quickly until she finds the contact details of her father's solicitor. She runs to the phone, with the book in hand, desperately dialling the number which, thankfully, connects quickly.

"Yes, my name is Gemma Reese, my father, Dr Ken Burton, is a client, I need to speak with Harry Turner urgently."

⇒⟩⟩⟩ ⟨⟨⟨⟵

In Cobar, New South Wales, Police Constable Glen Standen is sifting through the evidence he's gathered in relation to the hunt for Michael Stewart and the possible abduction of Dr Burton. Days before, he sent a request to the Western Australian Police asking them to follow up with Doctor Burton's daughter. He sent them copies of everything he had via telefax so they would know as much as he did about the case. However, it's been ten days and he's yet to hear anything back.

He wasn't even sure the doctor had been abducted, but he needed his colleagues to check. He wasn't going to make the same mistakes he made at the crash. No, from now on, he is going to be thorough.

All he had was a vague report of a similar Landcruiser driving erratically through town with a bearded man, which is half of this town on any given day. However, he knows from police files that the man he's hunting also had a beard and he believes it's worth checking out.

He finds the details of the written request, and the name he was given as the primary contact. He picks up the phone and dials the number on the sheet, hoping there is some good news.

⤜⤜⤜ ⤛⤛⤛

Senior Sergeant Tom Johnson returns to his office, having just arrived back to the station. He's relatively pleased with himself, having made the arrest as he was instructed to do, but finding the drugs, well, it made it a whole lot easier. It was almost legitimate. Sure, the doctor may well be completely innocent but he stopped worrying about such matters a long time ago, it's not his concern. His only concern is to do what he's told. In the quiet of the room, as he begins writing notes, the voice re-enters his head.

"You have taken another criminal off the streets, congratulations Tom," it says, praising the human.

"Thanks." he replies flatly, through some kind of telepathy.

He's never really sure what his master's reasons are when it comes to people, and, to be honest, he's given up caring. But he certainly knows who his master is; he knew that the first time they met.

It started when he was a teenager and a local kid called Billy, a small-town bully, made his school years a plain and simple hell. For years, he was the subject of regular school beatings dished out by this kid and his band of followers.

He asked his father, a mean-spirited man, for help but his appeal fell on deaf ears. He couldn't care less about his son who he regarded as an inconvenient mistake. The police didn't help him either and at school they told him to toughen up. He was on his own.

But one day, everything changed.

On this day, Billy and his friend had cornered him and were beating the living hell of out him. He fell to the ground, curled up into a ball, protecting his head, as kicks were fired into his body like missiles. He laid there, praying for the beating to stop but like the previous times, no one answered his prayers.

As punches rained down on him, he begged the universe for help, desperately reaching out into the ether, hoping someone, anyone, would end his suffering.

That was the first time he heard it.

"Would you like me to end this beating?" The eerie male voice asked, "Because I can end it for you."

He hears the words, spoken inside his head, a strange sensation, but before he accepts the help, he wants to know who it is. Before he can verbalise his question, it answers him.

"I'm a friend," the voice replies, as if it was talking directly into his ear, "you need only to say 'yes,' and I will help you. I will make you strong and no one will ever hurt you again, not even your father."

Just then, Billy punches him so hard he cannot see anything but darkness and nearly passes out.

"Stop it!" he screams, "Please!"

"You hear that, baby wants it to stop!" Billy yells, laughing sadistically to his friend, as they both revel in their victim's distress. Billy's pleas only escalate the attack, which becomes more frenzied as more punches and kicks find their mark on his bruised and battered body.

"Just say yes, and this stops now, I will protect you," the voice silkily promises, offering the boy respite from his persecutors. Fighting to stay conscious and feeling death's hand on his shoulder, the boy is left with only one option.

"Yeeees!" he screams, "Help me!"

"Then I will help you, my son."

At the time, Johnson had no idea who was offering to help him but he could sense an immense power in its words, an indescribable force.

His body is battered so badly, it's a couple of minutes before he realises the beating had stopped. He no longer felt the pressure of Billy's knees on his back. He couldn't hear the jeering of his chubby friend but he did hear something else that made him curious.

At first, he was too afraid to look for fear of coping another punch in the face but the whimpers became louder, and eventually he had to look.

As he struggled to his feet, he saw Billy and his friend lying on the ground, moaning and squirming in pain as if they were dying.

Johnson heard a sound from behind him and he knew it wasn't good. He turned around to see a giant black snake, coiled up, and rearing above the ground. It was huge, bigger than an anaconda, with a thick, human-sized head, and as tall as he was. He could feel a powerful coldness, coming from it, reaching out to him. The worst thing was it didn't scare him; actually, he felt safer than he had ever felt in his life. That was the moment when he knew who and what the snake was.

"Fear me not, my son," it says, "I have saved you and now you will serve me." Even at the age of thirteen, Tom knows what he has done but his anger and rage encompassed his whole being and he didn't care. He possessed a very powerful ally who would protect him and those who have hurt him will pay.

"Help me!" Billy squeaks, paralysed by the snake's venom, "Help me, please Tom!" but like others had done to him, Billy's pleas will fall on deaf ears.

Incapable of showing his enemy compassion, he is filled with an uncontrollable rage. He looks at his tormentor, lying on the rocky dirt.

"Sounds like baby wants some help," he shouts back with the same viciousness he was shown, bending low to ensure the last thing Billy sees is his face.

Having manifested itself as a voice in his head and now a snake, the entity is well pleased. It feeds off Johnson's hatred and anger; it will accommodate his thirst for retribution.

"We are going to do so much together, my son, wait and see."

Tom looks towards the other boy who is already dead, before turning his attention back on Billy who is gasping through his final moments of life.

Johnson places his hand over Billy's mouth, denying him his last few breaths, whispering into his ear, "Die."

⇝⇜

Since that day, Johnson has spent his life in his master's service, completely at his beck and call. It is the price he's paid for a decision he made as a child. Through him, it has managed everything from corruption to murder, everything it has craved, everything it has lusted after, he has facilitated.

But now, some thirty two years later, he'd be lying if he said he wasn't growing tired of it. He is terribly tired of it, but what choice does he have? It hasn't been a one-sided relationship. Johnson has gained money, women, material wealth although he expected to hold a more prestigious position by now. Either way, he will have to pay the piper one day, a prospect he is reminded of constantly.

His thoughts turn to this doctor, he knows he's going to need more evidence to build a watertight case.

"I don't know how long I can hold him. I need proof of the murder," he tells his master.

Ken's comment instantly draws a command from his master: "This one can't be let go; he's far too important."

Johnson scoffs, "Is that right, tell me, what has he done to earn your interest? Did he scorn you, reject you, or is it something else?"

There is a lengthy pause, before the entity speaks again, "That's not for you to know, you just keep him where I can get at him."

"Then I suggest you find me some actual evidence because in this world, I need evidence, otherwise, I may not have a choice."

"You have no choice regardless, Tom, remember worldly matters are your problem."

Suddenly his desk phone rings loudly, startling him, sending his master back into his subconscious.

"Western Australian Police, Senior Sergeant Johnson speaking," he says sternly.

"Good afternoon, Senior, this is New South Wales Police Constable Glen Standen from Cobar Police, how are you, sir?"

"What can I do for you, constable?" he asks, getting down to business.

"I sent you a contact request for a Doctor Ken Burton ten days ago, I'm needing to update my file. I was wondering, if you have had a chance to make contact with the doctor's daughter to ascertain his status?"

"Well, your timing is impeccable, constable, as we have just taken the doctor into custody. We are processing him, as we speak."

"I'm sorry, senior, did I hear you right, did you say custody?" the shocked constable asks, "On what charge. sir?"

"Yes, constable, you heard right, we found a trafficable amount of heroin and cash in his vehicle when we executed search warrants on his car and caravan this morning."

"I don't understand, sir, it was supposed to be a welfare check?" Standen asks, sounding confused.

"You are a junior constable, are you not?" Johnson asks tersely.

"Yes sir, I am."

"Well, junior constable, I don't know what you people do in New South Wales, but here, when we find someone with a large quantity of drugs on them, we arrest them.

"Yes sir."

"We also have reason to believe the doctor murdered Michael Stewart, and we're investigating the matter."

"Murder?" Standen says, wondering how they jumped to this conclusion so fast, it's like things are spinning out of control.

"Yes, constable, murder."

"I don't follow, sir."

"OK, look, your doctor claims he was taken into the desert, at gunpoint, by a man who had just killed someone and nearly two others, and somehow dies himself. Your doctor said he buried him in the desert, but can't remember where, which is rather convenient, wouldn't you say?"

Standen can't help but think this is a far-fetched idea without any real evidence to support it. He doesn't believe for one minute the doctor has it in him to do such a thing, but he admits the story is odd.

"Sir," he asks, "this is a bit of a leap, wouldn't you say?"

"I beg your pardon, junior constable?"

"I mean, Stewart is a well-known, violent drug user and trafficker; and yes, he had already killed one man the day before the accident. However, he was believed to be in possession of a large amount of cash and heroin, the proceeds from that crime. I don't see anything to support the doctor's involvement in a murder or even of drug trafficking for that matter. I have to say it doesn't seem plausible."

"You mean other than the 1.5 kilos of heroin and $8,000.00 in cash we found in his possession? No, junior constable, it's more than plausible."

"But sir, with all due respect, it isn't even in your jurisdiction."

Johnson knows the upstart is right, but as usual he has an answer for everything.

"Let me tell you something, junior constable. A crime has been committed. The offender is in my state, the drugs are in my state. We have no idea where the body is, it could still be in your state, South Australia or Western Australia, we don't know. So, when you have exhausted your search, we can begin ours."

"I understand, sir," Standen replies, determined not to be intimidated, "that is, if a crime has been committed at all?"

"Well, constable, I suggest you find me a body that a medical examination can prove died as a result of injuries sustained in a car crash, as the doctor claims, otherwise, he may well be charged with murder."

"I'll find the body, sir; I promise you that," Standen states defiantly.

"Good luck!" Johnson says smugly, knowing there's no chance it will happen, his master has seen to it. He slams the phone down and shakes his head, the audacity of this junior officer to question him like that.

In cases without a body, it is generally the most believable story that wins. Sprinkled, of course, with some circumstantial evidence and enough doubt to lead a jury towards finding the person guilty which is what Johnson will be counting on.

> ⟫⟩⟩ ⟨⟨⟨⟨

Standen hears the phone go dead. He's surprised a senior sergeant of his stature would arrest the doctor on such an 'iffy' possession charge, which has somehow risen to murder. It doesn't make sense, he's more confused than ever. He looks down, his head in his hands, puzzled by what he's heard.

Standen's colleague, Anthony Harrison, comes out of the bathroom, he's been in the police for ten years. He spots that his young friend appears troubled.

"What's wrong, mate, did she dump you again?" Harrison asks, in reference to Standen's on again, off again relationship with a local girl.

"No, nothing like that," he replies, "I'm feeling confused about this case."

"In what way?"

"I dunno. I sent a request to WA police for a welfare check on the doctor who was abducted by Michael Stewart, after he caused that accident nearly two weeks ago."

"How could we forget that?" Harrison remarks, shuddering as he recalls the accident scene.

"The police over there just told me they've arrested the doctor on drug possession charges and are trying to get him for the murder of Stewart who, the doctor claimed, died as a result of his injuries."

"And where's Stewart's body now?"

"That's the thing, the doctor claims he buried him out in the desert and carried on to Perth, it doesn't make any sense."

"Do they have any evidence?" Harrison asks, also finding it strange the doctor would not have taken the body with him.

"They found the drugs and money in the doctor's car but it could easily be the same stuff from the Anderson murder scene which Dubbo police say Stewart did."

"So, what's the problem?" Harrison asks, struggling to share his colleague's bewilderment.

"We both know the difference between good people and shit people. Michael Stewart is or was, a shit person; the doctor is not. I can't see that he would be capable of hurting anyone else, let alone dealing in drugs."

"They never are, mate, it's always the ones you least expect," Harrison offers, but Standen remains unconvinced.

"If you had seen how he worked on those people, how he fought to save their lives, you wouldn't think he could kill a fly, let alone a person."

"What about the drugs, how do explain that and the missing person of interest?"

"The drugs belonged to Stewart. I found drugs and cash in the wreck at the scene; he could have easily taken the rest of it with him and left the bag in the doctor's car."

"True, and your evidence could support that, so the question now is where's the body?"

"Well, that's right, where is Michael Stewart?"

Harrison takes in a big breath while drying his hands with a towel.

"Well, junior constable, I suggest you stop mopping around and get out into the desert and look for Stewart. Otherwise, your doctor friend may spend the next 20 years in jail."

Standen agrees, only a body and a cause of death will reveal the doctor's guilt or innocence, and he's the only one who can prove it. He has to find Stewart!

⟶⟫⟫⟩ ⟨⟪⟪⟵

After going through the indignity of being processed through the police booking system. Ken is ushered into a holding cell where he is uncuffed, awaiting whatever comes next. The small concrete room is so cold that the plaster covered walls are like ice to his touch. He also is aware of the misery this room holds, countless dozens if not hundreds of people before him have sat in this cell, pondering their innocence or guilt.

It's a sterile place, there are no clocks or benches, just a bed, a bucket and a basin. He wonders how long he'll be here, but knows they can't hold him any longer than six hours. Harry told him that much when they spoke.

He's tried not to show much emotion, choosing to remain calm and compliant. Some may say it's a sign of guilt, but in truth, he doesn't want to give them more ammunition to use against him. He has already done that with his made-up answers.

Jesus said there would be more trials ahead, more things to face, obviously this is one of them. What he can't figure out is whether this is another one of God's tests of his character and resolve, or is it something else? Jesus knew this was coming, hence the warning. The wonders of being omnipotent.

He sits on the end of the bed near the exit, the officers leave the room, slamming the steel reinforced door behind them. Alone again, he closes his eyes and begins to pray.

"You said the trials were not over, I trust in you, completely, to resolve this matter on my behalf. I have faith you are with me."

Suddenly, the lights of the cell begin to flicker, off and on, repeatedly, as the walls shudder simultaneously. It was as though a small tremor had passed through the building. It was so quick, lasting only a few seconds, and was over before Ken realised what was happening. A foul, pungent odour wafts in his direction, offending his sinuses. It's a vile smell that is somewhat familiar to him. He realises he is not alone.

A strange sound comes from behind him. It is loud and disturbing, as though someone is taking a long, deep sniff of air. Hesitantly, he slowly turns around to see a man standing in the corner of the cell. Ken is startled and instinctively fearful and takes a defensive posture on the edge of the bunk.

The room was empty when he walked in and there isn't anywhere for a person to hide which means this person must have literally appeared out of thin air.

The man, who is dressed in a black suit, with slick black hair, stands there, looking at Ken with desirous intent and a sadistic smirk. He is gloating: the human is scared his fear intoxicating.

"Beautiful smell, isn't it, the human soul?" the man asks with a smile as he inhales deeply once more. Although Ken has never seen this man before, something deep within him recognises him and he somehow knows it's the creature that he and Jesus encountered, but in human form.

"He isn't here to save you now, is he?" he says, relishing Ken's shocked state, "I told you I'd see you again and look, here we are, alone, just you and me."

Jesus showed no fear towards the creature and its unclean spirits. Ken is not sure he can do the same, he's only human and he's terrified. He keeps his eyes averted from the creature-come-man who stands directly in front of him.

"Don't look away, your friend Jesus has abandoned you, but don't worry, I have come to save you from this terrible injustice...my son," he says contemptuously, holding his arms open wide, pretending to care.

Ken is speechless, he doesn't know what to do. Does he speak to this...thing, does he not speak to it, he doesn't even want to acknowledge its presence. He cannot treat it with the same distain that Jesus did. The creature is right, Jesus isn't here, he's on his own.

He does know one thing. if he allows his fear to control him, this entity will surely consume him. Somehow, he must stand his ground if he is to survive.

He steadies himself, physically and mentally, focusing on being calm and measured, not fearful and emotional, before looking directly at the man.

"What do you want?" he asks sheepishly, doing his best to keep it together, as his voice quivers.

"I'm sorry, did you say something?" the man asks with smart aleck bravado.

"What do you want?" Ken asks again, slightly louder this time.

"What?" the man fires back, "I can't hear you!"

"What do you want?" he replies, in a louder voice, almost shouting.

"Ah, finally, he speaks. Good to see you have found your voice, Ken, I was starting to get worried." He chuckles, walking around the cell, pondering the question, "What do I want, you ask? The answer is simple, my dear doctor, I want your sweet-smelling virgin soul! That's not much to ask, is it?"

"Well, I'm sorry, but it's unavailable." Ken says, slightly lifting his tone, trying to be more confident but his response draws the creature's laughter.

"Oh, that's right, you're a Jesus man now, you've turned over a new leaf, but let me tell you doctor, that path is highly over-rated."

"Is that right?" Ken asks sceptically, finding his voice.

"Yes, it is, now with me, well, I can make the rest of your life more interesting than he can. We can have some fun with your remaining time in this world without all of the rules and restrictions that 'He' places on you."

"In what way?" Ken asks, which appears to spur the creature on.

"Well, you could return to Africa and go back to giving people your 'comfort,' as you call it, like those old times," he says, excitedly, "except this time they come to me when you, shall we say, release them."

Ken takes instant offence to the suggestion.

"Those people were going to die anyway; the only question was if it would be in agony or with some measure of peace."

"Hey!" the entity replies, "Relax, I don't judge. You can tell yourself you're an 'Angel of Mercy' for all I care, if it helps you. But you and I, we know truth, don't we?"

"And what, 'truth' would that be?"

"That you were an 'Angel of Death,' of course!"

Ken is silently enraged, doing his utmost to maintain some measure of discipline. Satan is trying to bait him; he needs to remember that.

"You're a voice in my head, you're not even really here," Ken says, trying diminish its presence to an hallucination.

"Oh, but I am here, doctor, as far as you are concerned that is, and I can become anyone, I could be a nun," it says, as its image instantly transforms to that of a nun in a black and white habit, "or a priest." Again, its image transforms into that of a priest, standing there, pretending to pray before transforming back into the man, "I can come and go, I can appear and disappear, I can do anything I like."

Ken is astounded by the demonstration and afraid of its power. He feels out of his depth, drowning, terrified of spending his eternity with those souls he heard screaming in the desert.

"Now, I can make all of this misfortune go away, wouldn't you like that? You could go home to your daughter, drink yourself stupid, spend the rest of your miserable life in ignorant bliss?"

"And how would you do that," Ken asks, needing to stay engaged in the conversation, "I'm in jail?"

"I have my connections, you let me worry about that," the man replies, bending down, so he can look Ken dead in the eyes.

"I am much more than a figment of your imagination, doctor, all you have to do is to say yes, willingly, accept my offer and I'll take care of the rest."

Being so close, he can feel the energy being drawn from his body, a strange feeling. It was as though it was taking a sample of his soul. In turn, he could feel the evil within this man, gushing out.

"Think about it, I'm a patient man, doctor, I'll be back later, maybe I'll pay your daughter a visit!"

In the blink of an eye, the entity vanished as Ken involuntarily vomits onto the cell floor. The smell of this thing and its energy made him sick. He gasps for air, trying to catch his breath, after coming face to face with pure evil. He was lucky this time but when it returns, how is he going to protect himself?

CHAPTER SIXTEEN

In Cobar, it's almost 2 p.m. and Junior Constable Glen Standen is getting ready for another search of the desert. Despite having grown up in the region and knowing the area well, he is worried about finding this man in the vastness of the outback. He might get lucky and stumble across it, or there may be some signs to indicate where the remains are which he missed before; either way, he wishes he had some help. He knows he's up against it.

Packed and ready, he sets off from the station and drives through the centre of town, waving to the various locals as he goes past.

Just before leaving town, he pulls over to check his maps once more, to be sure of his route. He's spent the last week, meticulously creating a map of the search area, up to and including the place he found the bloody blanket which is where he will recommence his investigation.

On his last trip, he pegged out a trail with star pickets and yellow ribbons every couple of kilometres; he hopes they're still there; it will make things easier and quicker to find his way back.

The wind blows through the cabin of the vehicle, making it difficult for him to hold onto the paper. As it flaps around, it looks like he's fighting a dragon.

A tingling sensation, the hairs on the back of his neck stand up. 'What's going on?' He looks around, scanning the area and sees an Indigenous man across the street leaning against a pole outside a shop.

His eyes are fixated on the young officer which is making Standen uncomfortable. It wasn't so much that the man is staring at him but how. The man was in a trance, eyes not blinking, it was strange.

Standen returns the man's direct gaze. He appears to be in his mid-thirties, average size and build. He hasn't seen him around here before.

He signals for him to come over to his vehicle, curious to know what his problem is. The man maintains his eye contact as he approaches the car, now within speaking distance.

"Can I help you, mate?" Standen asks in an official police tone.

The man shakes his head.

"No sir," he replies calmly.

"Is there something wrong?" Standen asks, and again the man shakes his head.

"No sir, nothing is wrong with me, why do you ask?"

"Well, you were staring at me for some time."

The man begins to laugh.

"Something funny, mate?" Standen asks, annoyed his words have provoked such hilarity.

"No sir," the man says, still giggling, "It's just I saw ya pull up and havin' trouble with the map. I was thinkin' if I should come and give ya a hand, that's all."

"Give me a hand," Standen replies, "I'm not sure how you could help me, what do you do for a job?"

"I'm a tracker."

"A tracker, who do you work for?" Standen asks, thinking he could come in handy.

"I've worked for the mines, off and on for years, goin' out with surveyors and geologists, makin' sure they don't get lost, that kind of thing. Where ya goin'?" the man asks.

"Out there, mate," Standen replies, pointing towards the desert, "I'm looking for someone."

The man thinks about it for a moment before asking another question, "And this someone you're looking for, are they a good or a bad person?"

Standen is honest. "A very bad man," he replies in a serious voice.

"Ya can't go out-there alone, ya know that?"

"Yeah, I know, but I don't have a choice."

"Hmmm, I better come with ya then hey, you'll need my help to find this fella."

"I can't pay you," Standen cautions, "If that's what you're looking for?"

Again the man smiles, "I don't need yar money."

Standen has a funny feeling about this bloke, somehow, he knows he can trust him and that he can help, he can feel it, as sure as he's sitting there.

"Alright then, so long as you're sure, get in," he says, gesturing to him to throw his gear in the car, which he does, before jumping into the front passenger seat with Standen.

"What's your name?" Standen asks the man, who is smiling from ear to ear.

He extends his hand towards the officer. "My name is Henry."

Standen accepts his hand, shaking it warmly. "Pleased to meet you, Henry, my name is Glen."

⇶ ⇷

Ken is trying to calm his nerves and recover from his encounter with Satan who is clearly the force behind his incarceration.

"It said it has connections, it has influence, but with whom?" he asks himself. The only logical answer is the police, but who and which one?

The sergeant had taken an instant dislike to him, he could feel the tension between them. He remembers what Jesus said, about there being no such thing as coincidence, how generally all things happen as part of

God's plan. It follows that evil must also have plans for people and this entity must be the orchestrator of men as well as circumstances.

At one time, Ken blamed God for the evil in the world. When he witnessed atrocities being committed in those other countries, he prayed and prayed. When no help came, he gave up asking. The resentment he harboured built to the point he was certain there was no God.

"How could there be?" he would continually tell himself, when day after day, more people needlessly died. From that point on, he decided mankind was inherently evil, actions were choices of men and men alone, made in their own right. He now knows he was wrong.

Never did he guess there was this 'thing' out there, all day, every day, influencing men and women with power and money, relentlessly creating a world of chaos and discord. Everything makes sense to him now.

The evil one created this situation to get him into a position where he would say or do anything to get out; it was expecting him to buckle. That's why it mentioned 'paying his daughter a visit,' knowing his vulnerability lay in his love for Gemma. He cannot bear the thought of his precious daughter being threatened by this vile entity. He has to trust Jesus will support him, as he said he would.

His thoughts are broken by the sound of clanking keys coming down the hallway which stops outside his cell. The door opens, and two large, fit-looking officers instruct him to stand, face the wall and to place his hands behind his back. He is handcuffed.

Ken is led out of his cell down the narrow hallway towards another room of some kind where he is seated at a white table. The officers handcuff him to another chain, directly underneath him, which is anchored into the concrete floor, prohibiting him from standing. The two officers stand together in silence, watching him, while they all wait for whomever is coming.

⋙ ⋘

Gemma sits patiently next to the phone, drinking a coffee, waiting for her father or his lawyers to call her back. She would be grateful to hear from anyone at this point, feeling completely helpless. The 'ratta-tat-tat' sound of someone knocking on the front screen door snaps her out of her daydream. Getting up from the table, she wonders who it could be, hoping it's some good news. As she approaches the door, she sees an older man, dressed in black, standing with his back towards her.

"Can I help you?" she calls out as she rushes down the hallway in her hospital shoes. The man turns around, through the screen she sees he is wearing a white collar. "A priest?" she asks herself, wondering why a priest would be visiting her.

"You must be Gemma?" the man asks warmly with a big smile.

"Yes, I am, can I help you, Father?"

"The police sent me over, to see if I can do anything for you while your father is away?" he says in a creepy tone that goes straight over her head.

"Do you have news about my father?" she asks excitedly, "Is he OK?"

"Oh, he's fine, but it's you I'm more worried about, my child, are you alright?" he asks, noticing a crucifix hanging on the wall next to hall entry.

"I'm fine, thank you, Father," she replies cautiously.

"Are you sure, my child, you look like you may need some spiritual comforting." he replies, licking his lips and pushing his hips forward in a suggestive manner. Gemma has a sudden and overwhelming feeling of dread; all she wants is for this man to leave.

"Well, as you can see, Father, I am perfectly fine, and in no need of any spiritual comforting. But thank you for stopping by," she replies, trying to fob him off. She is closing the door when he plants his foot in the way, keeping it ajar.

"I beg your pardon," she says, 'do you mind?"

"Come on, Gemma, let me in, let me give you my blessing," he says in a different voice, sounding more like a deviant than a man of God.

"Who are you?" she asks, but he doesn't reply, he just stares at her, grunting in a sexual way, but she's had enough and is starting to lose her patience. "I think it's time you just fu...-"

But the strange visitor cuts her off.

"What are you gunna do, call the cops?" His appearance begins to change in front of her eyes. A redness develops around his eyelids and the veins in his face and forehead become more visible.

"Let me in!" he demands in a distorted voice, trying to rattle the screen door from her grasp. For a few seconds, they wrestle for control, with Gemma using the high ground leverage to push the man down a step or two. This gives her a chance to slam the main door shut, placing her body firmly against it, in case he tries to force his way in.

"What the hell was that?" she asks, gasping. After she regains her breath, she turns to go back into the kitchen. The priest is standing in front of her, blocking the hallway entry, smiling devilishly.

Next to her right hand is a small writing desk, adjacent to the door. On the top is a metal letter opener. She uses the tip of her index finger to locate it. She has it. The man walks towards her, slowly, making indescribable noises that strike fear into her. Moans and groans, the same sounds her father described to her which she dismissed are now inside her home.

The priest charges her and, without a thought, she grabs the letter opener, thrusting it into the man's chest, directly into his heart. They both stand there, looking at the implement protruding from his sternum. He lets out a maniacal laugh, showing no indication of pain or even discomfort. He slowly pulls the letter opener out, dropping it on the floor. He holds his finger up, waving it at her like a misbehaving toddler.

"You're a naughty girl, Gemma, and I like naughty girls."

She lets out the loudest scream that pierces the quiet neighbourhood. When she stops, she opens her eyes to find that the man has gone, vanished from sight!

She looks at the letter opener, sitting on the floor, it's completely clean, there's no blood. She knows she stabbed him; she felt the resistance that a human body offers, as she drove the tool into him.

Just then, she hears the 'ratta-tat-tat' sound of knocking on the screen door once again, and she grabs up the letter opener, readying herself for round two. In that moment, she hears the friendly voice of her neighbour, Mrs Johnstone, "Gemma, you right, luv?" the old lady calls out.

"Thank God!" she says, breathing a sigh of relief to hear the voice of their resident busybody.

"Gemma!" The old lady calls out again, banging on the screen door. The sound of the latch opening the main door is heard, as Gemma slowly sticks her head out, looking around, making sure the coast is clear.

"We heard your scream, luv, is everything alright?" her neighbour asks.

Gemma nods, "Yes, sorry to alarm you Mrs J, I saw the biggest rat I've ever seen and it scared the 'you-know what' out of me."

The old lady chuckles. "Oh, they can be bastards of things, luv," she says, having had the same unfortunate experience, "Were you able to get rid of it?"

"I dunno Mrs J, I hope so."

>>>>> <<<<<

Senior Sergeant Tom Johnson bursts into the interview room with the confident swagger of a master of his domain; at least, that's how he sees it. He takes the seat on the other side of the table, having kept Ken waiting a good fifteen minutes. He's in control and loves to see them sweat and squirm. Everything is on his timetable and not the offender's.

"Good afternoon, doctor, sorry to have held you up," he says, dismissing the other officers from the room with a wave of his hand.

"It's quite alright, senior sergeant, it's not as if I have anywhere else to be, unless you are going to tell me this craziness is over?" he replies, returning the sergeant's sarcasm.

Johnson smiles, he detects the doctor's angst about being here and he's enjoying it.

"Absolutely not, doctor, you were found to have in your possession a trafficable quantity of heroin, together with a large amount of cash. So, to answer your question, no, this isn't over, we're just getting started," he replies, making notes in his pad, "I'd like to dive straight into it, if you don't mind?"

"That would be preferable," Ken replies, wanting to get it over.

"Do you own a gun, doctor?"

"Yes."

"And what kind is it?"

"A 38-snub nose, why is this important?"

The police officer ignores the question and proceeds with his next one. "And where is it now, doctor?"

Ken shrugs his shoulders. "At home I suppose, in my safe."

"And you didn't bring it with you on this trip?"

"Why would I?" he replies. It is a lie. In fact, he doesn't know what Jesus did with it, if it's in his safe at home or somewhere in the universe.

"Why do people do many things, doctor," Johnson remarks, furiously making notes, "What did you do with Michael Stewart's body."

"I told you; he died; I buried him out there somewhere."

"Yes, so you said, but you can't tell us exactly where out there either!"

"No, I can't."

"So what was your thinking? Were you going to inform any of the authorities of his death and the location of his body, or did you just hope no one was going to know?"

"I got busy. I was flagged down by a young woman who needed help to get her sick uncle to the Lake Carnegie area."

"And what was wrong with him, the uncle?" Johnson asks inquisitively.

"Advanced lung cancer."

"And what was his name?"

"Henry."

"Henry what?"

"I don't know," Ken replies, trying to find answers that sounded plausible.

"And the lady who flagged you down, the man's niece, what was her name?"

"Maisy...I didn't ask her surname either."

"Really? Pretty convenient she just happened to flag down the only doctor within hundreds of miles. And what happened to him, the old man?"

"He died, of his illness."

Johnson erupts into laughter. "You are kidding, aren't you?"

"No, of course not." Ken replies. Why was the sergeant laughing? Did he say something funny?

Johnson struggles to get control of his laughter and return to the interview. The more he laughs, the more frustrated Ken becomes.

"What so funny?" he asks in a sour tone as Johnson reins himself in.

"Oh, I'm sorry, doctor, but that was funny."

"Glad I've entertained you."

"Oh, you did with that one," he says, as his laughter trails off. "You see what the problem is, don't you?"

"What?"

"Well, beginning with the death of your wife, then Stewart, almost the two ladies in New South Wales, and now this...Henry, who you say had cancer, all of whom have died around you from sickness or injury.

You know what that makes you ...a suspect, you may well be a serial murderer!"

Ken shakes the chains, protesting his innocence.

"I didn't kill those people, they died of natural causes," he says, raising his voice.

"What about Stewart, his death wasn't natural, was it?"

"Either charge me, or let me go!" Ken insists, having lost his patience. "You have kept me for nearly three hours, without food, water or even a damn phone call. I also know, unless you are going to charge me, you have to let me go after six hours, so get on with it!"

Again, Johnson chuckles, finding the comments amusing.

"That's very good, doctor, however in Western Australia, a suspect can be detained for up to 12 hours, once approval has been given by the senior officer in charge, which in this case is me, which, of course, I will do. So, you may as well settle in, you could be with us for some time," he replies, making it crystal clear who's in charge.

Ken sees how the police are playing this game; so will he, to the letter.

"Very well Sergeant, if that's the case, I have nothing more to say until my solicitor gets here, you can take me back to my cell now," Ken says sharply and tries to stand as if to leave, "and I'll have my bloody phone call as well thanks." But he is yanked down by the chains. He'd forgotten about them.

Johnson takes his statement as a direct challenge, and stands purposely to get into the doctor's face, arrogantly staring at him. Ken can smell the same stench as the creature had, he knows that vile odour anywhere, as it seeps from the man's mouth. Unintentionally the policeman has betrayed himself. He now knows who's who.

"I'll let you know what you can and can't have in here, doctor, don't forget who's in charge," he is speaking with extreme menace, stamping his authority on Burton, in case there was any doubt. The men square off for a few seconds before the senior knocks on the door. Within moments, the guards return.

"Take the prisoner back to his cell, and see that he gets some food."

"Yes sir." the guard replies, forcefully re-cuffing Ken, before bundling him back to his cell.

From his brief chat, the senior sergeant knows there is only one way to get the outcome his master wants: a confession.

⤜⟫⟫⟩ ⟨⟨⟨⟨⟵

The police vehicle has been battling its way over the rough terrain for hours. They have made good time, thanks to the star-pickets and yellow ribbons Standen left out on his previous trip. This time, it was far easier to find his way, which had initially taken him more than eight hours. The wind has been increasing; the closer to their destination, the stronger it is. Now, as they arrive, it's almost cyclonic, engulfing them in clouds of fine red dust.

"Where has this come from?" Standen asks, surprised by the sudden ferocity of the wind storm.

"Dunno, mate, but lucky we're in the car, it's not real good out there," Henry replies, looking out at the wash of dust as it smacks against the windows.

"How long do you think it's going to last?"

"Can't say," Henry replies, "better for us to wait a bit."

Standen replies with a nod.

For nearly fifteen minutes, the men sit quietly in the car as it is buffeted. If they were outside, their skin would be blasted off by the sand.

Standen's mind is focused on his mission; he is keen to get moving, he has a point to prove. Henry, however, decides to meditate and doesn't move an inch. Standen even thought he might be dead, and had to make sure he was still breathing a couple of times. As the storm dies down, his companion finally opens his eyes.

"Good sleep?" Standen asks, whose map is spread out across the dashboard.

"Yeah, not bad thanks. Hey, who's this fella we're lookin' for?" Henry asks.

"What do you want to know?"

"What's he done?"

"Well, he murdered a man, and nearly killed a young girl and her mother in car accident. He fled that scene by abducting a doctor who had stopped to help," Standen explains.

"Oh, a real charmer hey?"

"Yeah, and if that isn't bad enough, the doctor, who escaped somehow, is being held by police in Western Australia as a suspect in this bloke's disappearance."

"So, is this fella dead or alive?" Henry askes,

"No one knows, the doctor said he died and he buried him somewhere out there, that's why we're here, to find out."

"You think the doctor killed him?"

Standen shakes his head, "The other police do, I don't."

"Why not?"

"I only met the doctor once but the way he cared for that lady at the crash scene, I don't see it, he isn't a killer."

"So it's a mystery what happened to this bloke?" Henry proposes.

"Yep, and it's one I've got to solve quickly, otherwise the doctor may go to jail for something he didn't do."

As if on cue, the wind drops sharply, the dust and dirt fall to the ground, revealing the surrounding desert country. The men exit the car which is covered in a thick layer of red sand, a striking sight against the powder-blue sky.

"How far do we have to go?" Henry asks.

Standen reaches for his map and walks around the front of the car, clearing the dust off the bonnet, and spreads the map out. Both men study it intently, looking for where he marked the position.

"According to the map, this is where I found the blanket which is where we will start the search."

"Are we in South Australia?" Henry asks.

Standen takes a closer look at the map.

"Just," he replies, "but out here, no one's going to know. The question is where to start looking, everything is covered over, thanks to the storm."

"I don't think we have to worry about that," Henry says pointing to a spot around a kilometre away.

A large flock of birds are flying in close formation in a circle, how buzzards circle when they find a carcass to feed on.

"I've never seen anything like that before, not that many at least," Standen remarks, surprised by the enormity of the dark mass of birds floating in the sky.

"Birds circling like that means one thing, Glen, food. We better get up there to see what they're feeding on."

The two men race off towards the location at breakneck speed, gliding across the landscape like a skiff on the ocean. They draw close enough to see what kind of birds they are, and stop the car. It's a murder of crows, bigger than either man has ever seen.

"I wish had my camera handy," Standen remarks, "no one would believe it without a photograph." However, Henry looks worried, this strange mass of birds means something to him.

In some cultures, the crow signifies a trickster, an old soul carrying knowledge; in others, it's a symbol of evil and is often associated with death. Standen observes his new friend's trepidation and starts to feel uneasy as well.

As they get closer, the men realise it's even bigger than they first thought. Hundreds, possibly thousands, of birds all flying in unison above whatever it is on the ground.

Standen is surprised that none of the birds are on the ground, feeding.

"Why aren't they eating what's on the ground, it's not like a crow to pass up food, especially out here?" he remarks, confused by the birds' strange behaviour.

"Because they're not here to eat whatever it is," Henry replies ominously.

"Then, what are they doing?"

"They're protecting something, I reckon."

⟫⟫⟫ ⟪⟪⟪

Ken was given food and water. Somewhere along the way he has lost his appetite, however the water was welcome. He still hasn't heard from his lawyer or their Perth people, they should have been in touch with him already, this 'detention' is starting to wear him down.

"Where are you, Harry?" he murmurs to himself, surely a lawyer of his stature would have people he could call upon immediately even if he is on the other side of the country.

"Be patient," he tells himself, reaffirming in his mind that this ordeal is another test.

"You know if you keep talking to yourself, people will think you're going crazy," a voice from behind him says. He swings his head around to see that Satan has returned. He's unprepared for another round with him, but somehow he has to find the strength, and quickly.

"I told you I'd be back, doctor; I want to see if you've thought about my offer?"

Ken shakes his head, "No, not really, I haven't had a chance."

"Well, that saddens me, it really does, because you're going to spend your best, the final years of your life, in jail for a crime you didn't commit. Hardly seems fair, wouldn't you say?"

"No, it doesn't, but I would say when it comes to you, fairness has little to do with it," Ken states.

"On that, we can agree!" Satan points gleefully at the stain on the floor from Ken's earlier vomit. He knows his first visit had the desired effect, that he terrified the human. They look at each other, knowing what this means without the need to exchange words.

"Perhaps you can help clear something up for me, doctor, something I'm unsure about?"

"And what would that be?"

"What I don't understand is, why God, would send the Son, to you, a creature that is nothing more than a bald monkey, I don't understand it?"

"Why do you care?" Ken asks in return, wondering why the creature is so interested in his relationship with Jesus. Perhaps if he downplays the relationship a little, the creature will get bored with him and leave.

"I must say, I'm curious. Ever since I smelt your soul, back out in the desert, I knew that if he's interested in you, I should be as well, he doesn't come back for just anyone."

"Just lucky I guess." Ken replies, "It wasn't only me; you know."

"Oh yes, the old man he cheated me out of. But come on, doctor, seriously, why are you so special, huh?"

"It's a mystery to me as well."

The creature stares at him, penetrating past his eyes and into his mind. Ken tries to break the eye contact but cannot, he's compelled to look. Something is pressing down inside his head, it moves around to different parts of his brain. It's like someone is rummaging around, looking for something. The creature is probing his mind, he is on the border of discomfort and pain. His head is hot and starts to ache.

It only lasts for a few moments but feels like many long minutes. The demon smiles and releases its hold. Ken's discomfort and pain disappear. It has discovered something important. "You see doctor, rarely does the Son himself return; usually it's the angels that come back and stick their noses into my business."

"Really, and how do they do that?" Ken asks, curious to hear its answer.

"In the beginning, I was told it was my right, to tempt and try to corrupt mankind, to test them, to see that they are worthy. But these...angels, which are nothing more than sycophants, keep coming back, trying to save people. The drug addicts, the prostitutes, the murderers, they are constantly interfering with my people!"

"Your people? I thought we were God's children?"

The man smirks.

"And they are, but once they turn their backs on him, they are mine, and that's my job, to get them to turn their backs. I'm not responsible for what grown people choose to do."

"But you manipulate circumstances to ensure their downfall."

"No, I only present the options, alternatives. It's not my fault that some are weak and lazy; I give them the choices," Satan says, absolving himself from any wrongdoing, but they both know how it works.

Ken needs to know how the creature engineered his arrest and who is pulling the strings while the man is still talking. Who knows, perhaps he can use that knowledge somehow.

"How did you manage to get me in here?" Ken asks, "You're not allowed to directly affect things here -"

"Is that what your bible tells you?"

"It's what Jesus told me," Ken replies.

"Well, he's right, of course, but, as I just told you, I'm allowed to influence, and that, my dear doctor, I do. It's too easy you know, corrupting humans. All I have to do is promise you money, power, fame or sex, and you will agree to anything, give me anything, so that you can live your miserable, short lives better than the next man."

"So, who's the person you influenced to get me in here?"

The creature shakes its head, "Why would I tell you?" he replies, grinning, enjoying this game with the human.

"The senior sergeant?" Ken asks, throwing out a name he's sure is the one.

Satan's grin widens, giving the answer away. "I was never very good at keeping secrets, doctor. Now you know, so what? There's nothing you can do about it?"

"So, is your plan, to have me stuck in here, so that I will make a deal with you, freedom in exchange for my soul?"

"Something like that, but let me tell you about what could happen if you say no, and I'm sorry to say, it isn't pleasant."

Ken gestures with his hand for the man to continue laying out his plan,

"I will ensure every day of your life in jail is a living hell. Imagine doctor, being raped every single day by dirty men who just want to reduce you to nothing. For no other reason than their own gratification, and, if that isn't enough, you will be beaten to the point of death every day by people who enjoy that kind of thing. When you can't take it anymore, you will take your own life, but that's not all. I will keep bringing you back again and again until you give in to me, and when you do, and only then, I may let you die."

The creature calmly paces the room.

"Let me ask you this: how hard do you think it's going to be to influence people in jail, huh? The right word in the ear of the right person, anything can happen? Desperate and disturbed people will agree to anything to survive, you should know that."

Ken is defensive, convinced what the creative has described will not be his fate but he would be lying if he said the thought of it didn't terrify him. He knows this evil one has the power to make it happen.

But Ken cannot budge. In his mind, there is no way Jesus would ever let that happen. He will not say yes, and he never will. There is no coercion powerful enough that would make him change his mind.

However, the entity has different ideas. When he probed Ken's mind, he found out the one button that will make him capitulate and forsake God. Now is the time to press it.

"And of course, there's your beautiful daughter, Gemma, lovely girl, gorgeous woman, nice house. I like that touch of the crucifix above the hallway."

Ken's parental instincts immediately go into overdrive, anger sky-rockets in him as he stands to face the hideous creature.

"You leave my daughter out of this, you mongrel bastard. This is between you and me," he warns, shaking his fist defiantly, giving the demon what he's been looking for, a way in.

"Relax, doc," he lets out a sinister laugh, finding his captive's reaction entertaining, "I won't touch one hair on her pretty little head, unless of course, you give me no choice," he replies, twisting the dagger deeper into Ken's spirit, opening the gap a little further.

The man has him right where he wants him, arrogantly making a gun-like gesture with his fingers, mouthing the word, "BOOM!" as he pretends to pulls the trigger.

Ken sits back on the bed, with his face in his hands, trying to wrestle control of his emotions, but he's struggling. The thought of this thing getting its hands on his precious daughter is too much to bear. He only has two courses of action; either he gives in and gives the creature what it wants, or he has to find a way fight it.

When he was a child, he read somewhere that, when Jesus called a demon by name, he forced it to leave a man alone. If Ken could find out Satan's real name, could he banish it from his presence by evoking God's power? Was it possible? Could be remotely strong enough to do something like that, would it even work? He has no choice but to try.

"Who are you, exactly, Satan, Beelzebub, or is it Lucifer?" Ken asks, to which the man immediately shakes his finger, warning him he's treading on uncertain ground.

"Be very careful, doctor, that is a very dangerous game you're not equipped to play. You think that if you know my name you can control me, like Jesus did? You don't have the authority, little boy, let alone the power!" Satan replies, angered by Ken's question. He walks over and leans into the human's face, far closer than before, lowering his voice, as if to share an important secret. Ken can feel that draining sensation again.

"I'll help you out here a little, doctor, I'll tell you who I am," he steps in even closer, putting his foul-smelling mouth directly on Ken's ear:

"I am the Devil."

The creature vanishes. Ken knew who it was, but needed him to say it, and now realises it was a potentially fatal idea.

⇒⇒⇒ ⇐⇐⇐

Henry and Standen are now a hundred metres from the crows, it's hard going, the cyclonic winds have returned. The closer they get, the more difficult it becomes to reach their destination. It's a strange sight, as dust once again encompasses everything in its path. Still, the massive formation of birds flies peacefully above. The vehicle has battled hard against the winds, grinding forward, inch by inch, until finally the four-wheel drive comes to a stop. Standen tries turning it over again and again, but it won't kick.

"Looks like we're on foot from here, mate," he says.

Henry is still on edge.

"What's wrong, Henry?" Standen says.

"Many of the world's old people say the crow is a sign of the supernatural," Henry's voice is low and soft.

"And you think that's what's happening here, something supernatural, should we be worried?" Standen snickers at the suggestion.

"Yeah, I'm worried, for you."

The smirk disappears from constable's face.

"Let's just go." he orders, opening the car door, stepping out into the storm, scrambling to grab his kit from the rear of the truck.

Henry's already walking off, towards the flock, leaving Standen to chase after him.

"You know what's going on, don't you?" Standen yells, trying to be heard above the wind but Henry ignores him and continues on. Standen catches up and touches him on his shoulder, stopping him.

"Someone doesn't want us to find the body! Henry yells over the shrieking wind, 'but we got to keep goin'!"

"Who, who doesn't want us to find the body?" Standen demands, tired of all the riddles.

Henry gives him a stern look, saying "The evil one."

If it wasn't for the seriousness in his companion's voice, Standen would have thought it was a joke, but for some inexplicable reason, he believes him.

"What's your involvement in this incident?" he asks, as the sand tears into his clothes and body.

"We don't have time, Glen."

"Tell me who you are, or I won't go another step!" Standen demands, giving Henry little choice.

"All I can tell you, I'm a friend and I've been sent here to help."

"By whom?"

Henry remains silent, not wanting to reveal the truth in fear of the young man rejecting the answer.

"Who sent you?" Standen yells impatiently.

"God," Henry replies, "God sent me."

Both men stare at each other while the young officer processes the answer, it wasn't what he was expecting.

"OK then," Standen replies, "let's go."

They continue the grind forward, pushing all their weight into the wind to gain a mechanical advantage. Standen has been silent, thinking about their conversation and the validity of Henry's answer. It's a hard one to accept but deep down he knows it's true, but he can't explain it. His face and arms are showing signs of wind damage; he only has his hat and sunglasses for protection.

It's a struggle to keep putting one foot in front of the other but they are close. The birds are an impressive, yet intimidating sight, there are so many of them, the sunlight cannot penetrate to the ground below.

They cross over a small hill. The wind instantly stops, causing Standen to fall heavily. The full weight of his army-style backpack aids his rapid decent to the desert floor. Henry helps him to his feet, fearing injury, as Standen spits out a mouthful of sand. His reaches for his canteen, taking a mouthful of water before spitting it out, cleaning his palate.

"Bloody hell!" he exclaims, taking another mouthful, swishing it around, and spitting it onto the ground. He repeats the process a few times until all the grit and sand is gone from between his teeth.

"You alright?" Henry asks.

"Yeah, I'm fine," he replies, "we should push on, wait, were you telling me the truth about what's going on here?"

"What's your heart tell ya?" Henry asks, as the young man searches his feelings.

"It tells me that you're telling me the truth."

"Then let it be your guide."

Without warning, the birds break formation and start their attack, diving straight for the men at high speed.

"Take cover, Glen!" Henry shouts the warning as they crouch between large rocks on the edge of the hill.

Within moments, the crows have swarmed around the men, nipping with their sharp beaks to tear their skin. Standen picks up a large stick off the ground and wields it to deflect the avians. He bashes into one gigantic crow which spins off at ninety degrees to his right, a perfect shot. He tries to hit as many as he can but is quickly overwhelmed, it's a futile exercise.

As the attack escalates, it plunges the desert into darkness. The birds are invisible in the dark, they pummel Standen from every direction, tearing into his skin as he cowers on the ground, screaming frantically for help.

Henry stands calmly on top of a rock amongst the sea of crows; they are giving him a wide berth. He holds his hands up to the sky, closing his eyes, and summons God. He turns his palms skyward before revealing his eyes which are glowing with a purple hue which pierces the darkness and illuminates a wide area. Standen is momentarily distracted from the birds and transfixed in wonder. The purple light is the most beautiful thing he has ever seen.

Henry brings his hands together, chanting words over and over again, each time the pace of his chants quicken, as the intensity of his words reach a climactic point, when a wave of energy erupts from his hands in the form of a brilliant, white light which fills the sky in every direction.

Standen dives back behind the rocks, covering his eyes, as the light strikes the birds, causing them to vaporise, disappearing from the sky. Feathers fall from on high as the darkness slowly makes way for the light of the sun.

Standen stays covered until he feels the warmth of the sun on his body.

Cautiously, he opens his eyes and sees hundreds of thousands, if not millions, of black feathers fluttering towards the ground. He sees Henry, standing there, bringing his palms back together, ending his prayer.

Standen is aware of something else: his injuries from the wind storm and the birds are gone. He looks at his arms and clothes and finds no trace of damage. He remembers a fleeting, warm sensation, as he was basked in the white light. He is stunned.

Rising to his feet, dusting himself off, Standen looks at the man who said he was sent by God. No doubt remains in his mind about the truthfulness of his statement. Their survival was truly miraculous. "What just happened, where have the birds gone?" he asks, seeking a rational explanation.

Henry walks over to his younger companion, looking around the desert and the sky in all directions. "I guess they all flew away," he says coyly, shooting the officer a cheeky smile.

"Are you an angel, Henry?" Standen asks gently, wanting to know his friend's true identity.

"I'm a helper, I promise ya these evil forces won't give up that easily. This attack was just the beginning!"

Standen nods, again he experiences that sensation of truth.

"Righto, where do we start looking?"

"What's there? What were the birds hiding?" Henry suggests.

CHAPTER SEVENTEEN

Tom Johnson sits at his desk attempting to make his case against the doctor strong and compelling. He's pondering the infinite number of possibilities and ways to spin it in order to lock him away, as his master ordered. His hopes of charging him with murder rest on finding more physical evidence other than the drugs. He knows the case is light on, which is why he needs the gun. He couldn't believe his luck when the doctor said he owned one. Of course, it doesn't necessarily have to be the doctor's actual gun, but a gun fitting the bill; which is sufficient evidence for a jury to convict.

Conversely, it won't be hard for the doctor's defence team to beat the drug charges, not when that little upstart from New South Wales police will surely help. All they have to do is to create enough doubt over the case as a whole for him to walk free.

Johnson's story is different. A local GP of 30 years, pillar of the community, suddenly snaps and kills a criminal after the death of his wife. It's not such a far-fetched story. Not having Stewart's body helps, it keeps the waters muddied, not proving murder one way or the other, which brings it back to who has the best story and evidence to fit.

He often thinks about what his master will do if he doesn't succeed. In the rare times he's failed, he comes up with some short-term punishment, however it is not only the here and now that concerns him, but eternity.

Satan promised him an afterlife, not one of torment, but one of resurrection. He promised Johnson an afterlife in which he would be allowed to return to Earth to influence other men as his master's agent rather than burning in hell with everyone else. This is why he can't let the doctor slip away, it's no longer a matter of choice, it's a matter of his own spiritual survival.

Nevertheless, the years of being in the demon's service have taken their toll. Johnson has grown weary of the demands placed upon him, of causing innocent people pain, and having no real life of his own which, in itself, is his torment.

He wonders if immortality is worth it? Leveraged into a choice he made as a desperate child by an entity he had no concept of. He often finds himself contemplating if there's any way out of this bargain with the Devil. Is there any place where he can escape his life of violence and servitude? However, he tempers those thoughts with the belief he has performed too much evil, gone too far, that it's too late for him, but is it? For now, he has to push on.

He picks up the phone and dials the forensic team that took possession of the doctor's car and caravan. They have been searching it all day without a word; he can't wait any longer, he needs to make something happen.

After a few moments, the phone is answered, "Forensics, Sergeant Jacobs."

"Yes Sergeant, Johnson here."

"Yes Senior."

"How have you gone with that four-wheel drive and caravan we brought in today, found anything?"

"No sir, nothing yet," Jacobs replies, "Everyone has been on it today and we've pulled everything apart. All we found is food, camping and medical supplies, some clothes and personal effects. No weapons or drugs."

"Fark!" Johnson is ready to blow a gasket. He was certain they would find something else to put the nail in the doctor's coffin. Now he has no choice but to take matters into his own hands.

"There's a gun there, the offender told me so himself, I'm coming down," Johnson says.

"Sir, we don't need to bother you with coming downstairs, we'll redouble our efforts." It's the last thing they want, no one can stand Johnson and his attitude, especially when he's looking over your shoulder.

"I insist, I'll be down in a couple of minutes," he says, flexing his authority and abruptly ending the call.

He grabs his set of keys and opens the bottom drawer of his desk. Inside the drawer, there is something wrapped in rags. He grabs the bundle, unravelling it, revealing a black snub-nose pistol, identical in model to the doctor's.

Using another rag, he wipes it clean of any prints, before rewrapping it. He stands up from the desk and places it in his pocket. It barely fits but all he has to do is to make it downstairs without being seen and plant it somewhere in the caravan.

He makes his way to the forensic garage, taking the fire escape to avoid being spotted, bounding his way down the stairs, before exiting the escape door. He sees the men working diligently and makes a B-line straight towards them.

"Jacobs!" he calls out, who has his back to him. He rolls his eyes, uttering something uncomplimentary under his breath, before turning to greet his superior officer.

"Yes sir," he replies, standing smartly as Johnson storms over to him.

"Update, where have you and where haven't you searched?"

"As I said on the phone, sir, we have had all teams working on this today. We have stripped both vehicles apart and found nothing of consequence."

"I'll let you know what's of consequence in this investigation, Sergeant." Johnson instructs, walking into the cabin of the caravan which is half deconstructed. He has to find a place to plant the gun, somewhere hidden and out-of-the-way.

"I'll have another look through here, you blokes carry on out there."

"Sir, we have already searched that area, we've pulled everything apart."

Johnson cuts him off. "You have your orders, Sergeant, carry them out!" he commands, keeping the forensics team distracted from noticing the bulge in his pocket.

"Yes sir," Jacobs replies flatly, as they return to their work.

Johnson wastes no time and reaches into a cabinet that is close to the ground. It has seats on top to make a secondary bed, if need be.

He lifts the lid of the empty storage space, spotting a little crevice at the bottom, it's not a large space, but big enough

He removes the gun from the rags and places it in the gap, jamming it in, making it appear as though it's been there all along.

He sits there for a few minutes, so as to not arouse suspicion, timing himself with his watch, making it sound like he's searching the van. The arms of the watch tick over, four minutes, that's long enough.

"Jacobs!" he bellows.

Jacobs comes running, "Yes sir?"

"You told me you searched this area?"

"Yes, we did, thoroughly." Jacobs responds confidently,

"Then what the fuck is this?" Johnson demands, pointing towards the cabinet. Jacobs lifts the lid, revealing the gun, slightly poking out from the under the ledge. He's lost for words.

"That's bullshit, we already searched there and nothing was inside."

Jacobs's second-in-charge, Bill Anderson, comes into the caravan and looks inside the cabinet.

"What the hell, that wasn't there before," he says firmly.

"I know," Jacobs agrees, "but thankfully the senior sergeant worked his magic, yet again, pulling us out of the shit."

Johnson takes exception to his smart aleck comment.

"Do you have something to say, Jacobs?"

He's tempted to unload on Johnson but he'll keep; they both know what happened here. The suspicions about Johnson have run through the place for years but no one could ever make anything stick.

"No sir," he says dryly.

"I didn't think so. you blokes are the deadest fuckin' useless lot. If I didn't come down here, you would have let a serial-murderer get away with it." He says ripping into them for all to hear, leaving Jacobs fuming.

"Bag it, admit into evidence and have it on my desk in 30 minutes, it's time to close this investigation," Johnson says, storming out of the caravan and back towards the elevator, muttering profanities under his breath.

Jacobs has had enough of his team being the scapegoats for Johnson's stitch-ups, and he has the audacity to call himself a cop. Everyone knows his forensics team is one of the best in the country.

He turns to his second-in-charge, "I'm not losing my pension for this bullshit," he says angrily.

"Me neither," Anderson replies, "what do you want to do?"

"Do me a favour, bag it and before you admit it into evidence, do a quick firing test, and bring me the casings. I have a feeling about this gun." Call it intuition, but something is sticking in the back of his mind about the make and model of this weapon.

"What are you hoping to find?" Anderson asks.

"Just do it, Bill, we don't have a lot of time, I'll explain later."

"On it, boss!"

Anderson places the gun inside a plastic bag before hurrying off to the lab.

→≫≫ ≪≪←

Once again Ken is being bustled down the hallway towards the interview room. Despite remaining compliant, he is being manhandled in a way that is totally not justified. However, he remains silent and does not resist.

"Where am I going?" he asks the guards who say nothing. Once inside, he can see the same small desk and chair he saw earlier when he was interviewed but also a phone.

"Your phone call, you have two minutes," one of the guards says, as they seat Ken in the chair, freeing his hands. One guard remains inside the room as the other exits.

He dials Gemma's number, hoping she will pick up, he's desperate to make sure she's OK. Thankfully, she answers the phone in quick time.

"Hello?" the sheepish female voice says on the other end of the line.

"Gem," he says, "it's Dad."

"Dad!" she exclaims, her voice bursting with relief, "Oh, thank goodness, I've been so worried, I've been sitting next to phone since they - "

Ken cuts her off mid-sentence.

"Gem, sweetie listen, I don't have much time, did you speak to Harry?"

"Yes, Dad, the guy he has in Perth is overseas on holidays and doesn't have anyone else. Harry's trying to get a flight over, but it's looking like tomorrow afternoon at the earliest."

"Blast!" Ken says, frustrated, but at least his lawyer is on his way, "It's OK, Gem, now listen to me very carefully," he says, looking at the clock, "They can only keep me 12 hours without charge, that's 12 a.m. midnight, I'll call you if they let me out."

"If they let you out?" Gemma asks, confused. The way the police were talking, she thought it was a done deal. He detects something in her voice, something not quite right.

"If they don't charge me by midnight, they have to let me go," he assures his daughter. "It's going to be alright, Gem, I have faith everything will turn out the way it's meant to, are you OK?"

"No, not really, Dad," she replies.

"What's wrong, I know this is stressful but we will get through it."

"It's not that, Dad, something happened today, something I can't quite explain."

Ken knows what it is, he was hoping the entity had made it up, about visiting his daughter. He is beyond furious but has to keep it together. "Let's just say, I believe your story, darling. Is Kevin far away?"

"Yes, he's still at the mine, I tried calling and left a message but he hasn't called back yet."

"I'm sorry I wasn't there to protect you," Ken replies, feeling helpless.

"There wouldn't have been anything you could have done, Dad," she replies, sobbing.

"This will all be over soon. I promise."

"I hope so." she replies softly.

"It will be, I love you, Gem."

"I love you too, Dad."

He hangs up the phone and looks over towards the guard watching him, "I'm ready when you are."

As they prepare to leave the room, the second guard hurries in, saying "Senior wants him taken to interview room one."

Both guards lead Ken to yet another room. This room is very different from the one he was just in. It's brightly lit with a white table, two chairs and a microphone in the middle. Ken senses the formality. He's directed to sit in a chair, with the guards threading another chain over his cuffs and fixing the chain to the floor. Once secured, the guards depart, leaving him alone in the room.

Forensic technician Anderson races down the corridor towards Jacobs's office, having completed the test fire of the gun Johnson found in dubious circumstances. He has the gun and the bullets in two separate plastic bags. He bursts through the door of the lab to see Jacobs standing over a cardboard box.

"Here it is," he says, eagerly passing the plastic bags to his supervisor.

"Excellent," Jacobs replies, snatching the bag out of his hands.

"What do you have in mind, boss?" Anderson asks inquisitively. Jacobs quickly ponders if he should share his hunch but if he can't trust his number two, who can he trust?

"Do you remember that unsolved shooting in South Perth three years ago?" Anderson shakes his head.

"Not really, no, there was a few in that time."

"Well, when I saw the gun that Johnson had found, it started me thinking. We identified the type of gun from the ballistics of the shooting but we never recovered the weapon, nor did they ever find the shooter," Jacobs explains.

"So?"

"It was the only crime committed with this type of gun over the last five years, and I think this could be the same gun Johnson planted in the caravan. Come with me."

They walk over the bullet comparison machine.

Jacobs explains, "This is the bullet taken from the victim three years ago, it's remarkably well preserved." Anderson has a quick look through the machine.

"Now let's load in the new bullets from your test," Jacobs instructs, taking the fresh test bullet from the bag and loading it on the right side of the microscope, taking a very long look at the striations on both bullets, hoping for a match.

Anderson can't contain himself; he has to know the result.

"Well?" he asks impatiently, "is it a match?"

Jacobs lifts his head from the scope. "Take a look yourself," he replies, as Anderson eagerly moves over to look. The evidence is clear and compelling.

"Bugger me!" he exclaims softly, raising his head to look at his boss with a stunned expression, "You know what this means?"

"I do," replies Jacobs smugly, "we've got the bastard!"

"So, what do we do now, who do we tell?" Anderson says, excitedly.

"Listen to me, Bill, this is very dangerous information, say nothing to anyone about it, just give the gun to Johnson, and don't let on anything. I'll handle the rest," he orders quietly, not wanting to generate attention.

"Alright boss, how will you handle it?"

"I've got a phone call which I've been waiting for years to make."

Anderson leaves to deliver the gun to Johnson while Jacobs walks straight to his desk, located in a small room at the back of the lab. He reaches into his desk drawer and takes out a small leather-bound notebook.

He opens the notebook. There it is: the number he has been waiting to dial and finally that time has come. He knows it's late, but dials the number regardless, hoping he's still in his office. It rings several times before being answered.

"Clarkson." The stern voice says on the other end of the line.

"Commissioner, it's Jacobs from Forensics here."

"Yes Jacobs, I was on my way out, what can I do for you?"

"Do you remember telling me if I ever had proof on Johnson, I was to let you know."

"Yes, I do," the Commissioner replies, a hint of excitement in his voice at what Jacobs has to tell him.

"We've finally got him this time!"

He doesn't know if it's due to his exposure to the entity or not, but Ken felt the sergeant's presence before he entered the room. He felt the darkness hanging over him, it causes a nausea-like sensation. Johnson strides to the table, carrying his notes, folders and something else, a package of some kind. He places everything on the table, ordering it neatly so that both men can see the exhibits. Ken spots a gun inside the evidence bag which is not a surprise, he was expecting something like this to happen.

Johnson presses a button next to the microphone, which starts a machine somewhere in the room, and begins dictating;

"Interview of Doctor Ken Burton in relation to the disappearance of Michael Stewart. Interview conducted by myself, Senior Sergeant Tom Johnson, Western Australian Police, Perth City Station, at 6.30 p.m. The date is April 15, in the year of our lord 1979.

Doctor Burton, you have been arrested for possession of a trafficable amount of heroin that was retrieved from your vehicle today, as well as a large amount of cash, totalling $2,900 that was also found in your vehicle. The search was based on our investigation into the disappearance of Michael Stewart of Dubbo at the behest of New South Wales Police. It is our contention that you have, in fact, murdered Mr. Stewart in relation to his role in an accident and a previous murder. Would you care to comment on these allegations?"

As before, Ken won't be playing this man's games, he'll play his own, to the letter of the law, "No comment," he calmly replies.

The sergeant already looks agitated.

"Based on reasonable suspicion, Western Australian police officers executed a search warrant for your vehicle and caravan where we located a firearm. A 0.38 calibre snub nose revolver was recovered from within a cabinet in the caravan. Doctor, is it not true you own a 0.38 calibre revolver which is registered to you in New South Wales?"

"No comment," he replies, once again, further irritating his accuser.

"Is your weapon not identical to this one?" he asks, holding up the bag containing the gun.

Ken will answer this one. "No, it's not. It may be the same model, but that's not my gun."

"Doctor, we are in the process of running the registration number of this firearm against the one which is registered to you. Why don't you save everyone a lot of trouble and admit that it's your gun." Johnson asks, hoping to bluff his way to a confession.

"My gun is silver, not black, sergeant," Ken replies flatly, looking him straight in the eye, hoping to throw a cat amongst the pigeons.

Johnson looks panicked.

"I beg your pardon, doctor?"

"My gun is silver, not black, you have the wrong gun."

It didn't occur to Johnson the gun could be a different colour. Even though this mistake is embarrassing, it is not terminal to his plans. He'll make an adjustment to his brief of evidence when the time comes.

"Doctor, did you kill Michael Stewart?"

"No." Ken replies, tired of this merry-go-round, "As I said before, I will not answer further questions without counsel."

The Sergeant takes a deep breath before letting it out as a frustrated huff.

"OK, doctor, again have it your way. Interview is suspended at 6.35 p.m., suspect has invoked his right to counsel." Johnson says into the microphone, before ending the recording.

He begins to pack up his files of contrived evidence and looks sternly at Ken, frustrated he isn't able to intimidate him as easily as he has many others over the years.

"You know, it doesn't need to be this hard, doctor," Johnson says, trying to sound like he's wanting to help him, but in return Ken gives him a look of contempt.

"It does when you're trying to frame me for a crime that didn't happen. All I've done is invoke my legal rights."

"Yes, of course you have," Johnson says bitterly.

It occurs to the doctor he may not be able to stop the entity directly, but perhaps he can try some influencing of his own. This is his chance to stir things up.

"I know why you're doing this; it's not up to you, is it?"

"What do you mean, doctor?"

"Your friend keeps visiting me and telling me he can make all of this go away if I give him what he wants."

The comment gives Johnson pause, not once has a suspect been directly visited. For the first time in his life, he feels nervous about being discovered, but he'll bite, he wants to know more.

"And what does this so-called friend of mine want from you?"

"My soul," Ken replies, staring the policemen down.

His answer sends shiver down Johnson's spine. "I have no idea what you are talking about," he replies coyly, quickly gathering his papers, intent on making a hasty exit

Ken pushes the topic further. "I think you do, senior sergeant, you've been doing what he wants for so long you've forgotten what it's like to have a mind of your own, haven't you?"

Johnson feels like he's about to explode, feeling betrayed, his master has been trying to cut a side-deal, keeping him out of the loop. He feels like an idiot, allowing himself to be so callously used. He'd been instructed to lock this man up, incarcerate him, at any cost, and now he finds out the demon has been going behind his back.

Ken senses he has struck a chord, the look on his adversary's face says it all, but he isn't finished yet.

"There is a way out of this, Sergeant: ask to be forgiven, and you will be."

Johnson stares at him. "I don't know what goes on in your head, Dr Burton, but I don't need forgiveness from you or anyone."

Ken can sense his anguish and anger. It's working.

Johnson stands to leave the room, dismissing the comment, but Ken has one final parting shot.

"Let me ask you one more question, senior sergeant, what you've received for selling your soul, was it worth it?"

Johnson wants to strangle the doctor, right there and then, for being so brazen with him, so presumptuous, but thinks better of it. He opens the door, "Take him back to his cell," he orders the guards, before exiting the room, racing down the corridor and into the men's room.

Without thinking, he drives his fist into the hand towel dispenser, putting a massive dent in its rounded shell. He turns his attention towards a cubicle door, kicking it so hard that a crack appears down the length of it as he continues to vent his rage by punching and kicking. The door eventually splits in two.

He stands in front of the sink, panting, running cold water over his swollen hand, 'What's next? What's he going to do?'

He looks into the mirror, a figure of a man, dressed in black, stands behind him. The demon has returned.

"If I didn't know any better, I'd say your losing your touch, letting him get to you like that," Johnson had never let anyone get under his skin before, but then again, no one ever knew the truth about him either.

"He threw me," Johnson replies angrily, "no thanks to you."

"Oh, so I told him about us, big deal. I didn't mention your name but the doctor, he's smart, I guess he figured it out," Satan says, knowing full well he threw his servant under the bus.

"Why would you risk exposing me like that?"

"I don't know...to spice things up a little, to keep you on your toes. You said, you don't have the evidence, so I had to cultivate other options, in case you couldn't get him over the line and so far, you haven't?"

"I'm just a tool to you, aren't I?"

"Of course," the creature replies, "that's who I am, you knew that. You knew exactly who I was and what I wanted when I saved you, so don't act like you didn't know."

"I was a scared kid and you took advantage of me," Johnson spits out.

"Boo fucking hoo...you would be dead if it wasn't for me, and this is the thanks I get?"

Johnson wants to strike his master, but knows that would be futile, however, his master can sense his intent; his anger only excites him. Instead, he says "I wish we had never met."

"Like I said, Tom, you would be dead if we didn't."

"Perhaps death would have been better than what I've lived through."

"All the choices you've made since I saved you have been of your own accord. You did them because you wanted to, so don't you blame me if you're unhappy. This is your doing!"

Satan paces the bathroom, thinking, and asks "Do you want to end our arrangement, Tom?" to which there is no reply, as Johnson decides to keep his mouth shut.

"That's what I thought... now, we are running out of time."

"You need to tell me why, why you want this one so badly. Why are you infatuated with him?"

Satan continues pacing.

"You have no idea of the powers at work here, but when God himself sends his Son back to Earth, to save one soul, you have to think to yourself, there is something special about that soul, and I have to have it."

"So you're doing it to spite God?"

"Tom, you make me sound so petty...but yes, that's it, exactly."

For the first time since making his own covenant, only now does he realise how big of a mistake it was and that there is no way out for him, no happy ending.

"I have given my life to our agreement. I have done things on your behalf that have served no other purpose than your entertainment." He scoffs at his own naivety, "Stupidly, I would tell myself you were like a father to me, I suppose in some twisted way you were, the only father I've known. I believed if I did the things you asked, perhaps, you would be, proud of me..."

The demon cuts him off.

"And I am proud of you, Tom, and we are a glorious team," the demon says, touching his shoulders, staring deeply into Johnson's eyes, sensing something in his prized pupil that wasn't there before...doubt.

He knows he's losing him, and that's something he cannot allow; this kid has been a lifelong investment.

"I tell you what, Tom, you're right in everything you've said. You've been a faithful servant to me for all these years and you deserve to be rewarded. How about this…get this last one for me and I will let you out of our agreement, I'll leave you alone and you can live out the rest of your life in peace, without me. How does that sound?"

Johnson is surprised by the offer but he knows he can't trust a word his master says; he knows it will never let go of him.

"And what happens when I die here and come to you to be tortured for eternity?"

Satan shakes its head.

"I'll let God judge you on your life, and let him decide if you're worthy of salvation?"

It sounds too good to be true, and of course, he's sceptical. He needs more time to think about it, but will have to continue playing the game for now.

"Sure," Johnson replies, but this entity is old and cagey, he knows his response is a lie, just as his promise is.

"Great, it's a deal!" He says, clapping his hands together, "I'll be seeing you soon then?" Johnson nods, knowing full well that, one way or another, their arrangement is coming to an end.

The light is fading fast, it's nearly the blue hour, the time when the sky transitions from day to night and incredible shades and tints of blue and purple transform the land into some kind of alien world. The two men reach the top of the small hill which looks down into the rock gully where they see a body lying face down in the red dirt. This is what the crows were protecting. The body is dressed in the same clothes as Michael Stewart was last seen wearing. It's him.

They stand there for a few moments; it is a solemn moment, finding a body.

"It's a pity he won't face justice for his crimes," Standen says, "death is too good for a man like this."

"No one escapes judgment, Glen; we all face it, one way or another," Henry replies, assuring him his sense of justice has been fulfilled.

"I hope you're right. Come on, we should get down there. Let's do what we have to do and get the hell out of here before it gets too dark."

Henry nods, as they both descend into the gully.

Once down, Standen knows they have to work fast while they have the light. He takes out some rubber gloves from his backpack, and a pair for Henry. He also removes a black body bag, as well as a camera to process the scene.

He snaps pictures of where the body lies in situ, doing measurements and scouring the area for any other evidence, before moving on with the grim task of identifying the corpse.

"Let's turn him over, make sure it's who we're looking for." Standen orders, as they both crouch and gently roll the body over onto its back. As the body turns, they can clearly see who it is. Based on the photos he's studied. he recognizes Stewart's face instantly.

Standen can't believe how well-preserved the body is, despite having been left out in the elements for nearly two weeks. Stewart's poor health is obvious, however, they find it strange that the body hadn't begun decomposing, as it should have by now, the body isn't even bloated, probably due to the gaping hole in his stomach.

Standen begins a closer examination; the front of the shirt is soaked in dry blood, with white powder mixed in, it's all over his shirt, shoes, hands, everywhere.

"It's him," Standen confirms, covering his mouth trying not to gag, "No sign of gunshots, stabbing wounds or strangulation; the only signs are consistent with major stomach trauma. We'll need a full autopsy to confirm cause of death, but I think it's pretty clear how he died."

Henry focuses skyward, staring intently as though he heard something or is listening to something. The wind, begins to pick up again. Standen, continues to take photos. Henry is restless, his eyes darting around him, and begins his prayer ritual.

"You with me, Henry?" Standen asks, wondering what Henry is sensing.

"We need to get back...quickly," Henry replies, his voice is loaded with fear and urgency.

"And we will, just as soon as I finished with the photos," Standen says, knowing the importance of correct police processes.

Over the next few minutes, Henry continues watching the skies, while Glen completes his business of documenting the scene. There isn't much to do compared to other crime scenes, but regardless, he concludes his work and begins to pack everything away, albeit in a hurried fashion.

"OK, let's get him into the body bag and back to the car," Standen says, but his friend is more concerned with something else.

"You get the car; I'll bring him back."

"Don't be silly," Glen says, "he'll be too heavy for you to carry, besides what's the rush?" Standen asks, unaware of any looming danger.

Henry points to a dark cloud coming straight towards them.

"What's the hell is that?" Standen blurts out, "Not more birds surely?"

Henry shakes his head as lighting flashes within the ominous formation. "Glen, get the car, now!"

Standen picks up his gear and begins running as fast as he can toward the police vehicle, hoping it will start when he gets there.

Henry turns his attention onto the body on the ground, placing his hands gently over it, patting it, as one would a dear friend.

"Don't worry, we'll get you home."

It takes Standen some time to sprint back to the car, the heavy backpack makes it even harder. The winds are increasing in strength and velocity. He arrives, gasping for oxygen, as his throat feels like sandpaper from the dry air. He stows his gear and takes a quick swig from his bottle to wet his mouth. He jumps into the driver's seat, looking back at the dark clouds which are approaching faster than before. Red and white flashes of lightening fill his windscreen's field of view.

He decides a small prayer is in order, after all, what can it hurt?

"If you've really sent Henry to help me, then please, let this car start," he prays aloud before inserting the key into the ignition. He turns it, the dash lights come on and, after a few nervous tries, the car fires, a puff of black smoke escaping from the exhaust pipe.

"Thank you!" Standen says with a huge sigh of relief. He engages first gear, setting off towards Henry, crushing the crow feathers littering the area.

Darkness engulfs them, as the winds return to their former ferocity. Lighting strikes, coupled with thunder so loud it causes him to think 'This is what the end of the world would be like.' He turns his front spotlights on. Henry is walking casually towards him, carrying the body bag over his shoulder. He turns on his flashing blue police light which acts as a beacon amongst the blackness. Hail is pelting into the windscreen. Tiny cracks appear in the thick glass. He accelerates towards his friend covering the ground quickly.

Standen pulls up next to Henry, before getting out to open the rear door, placing the body safely inside, as larger hail hits him in the face and body like vicious punches.

Standen and Henry jump back into the car, at once setting off for home.

"Go! Go! Go!" Henry yells, desperate for his friend not to get caught in the storm, "Glen, you gotta try to outrun it!"

"I'm going, I'm going, I've never seen a storm like this, it's not normal, is it?"

"No way," Henry replies, shaking his head.

The 4WD is bombarded with hail which slams into the sheet metal like bullets with such tremendous force they go close to penetrating the body of the vehicle. A large piece hits the windscreen, cracking it on the passenger's side. Standen finds solid ground and rapidly puts some distance between them and whatever is in those clouds.

"That was close," Standen gasps, watching the lightening in his rear mirror. A cut above his right eye is bleeding. All he wants is to lie down and go to sleep, but he can't, he needs to keep going. It will be at least another five hours before they get back, and something tells him this ordeal is not yet over.

CHAPTER EIGHTEEN

At this moment, all Ken can think about is Carol and he wonders, 'What would she think of this situation?' He hopes she would be proud of him, the way he's handled these extreme events. As well, the person he's become and the direction he plans to take, providing he can get out of this place. He allows his mind to wonder further, pondering how he will be able to live in this world, now that he knows what really goes on. 'If only Carol was here with him; though perhaps she is in spirit.'

He thinks about the senior sergeant, and is sure he broke through to him. As Jesus told him if anyone asks for forgiveness and they are sincere, they will be forgiven. Maybe Ken can convince him of that promise and he will turn his back on his dark master.

The lights begin to flicker in his cell again, Ken knows what it means, the demon is returning. A voice he has come to loathe booms out of nowhere.

"It won't work, you know; it's too late for him, the things he's done," Satan says matter-of-factly, reappearing in the corner of the cell. Ken is better prepared; he must be getting used to him.

"Reading my thoughts again?" Ken asks, which the creature ignores.

"I've corrupted him too much, he's too rotten, too far gone for 'God,' he's beyond redemption."

"It's never too late for a person to change, so long as the desire is there," Ken replies.

Satan wears an oily smile. "You've really bought into his message, haven't you?"

"Why do you keep coming back?" Ken asks, "I've said no, haven't you got better things to do?"

"I don't give up that easily; besides I bring you a new offer for your consideration."

Ken cuts him off, he doesn't even want to hear it.

"Not interested!" Ken says rudely, which angers the beast.

"At least give me a chance to tell you the offer!" he yells in a deep growling tone which rumbles through Ken's body. He must be careful not to anger it too much.

Satan takes a breath and regains his focus. "As I was saying, doctor, I have a new offer for you – don't say anything, not until I am finished."

Ken sits quietly, Satan fixes him in his intimidating eyes which have turned into a solid black colour.

"In two hours, our mutual friend, the senior sergeant, will come in here with a piece of paper. On this paper will be your confession. He's going to use every tactic he has to make you sign it, forcing you to take responsibility for what you have done. If you don't sign it, he will sign it for you anyway, so it doesn't matter," he explains, making it clear it's a done deal, "Or, you can say yes to me, right now, and all of this goes away."

Ken shakes his head.

"No thanks," he replies, denying the liar of all liars again.

"OK, let me sweeten the deal. How about I let you see your dead wife, huh?"

The demon's mention of his wife shakes Ken up and Satan knows it. His heart rate has increased, now who's struck a chord. Aside from his daughter, Carol is Ken's weak point and they both know it.

"Has that got your attention, doctor?" it asks smugly.

"You can't do that; I already know where she is; she's in heaven."

The creature shakes his head. "No, she's in purgatory, the in-between place you go to pay for your sins."

"I know what it is," Ken snaps back, "Jesus promised me she's in heaven and I believe him, so again, I say no to your offer."

"Is she really, he never did answer your question about whether she was there or not, you've just assumed she is. I happen to know better. Maybe he didn't tell you she was there, you know, being such a devoted woman and all, maybe he was worried you would see it as a betrayal?"

As much as he hates to admit it, the unclean spirit is right, Jesus never did answer his question. 'Could it be telling him the truth?' he asks himself, 'Of course not!' He dismisses the thought quickly.

He's come this far by trusting in what Jesus said to him. Despite his weaknesses, or how much doubt it tries to put into his mind, he can't take that chance. Jesus has no reason to lie, whereas the only thing this entity does is lie.

"No thank you," Ken replies, unmoved by the offer.

Instantly the lights flicker in the cell, the creature's rage builds, it doesn't like hearing 'No.'

"Think carefully, doctor, that was your last chance!" it warns, enraged, as several of the ceiling bulbs send sparks across the room,

"What is wrong with you people?" Satan screams. Ken is thrown from the bed to the wall, helplessly pinned there by the entity's powerful thoughts.

The lights continue to flicker rapidly, off, on, off, on, he can feel its rage building towards an explosive climax. Its face has changed, its eyes have transformed from black to blood red, veins, visible, running across its hideous head, bulging and pumping with demon blood.

Ken begins praying, desperately reciting the Lord's Prayer loudly, to which the creature responds in kind. The more Ken prays, the tighter its hold on him becomes. The pressure builds, his air supply is cut off, he is choking to death.

"I should rip you apart and consume your soul right now, you stupid monkey!" Satan screams in a distorted voice. Ken can hear those sounds again, the sounds of people begging and moaning for salvation, and he's terrified. He closes his eyes and continues to pray harder and faster, desperately hoping Jesus hears his call.

He can feel himself losing consciousness. Is it the end for him? He stops struggling against the invisible force holding him, and goes limp. In this moment, he lets go.

Suddenly Satan stops raging and ends the torture. Ken falls heavily onto the bed, gasping for oxygen as the crushing pressure is released.

Something has upset the creature.

"No!" he screams, the body has been found and his plans thwarted. He continues to remonstrate loudly, like a child, throwing a tantrum and its toys out of the cot, before abruptly stopping. Satan senses something else, a presence is nearby, something dangerous to him.

"Never say I didn't give you a chance, doctor, now we do it the hard way," issuing his warning before vanishing back into the unseen world.

Ken cowers on the bed, too afraid to open his eyes, unaware the demon has left. Suddenly, he feels a gentle touch on his forearm and recognises the voice.

"Open your eyes now, you are safe."

It's Maisy's voice. He opens his eyes only to find she is not there. Did he imagine it?

He pulls his traumatised body up on the bunk, holding his crushed throat. A pleasant scent of roses and lavender wafts through the cell, replacing the creature's foul odour. He notices something on the floor and bends down to find a small, white feather. He picks it up and examines it, smiling, deducing it came from his angelic friend. He places it in his top shirt pocket, close to his heart.

"Thank you," he says gratefully, knowing his prayers were answered.

⋙⃗ ⋘⃪

Standen looks at his watch, it's nearly midnight, which makes it close to 10 p.m. in Perth. It's taken him longer to get back to town; the storm has been chasing them, eventually engulfing their vehicle hours ago. Fierce winds and heavy rain have made it tough going, but now the men are finally within striking distance of Cobar.

As they draw closer, Standen notices how quiet the police radio has been. Even this far out, he should have been able to pick up some chatter by now but there's only silence. In fact, the whole trip back has been quiet, the companions have barely spoken. They have been continuously alert, watching the road for anything else that may impede them.

"This trip would have failed without you, Henry, especially with everything that happened, thank you," says Standen, greatly relieved to be nearly home.

"No worries, but it isn't over," Henry warns, "that's why I was sent, God knew you would need me."

Glen shakes his head and chuckles. "I've never been much of a believer in that kind of thing, guess I am now." He has another burning question he has put off asking since Henry revealed his true identity. But as they near the end of their trip, it's now or never.

"Henry, I need to ask you something," he asks, conscious he doesn't want to cause offence, "Are you alive, dead or something else?"

Henry can feel his companion's discomfort in asking the question. Truth be told, he isn't sure how to explain it, it's new to him too.

"I am both, yet neither," he replies, causing his companion to screw up his face in confusion.

"What does that mean?" he asks, frustrated by the riddle response.

Henry tries to simplify his answer. "I once lived the existence you do now, but I don't any longer, my existence is hard to explain."

"I bet," Standen quips.

They turn off the desert track and back onto the main road towards town. They can see the lights in the distance, only a few kilometres away. As they come over the last hill, the high beam of the vehicle cuts through the rainy night like a laser beam, revealing something in the middle of the road, blocking their path.

"What's that?" Standen yells, as he slams on the brakes and comes to a screeching halt to avoid a collision."

Henry is uneasy. Looking through the cracked windscreen, they see an old, grey-haired man, dishevelled, standing on the road, staring directly at them.

Standen instinctively turns on the blue lights of the police car, ensuring they don't get cleaned up by a truck that frequents the area.

Henry goes on immediate alert as Standen opens the door to investigate. "What're you doin? Don't get out of the car!" he cautions.

"Relax, I have to see what's going on," Standen replies, walking towards the man.

Henry can sense the presence of evil around them, it's overwhelming, and he knows what it is. He rushes out of the car behind Glen, sounding a warning, "Stop, it's not who you think – it's him, it's the Devil!"

Standen stops in his tracks, unclipping his service revolver and keeping his hand on it as he slowly moves closer.

"What's going on, mate?" Standen asks the old man, keeping a safe distance away but the old man doesn't reply. He beckons for him to come closer.

In the headlights of the car, he inches forward to get a better look.

"Grandad?" he exclaims.

Henry jumps into the fray. "That's not your grandfather, it's him, the deceiver!"

"What do you mean it's not him?" Standen replies, "He's right in front of me?" transfixed by the impossible.

"That's what he does, he comes when you're at your most vulnerable, that's when he gets inside your head."

His grandfather urges him to come closer, "Don't listen to him, it's me, Grandy, come give me a hug."

"How could it not be him, Henry, I know my old Grandy."

"Glen, you're exhausted, tired and weak, he's in your head. Focus, see him for who he really is!" he warns but the young constable is entranced. He moves closer.

"Yes, that's it, come to me, Glen, come to Grandy."

Henry has to try and reach Standen before it's too late. "Think, where's yer grandfather now, where is he?"

Standen pauses before he answers, "He's here, right in front of me."

He replies, "No! He's dead Glen, remember, he died 14 years ago, you were at his funeral, remember that day!"

Standen stops, staring with bulging eyes, about to hug his Grandy. The mist before his eyes begins to clear, "You're right, my granddad passed long ago, I was only a boy," he cries out. He stares as the old man's eyes turn red and his skin turns scaly. Only inches away, he jumps back from what is in front of him.

"Ignore the angel, you dumb fuckin' monkey! Give your grandfather a hug!" It commands in a horrendous voice and lunges at Standen who reacts swiftly, drawing his service revolver, firing several shots into the chest of the old man who slumps to the ground with a thud.

Standen backs up towards the car, gun still drawn, trained on the body on the ground. They stand side by side, looking at the steam rise off the body, unsure if it is dead.

"We have to get out of here, before it gets up," Henry urges.

"Get up? I just put three shots in its chest, it isn't getting up!"

But before he can add another word, a demented laugh rises from what is on the ground.

The body of the old man begins to move, twitching and wriggling, and before their eyes, it transforms into something evil and unholy.

The beast rises from the ground, they hear its guttural growling, smell its foul breath. Finally, it stands before them in its true form on two legs baring its fangs, its mouth open and drooling.

Standen is gobsmacked by the creature's size. It's bigger than the police vehicle.

"What the hell is that?" he asks, watching intently as this giant hell-hound walks up around the men, stalking and sniffing them. They can feel its aggression. He raises his weapon once more, discharging it into the beast, causing it to yelp and run off into the darkness.

Standen and Henry are in a state of panic, frantically running to the police car and taking off at high speed.

The police radio splutters into life. A venomous voice fills the cabin. "Give me the body, boy," the voice roars, "Give me the body and I'll let you live." They dare not reply.

"Watch out!" Henry yells as the giant beast rams the vehicle, striking it on the passenger's side, slowing their momentum but not enough to stop them.

They race into the main street, screaming around the corner at high speed.

Sipping their beers outside the pub, the locals see the damaged police car being driven manically and nothing else. However, the beast remains in Standen's rear-view mirror, and it isn't slowing down.

The car drifts sideways around another corner, the squealing of tyres echoes across the quiet town.

"Give me the body, boy!" the beast demands, "Give it to me!" it screams as the underworld howls rise around them.

"I have an idea!" Standen exclaims excitedly.

"What?" Henry asks,

"You said this thing is the devil, right?"

"Yeah, it is!"

"And it fears God, right?"

"That's right."

"So, let's go where the devil can't go."

"And where's that?"

"You'll see." Standen kicks the car into high gear and increases speed, taking the final turn into Barton Street where the police station is located.

"The police scare the devil, Glen," Henry says sceptically, as the police car flies into the driveway of the station, coming to a stop like a jet fighter landing on an aircraft carrier.

The lights of the building are on, he knows other officers are there.

He jumps out of the car, gun drawn, aiming at the top of the street, waiting for the creature to make the turn towards them.

"If that thing is really the devil, this is the safest street in the world," Standen says, allaying his friend's concerns, "Look around you."

Henry looks around the buildings to see three large crosses outside of three different churches, all in the same street. He smiles, impressed by the quick thinking of his young friend.

"If that doesn't keep us safe, I don't know what will," Standen replies, watching carefully down the sights of his service revolver, "Henry, as an angel, you should have known that."

"I told ya, I'm a helper, not an angel, not yet."

The men stand there waiting for the beast to continue its attack. They can hear it screaming, as it stops at the top of the street, visible only in the street light and only to them. It rises up on it hind legs, unleashing a blood curdling sound that reverberates across the land, expressing its displeasure, as it feels the presence of a much stronger entity nearby. Unwilling to risk itself, it will not come into the street with the three churches. Standen was right.

The beast continues to display its fury for several moments, street lights explode and powers lines short out, sending sparks flying in all directions, before it vanishes from their sight, slinking back into darkness from whence it came; once again, defeated.

The police radio suddenly bursts to life with the sound of coms chatter, it's loud, giving Standen a fright,

"Jesus!" he exclaims. He can hear his co-worker calling him. He walks to the vehicle where he casually answers the hailing,

"Yeah mate, I'm outside in the driveway, come give us a hand will ya?" he asks, replacing the mic into its dash cradle. He hears an odd flapping noise from the rear of the vehicle and walks around to take a look. It's nothing. Everything is peaceful. It dawns on him, he can't see Henry anywhere.

He grabs his flashlight and searches around the car, but there is no sign of him and the street is empty.

"Oi," Glen hears, coming from the front door of the police station, it's his co-worker Anthony. "Did you find him; did you find Stewart?"

Standen nods.

"Yep, he's dead, I've got him in the back, let's get him inside?"

"What have you done to the bloody car?"

Standen allows himself a smile, having no intention of telling his colleague the truth "Hit a big roo and a big storm on the way back in, sorry boss."

"Must have been big, look at the damage, I'm glad you'll be writing the report and not me. By the way, we just received reports of gunfire outside of town." Again, Standen smiles to himself,

"That was me, I had to put the beast out of its misery."

"Well, you better get rid of it in the morning, we don't want it stinking up the road," Anthony says,

"I wouldn't worry," Standen replies, "the crows will clean it up."

CHAPTER NINETEEN

Tom Johnson is typing furiously, trying to get the document finished before his deadline but he's preoccupied. He's been stewing on the conversation with his demon-master and the resentment he now has towards him. He's beyond angry that he allowed himself to be used all these years, and for what? The doctor was right, what has he gained out of selling his soul? No family, no wife, no children.

Sure, he has a house and a large stash of cash, but his lineage will not continue. He doesn't know what it is to love someone, to be loved, or to care for someone other than himself. He can't even enjoy his ill-gotten gains because he's always working, six days a week for this thing, feeding it souls and other sensations. He has paid a very high price: his own life.

He imagined a very different life than the one he has now, something better, more powerful; he should be police commissioner. The main thorn is he isn't free.

All this episode with the doctor has done is scratch away the skin, exposing the raw nerve of resentment that's always been there. He can finally admit it to it himself and no longer cares if he winds up in hell. He just wants it to be over.

He stops typing and thinks about what the doctor told him. If he was to ask God for forgiveness, would he bring him into the light after spending so much of his life in darkness. It couldn't be that simple, could it?

He looks at his watch, it's just after 11 p.m., less than an hour to go. He isn't that interested in destroying the doctor, but he would like some kind of indication of what to do next. Perhaps God will send him a sign? He dismisses the thought, as if he would receive such an accommodation after the things he's done.

The phone rings, he answers in his usual strident tone, "Johnson."

"Good evening, Senior, it's Junior Constable Standen from Cobar in New South Wales, you might remember we spoke earlier today?"

Johnson rolls his eyes, "How could I forget, constable, what can I do for you, it's been a long day?"

"I just thought I would let you know we have recovered the remains of Michael Stewart."

"What?" He was assured they wouldn't find it, but he's not surprised. He's been lied to about that as well.

"We found the body of Michael Stewart."

"And what else, Constable?"

"Our local doctor has issued a preliminary cause of death: Stewart died of injuries consistent with a car accident," Standen earnestly states, enjoying telling him that news.

"Well done, constable," Johnson says begrudgingly, trying to give the appearance of appreciation but the news has taken the wind from his sails.

But Standen isn't finished, "You should also know that heroin was found all over the body. It was on his clothes, over everything. I'm sure you'll find our report will match the heroin in the doctor's car."

Johnson is sunk. "I'm sure it will. Well, thanks for letting me know, I'll add it to the report, it certainly makes matters clearer," Johnson says, knowing there is no chance anything will stick now. 'Is this the sign he asked for?'

"You will release the doctor now, right?" Standen asks, wanting to be certain that justice will prevail.

"We'll let you know how it turns out, constable, thanks again for your help," Johnson replies, immediately hanging up the phone, not giving him the chance to ask any more uncomfortable questions.

Standen sits at his desk, smiling and savouring his victory. He feels satisfied but knows he wouldn't have been able to do it alone.

"Thanks, Henry," he says softly to himself, sitting at the table, finally beginning to drift off to sleep. He can't even think about the things he saw out there today, as he lays his head down on a phone book, content in the knowledge he has freed an innocent man. Everything else can wait.

Johnson's thoughts are on that telephone call. He asked for an indication of how to proceed and he received it, clear as daylight, that's what has him rattled, he didn't expect it. He looks at the typewriter, he would have to start all over again if he is to proceed with any of the charges, however, as he has always known, the drug charges were tenuous to say the least. At least this development has given him direction, as he pulls the paper out of the machine. Now he needs to think about the best outcome for him.

He feels as though he's being watched and looks up to see his master, sitting in a chair opposite him, dragging on a cigarette, blowing smoke into his face.

"You can't let him go," he says, staring with malicious intent, his ego bruised. Johnson stares back, no longer afraid. "We don't have the evidence, it was always going to be a battle, now it's impossible," he says gruffly, "unless of course you want me to go in and shoot him?"

"You've failed me, Tom, you owe me a soul."

"And you failed me," Johnson quickly retorts, "You told me they would never find the body but guess what?"

The creature is visibly annoyed. "Well, that young policeman had help I wasn't expecting...maybe I should recruit him next, he seems to have more drive than you," he says, disgusted with his agent, taking another long drag on the cigarette..

"My service means nothing to you, does it?"

"Results Tom! That's what matters, I need results," Satan snaps, "Just get him to confess to something, I can do the rest. Then things can go back to normal between us."

The phone rings again, interrupting their conversation. The creature immediately disappears but its message was delivered. Johnson is sick to death of the interruptions, and desperate to be left alone.

"Johnson!" He barks once more into the receiver.

"Senior, this is Clarkson," the caller says in an even gruffer tone. He knows the sound of the commissioner's voice. Clarkson has been after him for years, but thanks to demonic interference, could never lay a glove on him, that is until now.

"Yes sir, what can I do for you?"

"I require you to come to my office at 12 p.m. tomorrow, we have some matters I want you to help me clear up."

"Matters sir, what kind of matters, in relation to what?" Johnson asks, clueless as to what it's about.

"In relation to the South Perth murder investigation you were involved in three years ago, we have some new information we think you might be able to clarify."

Johnson knows what that means, it's another way of saying investigation!

He played a crucial role in that case, the death of a fellow officer and the subsequent acquittal of the suspect. The murder weapon disappeared and Clarkson rightly tried to point the finger at Johnson, which, of course, he couldn't prove.

He cringes, realising he made a terrible mistake, the gun he planted in doctor's caravan, he used the wrong one. Jacobs must have tested it, as a matter of course, and narked him. It's the only way this could have come up again. He was so focused on doing his master's bidding, he didn't stop to think. Sneaky bastard.

What makes matters worse, the creature would have known this was coming, it was just here with him, yet it chose to say nothing…this is his punishment, and now he's screwed.

"If you don't mind me asking, should I have my union rep with me?"

Knowing the answer will give him an indication as to which way the cards are going to fall.

"Probably a very good idea, Senior." Clarkson replies, "12 p.m. sharp, don't be late," he orders, ending the call. Johnson always knew this day would come; his dark endeavours would catch up with him, it was only ever a matter of time.

Finally alone, he looks around his office at all the plaques and awards he's received in his career. He snickers, knowing that most of them are undeserved. On the surface, he's a decorated career policeman but he knows how he got there, and there's no way he can go jail.

He asked for direction and he's received it, what he does next is his choice, there's only one option for him now. He picks up the phone and calls the guards.

"Bring the doctor back to interview room one, quickly," he orders, hanging up without delay. For the first time since he was a child, he's clear in his own thoughts. Finally, he is free.

➤➤➤ ◄◄◄

Ken sits patiently in the interview room, praying silently. If the demon is correct, this is when he is to be presented with the fake confession he is expected to sign or face the consequences. It's almost 11.15 p.m. so this is it, it all comes down to now, he's expecting the screws to be turned heavily on him. He looks around the room which is different to the other interview rooms. There are no microphones or cameras. It must the place where Johnson does his best work, out of view.

The door opens and Johnson strides in with his usual self-confidence like a man on a mission. He proceeds straight to the table and goes through his ritual of laying out his files neatly in front of him. Although Ken is mentally prepared, he feels the knot tighten in his stomach, unsure of what to expect.

Johnson pulls out a document, and lays in front of Ken.

"Do you know what this is, doctor?" Johnson asks, pointing to the paper.

"According to your friend, it's a confession you will try to get me to sign, by any means necessary."

"That's right, but make no mistake, doctor, he's no friend of mine." Johnson's reply is cryptic but it has Ken's attention. "The last time we spoke, you told me I should ask for forgiveness if I really meant it."

"That's right," Ken replies.

"And you believe we can be forgiven for the things we've done, even if they are bad or even evil?"

Ken thinks back to what Jesus told him about salvation, but a part of him is confused about where this conversation is going. This man has been hellbent on his destruction, and now, suddenly, he's changing his tune. Ken can't allow himself to overthink it. All he can do is give him the benefit of the doubt, answer his question and see where it goes.

"I witnessed a drug-dealing murderer be forgiven and sent into heaven. You're not the only one who has done unsavoury things in their life. So, do I think God would forgive you? Yes, I know he would."

Johnson thinks about those words and what his next action will mean for his eternal soul. "I hope you're right. doctor," he replies, "I really do."

He knows Burton didn't deserve this false accusation. His final act as a policeman can't be to condemn another innocent man to prison for a crime he didn't commit. He takes the document and tears it up before walking over to Ken's side of the table.

"Stand up, doctor," Johnson takes his keys out of his pocket, and immediately uncuffs him. He walks back his seat, regaining his official posture.

Ken is flabbergasted, and sits there with an open mouth.

"The body of Michael Stewart was found today in New South Wales; his injuries are consistent with those sustained in the car accident. While a formal post mortem still needs to be done, it is clear there has been no foul play. He was also covered in a white substance which New South Wales police has identified as drugs, and I am sure it will match the substance found in your car. I can advise that all proceedings against you, doctor, will be discontinued...I'm sorry about the inconvenience. You are free to go."

Ken exhales, he can't believe what he's hearing, it's over. The tension in his brain and body releases its grip and he is flooded with relief and euphoria. He doesn't know whether it was the finding of the body or if he reached Johnson on some level. Whatever the catalyst was, he's just thankful it is finished.

He looks towards the sergeant, who cuts a lonely figure sitting on the other side of the table.

"What about you?" Ken asks, concerned about the repercussions for the policeman, "Are you going to be alright?"

Johnson allows himself a small smile. "Don't worry about me doctor, whatever happens next is what I deserve, I made my bed." He stops by the door, looking at Ken one last time, "It will take a little time to process you out, the guard will bring you some food and coffee. You should be out of here in twenty to thirty minutes or so."

At this moment, Ken feels nothing but compassion for the man.

"Thank you, sergeant, would you mind asking someone to call my daughter to come and get me?"

"Sure...good luck to you, doctor," Johnson replies, exiting the room without another word. Ken allows himself a moment of thanks for the help he's received when it mattered most.

⋙⃗   ⃖⋘

Gemma stands at the front door of the police station, waiting, as she was instructed to do. She is over the moon. When she was informed her father was being released, she couldn't get there fast enough. Now, they can finally put these last few weeks behind them. She presses the buzzer several times until a tinny voice responds over the ageing intercom speaker.

"Can I help you?" a man's voice asks.

"Yes, I'm here to collect my father, Doctor Ken Burton."

"Just a minute, I'll send him out."

A few moments are like an eternity as she paces. Suddenly she hears the most welcome sound, the loud buzzing of the electronic locks being released from the door. She spins around to see her father coming out towards her, holding his paperwork and belongings in a plastic bag.

"Dad!" she shouts, running to him, crushing him in her embrace, as his belongings fall to the ground.

Without a word, he embraces his daughter before kissing her on the cheek, equally relieved to see his girl. There were times when he entertained the idea he might never get to hug her again. This moment is a precious gift.

"What the hell happened, Dad, what's going on, is it over?" Gemma asks in rapid succession, desperate to know the details.

"Slow down, slow down," he says, laughing at her exuberance, "I'll fill you in the details later, I just want to go home, but yes, as far as I know, it's all over."

He has decided to keep some of the details of his incarceration to himself. Gemma had struggled when he told her what happened in the desert and he doesn't want her to be further troubled by Satan's attacks on him in the cell. Better to let it lie.

"Of course, I'm just relieved you're out of there, safe and all of this...crap is over."

"I am too, Gem. I am too."

She hugs him again, "You must be exhausted, let's go home, hey?"

"You don't have to ask me twice; however I have an idea I want to ask you about."

"And what's that?"

"Seeing as we are both awake, why don't we go home, freshen up and then go and spread your mother's ashes at dawn, just you and me?" he asks.

"Sounds like a great idea, Dad." They give each other an affirming smile as they walk towards the car, before Gemma stops in her tracks.

"Oh no, your solicitor, Harry, he'll be here this afternoon, he would have made the trip for nothing," she says, holding her hand over her mouth.

Ken laughs, "Don't worry about Harry, I'll reimburse his costs, besides one would have thought that twenty-five years of free medical care would get me some measure of goodwill."

They laugh together as Ken places his arm around his daughter's shoulders, pulling her close to him, like he did when she was little.

⤜⟫⟫⟫ ⟪⟪⟪⤛

It's been a long day for Johnson. It's one he would like to forget, but unfortunately, he won't have that luxury. It's time to take responsibility for the life he's led, and at this moment, he's never been clearer in his thoughts. He could always sense his master's presence within him. Twenty-four hours a day, seven days a week, he suffered a slight underlying headache, a constant reminder he was Satan's possession. Now he feels nothing, Satan has released his hold on him.

He takes a long look around his office for the last time; he won't be back, why would he, jail beckons. He makes his way down to the garage, and looks over to where his new brown Kingswood SL is parked.

It's late, the new shift is in full effect and he doesn't see any colleagues hanging around. He sits behind the wheel, immediately starting the six-cylinder motor vehicle, warming it up.

He rolls the window down and lights a smoke, a habit he kicked years ago, but he always kept a packet nearby, in case he had days like this one.

After a few drags, he allows himself to relax ever so slightly, to reflect on his life when he hears the demon's voice coming from back seat, directly behind him.

"You owe me a soul, Tom," his master says in a demanding tone, displeased with the performance of his former protégé.

"I don't owe you a thing," Johnson snaps back, "in case you haven't noticed, things have changed." He positions the rear-vision mirror, all he can see is a man's silhouette and a pair of red eyes, glaring back at him through the cigarette smoke.

"Oh yes you do...you let this one get away, but, no matter, I'm not finished with the good doctor just yet."

Johnson scoffs at the demon.

"Well, do it without me, I'm out."

"Out?" his former master laughs, "There is no out, not for you."

"You think so?" Johnson asks defiantly, daring him to test his resolve.

"What, you're going to ask 'him' for forgiveness? Oh, forgive me father for I have sinned," he mocks, "As if he is going to forgive you... a thief, a murderer... and a rapist."

"I am beyond giving a shit, do to me what you want but your reaction tells me he might actually forgive me, you never know your luck in the big city," Johnson replies.

Satan is infuriated by the suggestion.

"You know what really annoys me, Tom? He's always forgiving people. He keeps moving the goal posts on me, but you, you are too far gone

265

even for him, and I will not let you go!" he warns sternly, trying to create doubt in his former apprentice's mind.

Johnson was right about one thing, he's well past caring. He reaches into the glove box and produces a revolver, cocking it and placing it against his temple.

"You wouldn't dare!" the demon squeals, he had no forewarning, and did not sense the human's intention. The creature panics, he no longer has control.

"You know where you're going if you do this, I can't begin to tell you the torture and horrors that await you," he says, desperately trying to dissuade the human, "besides, you haven't even asked for his forgiveness yet, for your rotten soul."

Johnson looks directly into his red eyes, "Haven't I?"

Without hesitation Johnson discharges the firearm, sending a lead projectile into his brain. His lifeless body instantly slumps against the side window, as the sound of the shot echoes throughout the garage.

The creature panics, it should be able to feel Johnson's soul but it can't; it should have been instantly devoured, but it wasn't.

Instead, a brilliant white glow comes from within the dead man's body and soon the light fills the cabin of the car. Judgment has been passed.

The creature howls in rage, his fury causes the lights in the garage to explode, sending glass flying in every direction as the building rumbles. Satan has lost, yet again, and the sad life of Tom Johnson comes to an end at his own hand.

To those who knew him, he will be remembered as the harsh, violent and sometimes psychotic man who would do anything to achieve his goals. But in reality, Tom Johnson was that scared little boy who only ever wanted to be protected from the nastiness of the world.

Dawn is approaching Burns Beach. The glow from the morning sun looms from the east, while the stars of the night gently slip west across the ocean. Father and daughter hold hands as they navigate the rocks and other obstacles on the shoreline. Gemma cradles the urn as carefully as one would a baby to ensure there are no accidents. This was Carol's favourite place, aside from her Cronulla, of course. At this time of the morning, without the hustle and bustle of day trippers, a parking spot was easy to find. The beach is also very popular with the early morning walkers. Today, it is unusually quiet.

They make their way onto the sand; discarding their footwear, feeling the sand's silky softness underfoot, ensuring a more intimate connection with the beach.

"Strange, isn't it? To see this place so quiet, it's normally packed with joggers at this time," Ken observes.

"Maybe they're all in bed, Dad?"

Ken laughs. "If they had any sense, they would be."

The sun has risen higher in the sky, revealing a thick, low cloud cover, diffusing the morning light and giving off an overcast hue. They pause at a spot on the shoreline and Ken stares blankly out to the ocean, breathing the sweet air of freedom and thinking about their reason for being there.

Gemma looks at her father, eyes wide open, full of admiration and pride. The father she knew as a young child has returned to her, free of the bindings that controlled him for much of her adult life.

But now, it's time for a new chapter.

She holds the urn up towards him.

"Shall we, Dad?" she asks. He looks at it, cognisant it is all that remains of his wife, the remnants of a life.

"Why not, it's time," he replies, knowing she is someplace better and the ashes are not the sum of her existence.

Gemma turns the lid of the urn, opening it, exposing the ashes.

"Do you want to go first?" she asks her father, who shakes his head.

"No, you go first, my love."

Gemma nods. She tips the urn down, taking some of her mother's ashes into her hand and spreading them across the water.

"Goodbye Mum, I love you," she says, tears filling her eyes, as she watches some of the ashes soar in the gentle breeze, "I'll see you again one day."

She turns towards her father.

"Your turn, Dad." She passes him the urn.

Ken looks inside and comforts himself by recalling what he has learnt, knowing the soul lives on. He lifts the urn with both hands and shakes part of the contents onto the waves as they gently lap the shoreline.

"Goodbye, my love," he says, knowing they will be together again.

"Shall we keep some for home, Gem?" he asks his daughter but she doesn't answer. He turns to repeat his question, but it is all different. He doesn't speak.

Gemma and everything around her are frozen, it is as though someone has hit a pause button on the world. Yet he can still move freely. He gently nudges her shoulder, but there is no reaction, her body is like stone.

He looks around him, the seagulls are suspended in mid-air, the ocean is like a shimmering mirror and all local sounds have ceased. No sounds can carry, it is so quiet, he can even hear his heart beating.

"What's happening?" he asks out loud, when it hits him. "This is like it was in the desert!"

In a matter of seconds, he hears a familiar voice.

"Hello Ken."

He spins around to see Jesus standing in front of him but he barely resembles the man he'd met; he looks similar, but not quite the same. His body has a radiance which at times appears translucent. It is as if he's here and yet he isn't, phasing in and out of this reality.

Ken puts out his hand to touch him, and Jesus takes his hand in return.

"You look so different, yet you are solid to the touch...amazing," Ken exclaims. He is thrilled to see him, but the question is why, what is the purpose of the visit? He knows it must be important, otherwise he wouldn't be here.

"Why have you come back?" Ken asks gently, not wanting to sound ungrateful for the heavenly attention.

"I have prepared this special place so I may see you, to tell you how proud I am of you; you kept the faith while facing the dark one; you stood strong and did not fear him. You knew the Father and I were standing with you."

"I did my best," Ken states bashfully, a little embarrassed by the praise.

"This is how people must handle dark times, by having belief in themselves, and not giving up. To stay true to the principles and beliefs that make them who they are, and having faith in them."

"I could never have accepted that teaching before, but now I do," Ken says humbly.

Jesus beams a smile of satisfaction at his friend who has come through a vital test of character. "You were lost, but now you are found."

"With your help," Ken replies with a smile.

"I never did answer your question about Carol, if she was with me or not, did I? I said, I didn't want to answer it, at the time."

"I assumed you would tell me when you were ready."

"Well, now I'm ready."

Jesus waves his hand and Ken closes his eyes, not asleep or unconscious, not frozen or suspended like his daughter, only his eyes have been closed.

A strange sensation flows through his body, similar to the tingle he experienced when Jesus first touched him, however this experience is far more intense. Suddenly, he's aware of everything around him feeling strange but wonderful.

It is as though mild electricity is running through his entire body and he is connected, to everything in this world, the trees, the sky, even the seagulls, he can feel their energy. He can feel Jesus's presence and his daughter's too without the need to look; it's almost indescribable.

His thoughts shift, something else suddenly grabs his attention, he can sense another presence nearby, he can feel its innocence and purity, then it comes to him.

"A baby," he exclaims, "Gemma's pregnant, a little girl!"

He can feel the embryo's heart beating inside its mother, she hadn't made any mention of it, but another thought pops into his head, 'She doesn't know.'

Ken can sense a fourth presence, it's familiar to him. He's trying to put his finger on it, to decipher the energy, when a voice enters his mind, a female voice, one he recognises instantly.

"Hello darling," she says, his heart instantly races with excitement, he knows that voice anywhere.

Unable to contain himself, he opens his eyes. "Carol!" he cries out, as his wife stands before him. Like Jesus, she has a radiance, a shimmer, as her skin is glowing, restored by God.

"Yes, my darling," she replies, "I am here, with you."

"Carol," he exclaims, "I have so much to tell you, and so much to apologise for." He reaches out towards her and she takes his hand.

He looks at his wife, his love for her flows out of him like a beam of energy. He has missed her so terribly.

"You're really here, aren't you?" he asks, pressing her hand to make sure she's real, feeling that same tingle and warmth.

"We don't have much time. I need to tell you some things that are important."

"Yes, my darling." he replies, desperately grateful to be with her again, completely preoccupied.

"Live your life Ken, you have so much more to give and so many people who need you. Don't waste it on guilt, sorrow or regret, make every day count."

"I'll try," he promises, nodding his head, not wanting to let go as tears of joy run down his face.

"Everything happened as it was meant to, to bring us here, to this moment. Everything you have experienced in your life has been to prepare you for the things yet to come, do you understand me?"

His head is full of emotion, he's struggling to comprehend her words. "I think so."

"Don't close your heart, my darling, there is time for you to live and love again."

"You want me to move on?" he asks.

"Live and love again my darling, live and love again."

It is hard to hear her say those words, but he knows she's right. He has to live in the now and not in the past, despite how much he misses her.

Carol looks at her daughter, standing there, oblivious to what's happening around her, as they are outside of normal time and space. Ken can feel her love for their daughter.

"She's missed you, Carol...she's been brave, but deep down she's been struggling without you."

"I know," she replies, turning towards her husband, "She will need you now more than ever, and so will our grandchild."

"Have you met her?" Ken asks.

"Yes, I've met her and the three of you will have your hands full."

Jesus approaches them as they gaze into each other's eyes.

"I'm sorry, we must return."

"No, wait, not yet!" he exclaims, as she slowly let's go of his hand,

"I love you Ken, I will always be with you and Gemma and our family," she whispers, as her image and the image of Jesus begin to fade out of sight.

"I love you, Carol," he says, as they both vanish from view.

"Dad!" Gemma yells, "Are you OK?"

Her piercing voice snaps him back to reality as the sounds of the world come flooding in. So too does the bright morning sun and the noises of the recreational users. It's quite a shock as he looks around and realises where he is.

He looks at his daughter, feeling confused as his senses readjust to the human world.

"Yes darling, I'm fine...why wouldn't I be?" Ken asks, unaware that tears are flowing down his face..

"You were really off with the pixies there for a bit, I couldn't get your attention for ages."

Ken breaks into gales of laughter.

He places his arm around her shoulders and looks lovingly into her eyes. "They weren't pixies, come on, let's go home."

ABOUT THE AUTHOR

Ray Doherty was born in Brisbane, Queensland, Australia in 1968. He attended a Catholic primary school and was, at one time, an altar boy at the behest of his aunt who was a nun. Ray has always had entanglements with religion and the paranormal, which have been a constant part of his life. In his first novel, "Jesus Can't Drive" © 2023, Ray explores the idea of a connection to a higher power that can influence our daily lives, and how events and circumstances work together to shape one's destiny.

Ray worked in the Australian media for over 20 years as a radio news journalist, copywriter and voice over artist, before moving into media management. In 2022, he returned to writing fiction and working as a freelance marketing consultant. Ray is a father of four.

RAY DOHERTY

For more information on Ray's next novels, you can find him on Facebook, Instagram and X, or email panda_press@hotmail.com